Quentin Dodd

The Blue Bear

A Dean Sherwood Supernatural Adventure

Snake Year Press

Copyright © 2024 Quentin Dodd

Snake Year Press
Crawfordsville, Indiana

www.QuentinDodd.com

ISBNs
Paperback: 978-1-7337291-5-4
Ebook: 978-1-7337291-6-1

Library of Congress Control Number: 2024918627

The Blue Bear

1

She was naked, with honey-blonde hair and classical curves that brought to mind both Botticelli's *Birth of Venus* and Ingrid Pitt in *The Vampire Lovers*. She had been tied to the old wooden table by her wrists and ankles. Finding her in the basement storage room of a well-respected fraternal service organization was surprising enough, but then I noticed she had a tail.

The tail was covered in short, tawny fur and ended in a silky tuft at the tip. It snaked out from under one hip and hung over the lip of the table, where it twisted back and forth, serpent-like, while its owner looked up expectantly at me.

It took me a few seconds to recover the power of speech. When I did, the first thing I managed to say was, "Are you all right?"

She didn't respond. She was probably thinking, with good reason, that this was the dumbest possible thing a person could say at this moment. I didn't waste any more time babbling, but instead stepped into the storeroom and closed the door behind me. With my penknife, I started cutting the thin nylon ropes that bound her wrists. When I got through both of them, she sat up and began to loosen the cord around one ankle while I took care of the other. She pulled awkwardly at the knot with her right hand while her left hand remained clenched in a fist, and I wondered if that hand had been injured somehow.

When she was free, the woman rotated around and hopped to the floor. I naturally offered her my jacket. She was as tall as I was, and the lightweight blazer probably wouldn't have covered all that much, but I imagined it was better than nothing. But she didn't reach out to take it. Instead, she stood and watched me, still not saying a word. She wasn't frightened and didn't seem the least bit embarrassed. I got the impression that she was evaluating me, waiting to see what move I was going to make next.

"Follow me," I said, then paused when she remained motionless. "Do you understand? 'Follow me'?" I began to suspect we didn't share a common language, so I pointed to myself, then to her, then to the door, but she still didn't move. I took hold of her wrist and pulled slightly, and she allowed me to lead her out into the multipurpose room.

Up until a few minutes ago, I had been setting out barbecue supplies in the institutional kitchen on the other side of this room. Since I'm not normally a food-service kind of guy, I had woken up today expecting to run a few errands for my uncle and then collar the comfy chair at the coffee shop, but then my friend Ken Weinbach had called. Ken's an assistant manager at Fox's Barbecue, and he was in a tight spot with the day's deliveries. So, as a favor, I ended up delivering a carload of miscellaneous barbecue supplies, including chopped onions, pickles, coleslaw, succotash, barbecue sauce, restaurant-quality buns, several gallons of Fox's world-famous barbecue sauce, and a large box of paper napkins. In retrospect, I should have steeled myself against Ken's pleas and tried harder to avoid this assignment. Much harder.

The woman and I were halfway across the room when we heard heavy footsteps descending the stairs. Before I could decide whether to make a dash for the other hall across the room or hurry back into the storeroom to hide, the stairwell door swung open and half a dozen beefy guys emerged. The one in front was somewhere in his fifties, with a square head, florid features, and a shirt and tie under an International Order of Peregrines fleece jacket. He held a large kitchen knife in one hand, and some of the others carried industrial trash bags and bunched-up garments that looked an awful lot like butchers' smocks. Instantly, I understood why these guys had ordered all the side dishes and fixings from Fox's, but no entree.

The beefy guy was just as surprised to see us as I was to see him. "What the hell are you doing?" he barked.

For an instant I thought about bluffing our way past them, pretending to be an outraged health inspector, a horrified janitor, or even this mysterious woman's brother. But there were a lot more of them than there were of us, and I decided to exercise the better part of valor. I ran for the hall, pulling my new friend along with me. This caught them flat-footed and gained us a few extra seconds. We raced past the kitchen, where I had set out all the supplies from Fox's, and where I had waited for ten minutes for someone to show up and sign my receipt. At that point, I got bored and started wandering around, opening doors and seeing what I could find.

That's what they're going to put on my tombstone, by the way: "He was easily bored."

A flight of concrete steps went up to the ground level. At the top, the steel door leading outside was propped open, and I kicked out the wooden wedge as we passed. It slammed closed. The woman remained silent as we ran, and I wondered if she might be in shock, or if she was simply waiting to see whether we actually escaped or not. I still hadn't completely processed the tail yet. It was definitely on my list of things to think about, but not quite as urgent as the knot of angry guys closing in behind us.

My Jag was parked in the gravel lot behind the International Order of Peregrines' building. I threw open the passenger door and helped the woman inside. Our pursuers arrived just as I was getting behind the wheel. The thick-necked, red-faced guy was still in front. He was apoplectic, with the kind of blind, hysterical rage you don't get to see too often up close. The rest, following closely behind, seemed more shocked and confused, as if somebody had unexpectedly canceled Christmas.

After whimsically refusing to start, the car growled to life on the second turn of the key. I slammed it into reverse and rocketed out of the parking lot before anyone could try jumping on the hood. Once we were a couple of blocks away, I ceased coasting through the stop signs and made an effort to drive like a regular person again. I didn't know what a police officer would do after pulling me over for a minor traffic infraction and discovering in the passenger seat a statuesque naked woman with a tail, but I wasn't interested in finding out.

She watched the tree-lined rows of houses pass by while I drove. She wasn't particularly concerned about her recent imprisonment, or even about her current nudity, and that continued to strike me as odd. When I've found myself in an inconvenient spot without the benefit of clothing—a condition that has, alas, happened more than once—my over-riding impulse has always been to find something to wear as soon as possible. Food, shelter, vengeance, alcohol, all other desires take second place in relation to finding a humble pair of pants. She, however, didn't even seem to notice.

I suppose the tail itself was pretty odd, too. Even if circumstances were different and this woman were soberly dressed, sitting in a restaurant and eating a Caesar salad, the presence of the tail would still provoke a great deal of attention from people, if not outright fear. But, the truth is, I've run into this kind of thing before.

My day-to-day employment is doing various jobs for my uncle Willard. He owns a couple of buildings in Garvinville, and now that he's retired he has delegated to me all the mundane tasks he can't be bothered with anymore. I deal with plumbers and electricians, I make sure the city paperwork is in order, and I organize all the receipts for tax time. I work with the tenants when there are problems, and I make sure that everyone's happy and has what they need.

But that's not all I do. Uncle Willard, over the years, had developed a local reputation for being the person to go to in the event of certain very unusual, very specific problems. For example, if you bought an antique Austrian writing desk, and you woke up one morning to see a translucent eighteenth-century cavalry officer writing letters at it, then the person to call about that was Willard Sherwood. If your nearest and dearest had been nipped by a mysterious dog and started acting a little funny during times of the full moon, you needed to talk to Willard. If you could suddenly hear the wails of the damned from behind your bedroom closet door . . . You get the idea. Now that my uncle makes a point of doing nothing outside of his hobbies, I've taken over the "supernatural investigations" as well. In the event of a mysterious manifestation in the greater Garvinville metropolitan area, the best person to talk to is now me, not him. You're probably a little disappointed about that, and I don't blame you.

So the tail—as a tail—was not as startling to me as it might be to other people. I didn't necessarily understand anything about it, or the woman it was attached to, but at least I could think about it without freaking out.

She sat there, eye-searingly beautiful, and gave the impression of complete relaxation, even bordering on boredom. The only exception was her left hand, which remained tightly clenched. The car was full of a scent I couldn't recognize. It was something animalistic, but at the same time related to the woods and the trees. The woman smelled like a forest, but a *sensuous* forest, for lack of a better term.

I tried again to make conversation. "Is there somewhere I can take you?" I asked. "The hospital? The police? I can drive you home, if you prefer."

At the word "home," she swiveled her head in my direction, and for the first time I got a good look at her eyes. They were the darkest blue I'd ever seen. They made me think of the icy waters of some cold northern sea, empty of all warmth but still seductively inviting. She didn't say anything, but I felt like a sort of communication had just taken place.

I headed north, navigating around the oddly-shaped blocks between downtown and the expressway. We passed people on the sidewalk and I idly wondered if they noticed anything unusual about my passenger. I tried to work out how much of her could be seen through the windows of a car, but was too distracted to handle the mental geometry. I passed the Carpenter Library and the garden store where Uncle Willard has me buy plants when they're in season. I turned left at the next light, heading west onto Franklin Street.

I didn't consciously decide to turn here. Somehow, I knew this was where I ought to turn, so I did. I wondered for a second how much of my mind was still under my own control. I made a point of taking one hand off the wheel and scratching my right ear. If I were under a type of hypnotic spell, would I still be able to scratch my ear whenever I wanted? I had to admit to myself that I wasn't certain.

We crossed the bridge, then passed the old brewery and the Art Deco tire store. This part of Franklin Street had been a shopping district back before the Age of the Mall, and I passed buildings that used to be clothiers and hardware stores and banks. Now many of them were restaurants and antique shops and vintage record stores that ridiculously jack up the prices on old jazz records in the mistaken belief that anyone besides me is going to pay that much. But there were still a few establishments along this street doing the same business they had done since Eisenhower. One of them was Hamilton's Hobbies, an old-fashioned craft store that sold fabric, art supplies, and model kits, as well as whatever other bits of kitsch happened to catch the eye of the manager.

The woman shifted slightly in her seat and I activated my turn signal. The more I thought about this, the more likely it seemed that she wasn't exactly controlling my mind. Instead, we were communicating on some unconscious level that I didn't recognize. I turned into the small parking lot behind Hamilton's and pulled the car into an empty space. There was a narrow back door with several small nameplates beside it, and I assumed they led to the apartments above Hamilton's.

The woman looked at me again and I felt a strange kind of fear. The idea flashed through my mind that, now that she had gotten a ride, there was no further need to keep me alive. She hardly looked violent, tail or no tail, but that didn't make the impression any less potent. However, all she did was hold out her clenched left hand, open it, and drop something into my lap.

It was a blue bear. The thing was about an inch tall, made of hard translucent plastic, depicting a bear sitting on its haunches. Its forepaws were up, almost like a dog begging for a treat. The eyes were two tiny black dots that regarded me with an indifferent expression.

When I tore my attention away from the blue bear, the woman was gone. I hadn't heard the door open, I hadn't heard her climb out, and I hadn't heard it close again, but she was gone. The door to the upstairs apartments was swinging back into place, and I saw one naked calf and the tufted end of a tail disappearing up the inside steps.

For longer than I care to admit, all I did was sit there holding the tiny plastic toy and thinking about the strange creature who had just gone out of my life. A wistful sensation washed over me, like I had met the woman who would have become the love of my life, but now she was gone forever. Obviously, this was ridiculous, but that's where my mind was. I instinctively knew that going after her would have been a bad idea, so I just sat there until my thoughts began to clear. Then I put the blue bear in my pocket and drove away.

2

I took the long way home, past the Episcopalian private school and the house with all the reproduction Greek statuary in the yard. I turned at the Civic Theater and followed Fourth Street under the expressway and around in a big loop until it entered the Riverside neighborhood. Reaching the house, I pulled the Jag up the steeply inclined driveway, under the porte-cochere, and into the garage. My car, which I love dearly, is a model that frequently turns up in sneering internet lists of the least reliable vehicles ever made. This fact is hard to dispute, given that my mechanic drives it at least as often as I do, and frequently jokes about listing the car on his taxes as a dependent. The Jag had been experiencing a protracted period of good behavior recently, which made me nervous. I suspected it was saving up something special for me. Escaping from the Peregrines would have been an excellent time for the electrical system to burn out, or for oil to start spraying around the engine compartment like a fountain. Since it didn't, I could only imagine that the car had even more spectacular antics in mind. But I knew I would forgive it, whatever happened. And the car knew that I knew.

As Uncle Willard's business manager-slash-apprentice-slash-houseboy, I shared the sprawling gray house with him. We got along surprisingly well, largely due to our unspoken agreement to give each other as much space as humanly possible. On the way in from the garage, I noticed that the small back yard had been festooned with stubby wooden stakes tied with ribbons of varying colors. Even though it was the end of September, Willard must have been planning for next year's garden, laying out hypothetical configurations and trying to visualize what things would look like in the spring.

In the kitchen, I flicked on the electric kettle and made two cups of lapsang souchong. One was to settle my mind, and the other was an attempt to bribe some advice out of my uncle. I let the leaves steep while I thought back on what had just happened. I gave myself a minute or two to be unnerved, then made an effort to put it behind me. No matter how many odd and unnatural things I run into (or vice versa) I never quite get used to it. I suppose that's what "odd and unnatural" means.

I poured the tea into a pair of sturdy mugs, then went around the corner and up the stairs. The first floor is largely open, unusual in a house this age, with a combined dining and living room in the front, and the kitchen and utility rooms behind. The second floor is smaller, filled mostly with bedrooms. In an upstairs corner, next to the narrow secondary stairs where the servants would have scampered up and down, a closet door was propped open by a fragment of cathedral masonry. A reinforced set of folding steps led up through the closet's ceiling and into the attic, and that's where I went, climbing gingerly and gripping both mugs' handles in one hand.

The attic had been extensively renovated by Uncle Willard, and it hardly resembled the bare, slant-ceilinged storage room it had originally been. Soft lights glowed from recesses overhead, and the visible rafter beams had been stained and polished, making the space look both rustic and sumptuous. A number of long, custom-built tables were arranged in rows and angles throughout the room, creating what amounted to a maze, although one with plenty of room for a large man to traverse with ease. On these tables, in a seemingly endless expanse, stood a miniature world. There were buildings and landscapes, rolling countryside and tightly packed urban centers, with silver ribbons of railroad track snaking everywhere. It was so complex and detailed I could easily imagine shrinking to the size of a chess pawn and happily exploring the terrain for years. I heard the soothing tick-tick of a model locomotive making its long rounds. An HO-scale steam engine traversed the table nearest the steps, pulling what looked like cars from the Erie Lackawanna Railway.

A massive dark form stirred at the other end of the attic. I threaded my way through the layout until I could see Uncle Willard sitting at his work table. He was painting a small building under the bright light from a gooseneck lamp. When he heard me approach, he took off his magnifying spectacles and spun around in his office chair.

"Got a minute?" I asked.

"Is it important?" he rumbled.

"I thought you'd like some tea."

He took one of the mugs and sipped. "Thank you," he said, then took a longer drink. "Do I detect a slight after-taste of obligation?"

"It's possible I'm just being nice."

"It's possible I'm the rightful king of France. However . . ."

I pulled the wobbly folding chair into the light and sat down. Uncle Willard keeps precisely one comfortable chair in his miniature domain, and it's for his own personal use. Guests have to make do with one that's on the verge of collapse. He does this on purpose, to make sure that visitors aren't tempted to overstay their welcome. If he could find a piece of furniture upholstered with spikes, or one that delivered electric shocks at intervals, he'd use that instead.

Behind him, the work in progress stood beside his extensive rack of paint jars. It was three stories tall and modeled to look like a late-Victorian storefront. Half of the back was still unpainted, revealing the corrugated cardboard and foam-core sheets that comprised its structure.

"Is that new?"

Uncle Willard nodded. "It's going to be a drugstore. I'm making a place for it over with the other Victorians." He pointed to an urban area in a distant corner of the attic. Some hobbyists were quite strict about the time period and details of the little worlds they created, but Willard favored the eclectic approach. He was perfectly happy working in whatever theme happened to catch his fancy, from the early nineteenth century up until more or less the present day, with plenty of digressions into sheer whimsy. With one finger, he pulled at the front of his new building. It swung open on a concealed hinge to reveal a delicate doll-house interior where one-inch people conducted business.

"The old drugstore didn't have an interior, so I decided to replace it." Willard said.

I whistled with an appreciation that was largely sincere. While I didn't share his obsession, I wouldn't be human if I couldn't at least admire the craftsmanship. In addition, a Willard who felt appreciated was a Willard who was more likely to give me advice without grumbling about it.

"Was there something else you wanted?" he asked, once I was through admiring his model.

"As a matter of fact, there was. Do you know anything about the International Order of Peregrines?"

Willard's brow furrowed. "Why? Are they having some sort of membership drive? Did they approach you?"

"Nope. Just curious. Their building's only a few blocks away, so I've been past it a hundred times, but I never really thought about what they do. What's their story?"

Willard put down the drugstore again and scraped some paint off of his finger with a broad thumbnail. "I don't know any more about them than anyone else. They're a social club. They organize events."

"What kind of events?"

"The same things other clubs do. They raise money for charities. They have clabber tournaments. I believe they stage a pancake breakfast at intervals, though I can't imagine industrial pancakes and canned syrup are worth whatever they're charging, no matter who it benefits. The building they have, it started out as a Shriners' hall, but the Peregrines bought it in the fifties and turned it into—" Willard looked thoughtful. "What do they call those? They have some clever name for their clubhouses."

"A perch," I volunteered.

"That's right. A Peregrine perch." Uncle Willard drank more of his tea and scrutinized me over the rim with undisguised suspicion. "All right, Dean. Where does this sudden interest in the Peregrines come from?"

So I told him. I told him how I'd done a favor for Ken Weinbach and brought the side dishes and supplies from Fox's Barbecue over to the Peregrine perch this morning, and what I'd discovered when I got there. Willard listened as he always did, impassively, only rarely giving the impression that he was even paying attention. When I was done, he digested this information for a few moments, then continued to gaze into the middle distance as he asked me questions.

"Is this why you brought me tea?"

"I was making tea and thought you'd appreciate some," I said. "The questions were secondary."

Willard didn't verbalize his disbelief, but he exhaled deeply and sunk into his chair. Now that he's retired, he loathes being drawn into other people's problems. Well, he *says* he loathes it, much like I *said* I brought him the tea out of pure altruism. Sometimes it's best not to dig too deeply for the truth.

"This creature, do you really think it had a tail?"

"I am positive she had a tail."

"Has someone asked you to investigate this? Is someone paying you to do it?"

"Not at present, no."

"Then there's nothing to do. Leave it alone."

"You honestly don't think this is worth looking into?"

"Not without remuneration."

"A woman with a tail, that doesn't seem the slightest bit odd to you?"

"It seems extremely odd," he admitted. "But the world is full of odd things. Don't waste your energy. The creature, whatever it was, has escaped, thanks to you, and the lunatics who were planning on eating it have been disappointed. Your part in this affair seems to be over. Personally, I think you should consider the matter closed."

"And yet . . ."

"Dean, there's no reason to place yourself in danger simply to satisfy your curiosity."

"There's no danger here," I said.

"One of the defining characteristics of danger is that you rarely see it coming."

"You only say that because you don't like the idea of having to train somebody new if anything happens to me."

"Yes. Precisely."

"Don't worry. I just want to find out more, that's all," I said. "It's not like I'm swamped with other projects at the moment. I can either look into this or I can go back to work on the estimated taxes, and if there's a choice between cannibals and tax forms, I'd much rather—"

"They're not technically cannibals. Whatever that creature was, it wasn't human. Therefore, the men trying to eat it weren't cannibals."

"All right. Fine. Not cannibals. But still pretty damn weird. And the Peregrine perch is about six blocks from the house. I'd like to make sure they're not planning on expanding their menu. After all, the gap between 'not quite a cannibal' and 'full-on cannibal' can't be very large."

Uncle Willard glanced longingly at the model building on his workbench and toyed with his magnifying spectacles.

I could tell that my time was short. "Do you think you could do a little research for me?" I asked. "See if you can come up with anything about a woman with a tail?"

Willard sighed. "I suppose I can consult the references. Perhaps send an email query. I seem to recall one or two specialists who might have helpful suggestions. But if I have to rescue you from this thing's clutches later, I am not going to be happy."

I thanked him and descended the stairs, leaving him to paint his little building in peace. I was pleased to have gotten a promise of assistance from him, grudging though it may have been. After all, he was right and I knew it. There was no reason for me to dig into this. All that was driving me was my insatiable curiosity, and a sense of indignation at seeing a bunch of whackjobs preparing to kill and eat a beautiful woman. Or, as Willard correctly pointed out, something that *resembled* a beautiful woman. It was possible that my knee-jerk act of heroism in freeing her had been completely misguided. There are, after all, lots of things out there that know the benefits of assuming a pleasing shape.

Even with all that being true, I wasn't ready to let this go. I went back to the kitchen and took a couple of slices of bread from the box. I had intended to make myself a ham sandwich, but somehow the idea no longer seemed appealing. Instead, I got out a jar of cashew butter and shoved the bread into the toaster.

While the bread toasted, I took the blue plastic bear out of my pocket and studied it again. I held it for a few seconds, trying to see if I could notice anything unusual about it. Nothing happened. My fingers didn't tingle. I set it on the kitchen counter and looked at it while I ate. Still nothing. The bear didn't move on its own and it stubbornly refused to glow. When I finished two pieces of toast and a glass of orange juice, I took the little plastic toy to my office and dropped it into the carved wooden box I kept on my desk.

3

My first task was to learn a little more about who had placed the order at Fox's Barbecue. Nobody orders only sauces and side dishes without knowing what the main course is going to be, so if I was lucky, the name attached to the order would be the leader of the quasi-cannibals himself. Once I had his name, I'd try to discover how he captured the tailed woman, and if he was likely to attempt something similar again. Then, finally, I could decide whether I needed to do anything about all of this or not.

The drizzle had come back, and one of the windshield wipers had developed an irritating squeak. I fixed this by turning up T. Rex on the car stereo. The pale gold Jaguar was far too old to have an aux port, let alone a Bluetooth connection, but the CD player worked pretty well. However, I knew better than to tempt fate, and made a point of never putting anything in the player that I wasn't willing to risk losing inside its mechanical innards.

Fox's Barbecue was in the lull between lunch and dinner when I arrived, with only a couple of tables occupied. The white tablecloths, patterned crimson carpets, and tubular mid-century chandeliers made the place look surprisingly upscale for a restaurant with the word "barbecue" in the name. A teenager in a white shirt and red tie stood at the podium by the door. I told him I was looking for Ken Weinbach, and he scampered off to deliver the message. I perused a menu for a few moments, then Ken poked his head through a side door and motioned for me to follow him. He led me to a little office near the kitchen, which held several gunmetal filing cabinets, their mechanisms oiled with decades of airborne barbecue sauce, as well as three tightly packed desks sporting well-worn computers and littered with papers. Ken sat on the edge of the nearest one. He was one of a trio of assistant managers at Fox's, all of whom knew that the elderly owner was going to have to promote one of them eventually. This led to a fierce but unspoken rivalry.

"Thanks again for running that stuff over to the Peregrines for me," Ken said. "Everybody wanted everything at exactly the same time today, and I just ran out of people. The Peregrines are a big account, and I didn't want to disappoint them. Do you happen to have the signed invoice for me?"

"As a matter of fact, I don't," I said.

He made a face. "Oh, well. That happens. It shouldn't make a difference. If there was a problem, they would have called already."

"Did you think it was weird that they didn't order a main course? Only sides and condiments?"

Ken thought about this for a second. "Not really."

"They've done this before?"

"The Peregrines? No, I don't think so, but we get orders like that every once in a while. Somebody wants to smoke their own meat, but they don't want to go through all the trouble of mixing sauces and chopping up a bushel of onions."

"Okay," I said. "I was just curious." It would only upset Ken if I described what I'd seen, but I still needed to get information out of him, so I approached the question from a different, slightly less truthful, angle. "Can you tell me who called in the order for the Peregrines today?" Before Ken could ask why I wanted to know, I launched into a story about getting a really nice tip and wanting to make sure the person in charge knew I was grateful. Ken wavered for a moment, then realized that a thoughtful follow-up like that might reflect well on Fox's. He flipped through some windows on his computer until he located the correct record.

"Rick Freeman." Ken scribbled the details on a blank order pad and handed it to me.

"Freeman Realty?" I asked.

"The same."

Freeman Realty always had big ads in "Garvinville Living" magazine, which Uncle Willard subscribes to for some unfathomable reason, and I occasionally read while eating breakfast. By sheer repetition, the name had penetrated my indifference and lodged itself in my memory.

I thanked Ken and let him get back to whatever it was that assistant managers did. I considered ordering a takeout sandwich, but decided against it. Eating a barbecue sandwich while driving is a recipe for disaster. You might as well douse your shirt and your upholstery with sauce and save yourself the time and uncertainty. I did, however, filch a handful of wrapped crackers from under the nose of the teenage maitre'd, who was not getting paid enough to care.

In the car, I took a look at the paper Ken had given me. The little logo in the corner showed a lip-smacking cartoon fox. Usually, I thought the Fox's Barbecue mascot was kind of charming, a goofy holdover from an earlier era. Today, though, he seemed lascivious and smirking, like he knew something awful was in store for me and couldn't wait until it happened. I took out my phone and punched in the number for Freeman Realty. Realtors kept odd hours, so I figured there was a good chance the office would be open on a Saturday. The woman who answered told me that Mr. Freeman was out on a showing, but he should be back soon. I decided to drive over and wait.

The office was in a band of small, pleasant-looking, green and brown commercial buildings that separated the neighborhoods on the east side from the retail sprawl along Green River Road. There were a lot of doctors, business consultants, insurance agents, and other people who didn't need huge parking lots. While I waited, a few yards away from Freeman Realty's front door, I checked their website for a picture of Rick Freeman himself. It wasn't difficult to turn up quite a few. It was that kind of website. Black hair brushed back, dark suit, plain sky-blue tie, smiling for the camera. He was stocky, but an athletic kind of stocky, like he had played football in college and managed to find ways to keep himself in shape ever since. I studied his face and I didn't like what I saw. This wasn't because of any supernatural insight, or even an indefinable subconscious suspicion. The truth was, I tended to dislike people around my own age who look like they've done a lot better for themselves than I have. This guy didn't seem like the kind of person who would be mixed up in capturing and eating a mysterious creature, but that didn't always signify much. The most successful weirdos are the ones you never see coming.

I watched the raindrops crawl down the windshield and let my mind drift back to the sixty-year-old blazer I'd found online last night. My affection for vintage clothes was deep, and I spent a substantial amount of my free time trawling through the internet and the local shops for new discoveries. I enjoyed things that had a little bit of history to them, and I wasn't averse to being the best-dressed person in the room. But was I the kind of man who could make sharkskin work? Was anyone? Was it worth two hundred bucks to find out?

Eventually, my patience was rewarded. A black Saab pulled up and Rick Freeman stepped out. I got out, too, and timed my steps to reach him just before he got to the door.

"Hello! My name's Dean Sherwood. Do you have a second?"

He nodded toward the office's front door. "Sure. Come on in and let's get out of the rain."

I didn't move. "It'll only take a second. I work for Fox's Barbecue, and I had a question about the order we delivered today."

"What happened?" he asked. "Was there a problem?" He wasn't happy standing still and getting rained on, but I wanted to make sure he was a little off-balance and uncomfortable, without much time to think about his answers.

"Oh, no. There was no problem. Just making sure everything worked out the way you wanted it. We don't get very many orders where the customer provides their own entrees," I said.

"Excuse me?"

This was what I wanted to see. Was there going to be denial? Bluster? Flight? Or genuine surprise?

"Wait, he didn't order any entrees?" The drizzle was beading up on Freeman's jacket, and I could see a drop of rain shake loose from his eyebrow as he frowned. He didn't seem suspicious or guilty, just bewildered. Either he honestly didn't know what had happened, or he had excellent self-control.

"That was the order." I made a show of patting my pockets. "I've got the sheet around here somewhere if you want to take a look."

"What in the world did he do this time?" Freeman muttered, more to himself than to me.

"You didn't place the order for the Garvinville Peregrine perch?"

Freeman shook his head. "I have a standing account with Fox's—business lunches, catering, whatever. I order and they send me a bill. I'm a member of the Peregrines, and there was a committee meeting today—one of the few committees I'm not on, thank goodness—and they wanted it catered, so I told them to use my account and we'd settle up later. Are you telling me he didn't order any food?"

I explained that they'd ordered everything but the main dish, and suggested they might have been planning to prepare something on their own. I left out what the main dish had been, and how I helped it escape.

"Like I mentioned, it's not something we do every day," I said. "It's no problem, but I just wanted to be certain everything turned out right. Would you happen to know who actually made the order?"

"It was El Stamper. Eldridge Stamper. He's the head of the catering committee at the Peregrines." Freeman thought for a second. "I'm not sure whether I've got his number or not."

The name was enough for me. I told him not to bother, and that I'd contact Stamper through the Peregrines. He nodded and hurried past me into his warm, dry office. I went back to the car and drove off, hoping the rain wasn't getting into the electrical system.

4

The next evening, I chose my outfit carefully. I wanted something that said "friendly and normal," but also "not out of place at a Peregrine clabber tournament." Perhaps unfairly, I felt that the safe zone between those two descriptions was fairly narrow. I settled on a V-necked sweater with a white t-shirt underneath and a pair of jeans that were beginning to fray around the edges. I hadn't seen Uncle Willard all day, so I left a note on the kitchen table, then drove the few blocks to Peregrine perch 47.

I hadn't been able to dig up a membership directory on the Peregrine website, but I did learn that the Garvinville perch was number 47 in the national organization, and their event calendar showed they were having a monthly clabber tournament tonight. For those who don't know, clabber is a card game, supposedly German in origin, similar to things like whist and euchre. The game is hardly played anywhere else, so it's become a point of regional pride to keep it flourishing. I had learned to play it on Boy Scout campouts and still remembered the rules, but I doubted I'd be able to hold my own at a tournament. That was fine, because I didn't intend to do any actual playing. When I saw the tournament on their calendar, I realized that the building was going to be full of unfamiliar people, giving me the perfect chance to sneak around unnoticed.

Peregrine perch 47 was a sullen-looking brick box, nowhere near as grand as Garvinville's other Masonic-type lodges, set in the middle of a residential neighborhood filled with Federal and Italianate houses. I wondered what chain of circumstances led to it being built here. It looked to my eyes at least a hundred years old, so it may have gone up when Riverside was experiencing its downswing in the early part of the 20th century, when this wasn't such a desirable place to live anymore.

The parking lot was full, so I parked on the street. The perch was close enough that I could have walked, but I wanted the ability to get away quickly if I needed to. Three or four other people were climbing the steps of the narrow porch to get to the front door, and I followed along behind them. We entered into a vestibule opening out into a main hallway, and beyond that was a high-ceilinged room filled with dozens of circular tables. I paid my entrance fee to the potbellied guy in a Peregrines polo shirt, who sat at a side table with a metal cash box. He gave me a red ticket, said there would be a raffle for a propane grill at the end of the night, then asked me if I already had a card partner. When I replied in the negative, he pointed me down the hall to where a pair of Peregrines were filling out a large bracket with the names of all the participants and their table assignments. I went to go sign up.

The interior of the Peregrine perch was decorated with the Fantasy Turkish elements you sometimes see in fraternal organizations of a certain vintage. The walls were a dark Moroccan red, with occasional cracks and bubbles showing they were due for a touch-up and a repaint. Arabesque traceries surrounded the windows and the doorframes, and the patterned carpets on the tile floors were worn in the center where generations of foot traffic had gone through. A pair of brass chandeliers illuminated the hall with not quite enough light. My first impression of the place was that I liked it. It felt lived-in. Comfortable. I could see myself sitting in one of the high-backed navy blue wing chairs in the side rooms, smoking cigars and reading the paper. In all likelihood, the idea was probably more pleasant than the reality, since membership undoubtedly required serving on committees and helping out at fish fries. Still, though, the thought of a pleasantly run-down club with like-minded compatriots was undeniably attractive.

With an effort, I returned my attention to the present. I was here for a reason, and that reason was not to consider membership. It was not to play clabber, either. Sitting at a table all evening, watching my randomly-selected partner pretend not to be annoyed at how poorly I played cards, was not going to teach me anything. The sign-up table was beginning to get congested, as a set of players tried to help the Peregrines arrange the brackets so they could play opposite each other in the first round. Six people were working through the permutations with the aid of some scrap paper, and no one was paying particular attention to the new arrivals. I caught the attention of the woman behind me. She wore a red sweater and carried a notepad and set of pencils wrapped in a rubber band, giving the impression she was a clabber-night veteran.

"Excuse me, do you happen to know where the bathroom is?" I asked.

She pointed. "Around the corner and go left."

I thanked her and gave up my place in the line, edged around the table, and turned left. Of course, around the corner and to the left turned out to be the women's bathroom, but it didn't matter. I didn't care about bathrooms. All I cared about was getting out of sight and having a good reason for doing so, so that no one would think twice about me wandering off. This little hall had several doors, and another angle led to a stairway reaching up to the second floor and down to the basement. I tried to orient myself with what I remembered of the basement from yesterday, and I guessed the utility room where I had found the tailed woman was somewhere below me. I decided to start my investigations upstairs. If I started at the top floor and moved downward, toward the rest of the crowd, it would be easier to sell the idea that I'd accidentally gotten lost.

Halfway up the stairs, I paused for a moment to quiet my mind. It's hard to explain exactly what that means, since I'm not completely certain myself. It was one of the few things Uncle Willard had taken the time to impart before throwing me, so to speak, into the deep end of the supernatural pool. I took a deep breath and let it out, trying to relax my muscles and at the same time bring my mind into something I can only call a state of unfocused alertness. The idea was to make myself receptive to anything that might be reaching out. When it works, I'm more likely to notice things that aren't "right." This often includes any beings or powers that don't fit correctly into our regular world. It's hard to do, and even harder to describe, but it's possible to get better at it with practice.

I didn't notice anything. That wasn't too surprising. The problem with this technique is that you never really know if there's simply nothing to notice, or if you're not as receptive as you need to be. It's even harder when you're anticipating a hand on your shoulder at any moment and a brusque "Where do you think you're going?"

Upstairs was another maroon hallway, with dark varnished doors at intervals on either side. A series of framed photos lined the walls. They showed the membership of the club from its founding until now, documenting a century's worth of trends in facial hair. The last pair of doors at the end of the hall were much more elaborate than the others. They were painted gold, with bits flaking away at the corners. I tried the handles. They weren't locked, and that was as good as an invitation.

It was a rectangular room with rows of theater-style seating, facing a raised stage to my right. Overhead, the plaster had come down in a few places, and everything was caked in dust. Several scenic flats, dark with age, were stacked up at the back of the stage. They showed murky views of forests and rolling, riverine landscapes. The doors clicked shut behind me as I stepped inside to get a better look. Clearly, this room had been used for plays or concerts, or even operas, back when the building was new. Despite the neglect, it was still beautiful. I wondered who had been in the audience, and who had been in the cast. I thought about people dressing up on a Thursday night to come and see a traveling theater troupe performing Gilbert and Sullivan. Maybe they had even shown movies here as the popularity of that new-fangled invention grew. I could imagine an enthusiastic group of Peregrines refurbishing this place, then inviting people in once again, to take in a show and mingle with any ghosts who might be waiting expectantly for the footlights to go up again.

While I stood hypnotized with the possibility, there was the sound of movement from somewhere in the hall behind me. I heard voices, so I put my ear close to the door and tried to pick up whatever I could.

"—didn't say anything. So I imagine it isn't."

"I can't believe that. It's not the kind of thing that's just going to disappear."

"Disappear is exactly what it's going to do. Why wouldn't it?"

"How do you know?"

"Just stop talking about it, all right? It's fine. Trust me. I know more about this than you do."

"What about that guy?"

"Don't worry about him. He was just some idiot who opened the wrong door. He saved us the trouble of getting rid of her."

"Well, is he going to tell anybody?"

They had moved on down the hall by this point, and I couldn't hear any more. But I didn't need to. These were obviously a few of the Peregrines I had seen yesterday, the ones doing something a little more unusual than clabber tournaments and fund-raisers.

This was the first piece of information I'd picked up tonight, and it probably made me a little too enthusiastic to learn more. If I'd been smarter, I would have hesitated a few more seconds before opening the door. Even though I really wanted to see where they were going, I wasn't going to learn much more if they saw me snooping around.

Which was exactly what happened.

5

It turned out there was still one guy standing at the head of the stairs. He might have stopped at the leaded glass window to admire the view down Oak Street, or he might have had a premonition that something was amiss. But whatever the reason, when I swung the door open and popped my head out, there he was. He was wearing a Peregrines polo shirt, which suggested he might have had to deal with wayward guests before. I tried to play into this.

"Excuse me," I said, taking the initiative. Trespassers never take the initiative, but people who are lost do it all the time. I pointed over my shoulder to the auditorium. "I'm pretty sure this isn't the bathroom," I said.

He nodded. "Down those stairs behind you and it should be on your right when you get to the bottom." He crossed the hall to join me, a tall guy with angular features and those squarish glasses with indestructible translucent frames, the kind that always makes their wearers look a bit like serial killers. His hair was cut short and combed over on top. "Here, let me show you. Did somebody tell you to go up this way?"

"I thought I knew my way around enough to take a shortcut, but I must have outsmarted myself," I said.

A voice called from down the other stairs. "Hey! You still up there?" Two more Peregrines appeared a moment later, looking for their missing member. One was a younger guy with a thin, scruffy beard that would have raised snorts of derision from any number of his Peregrine ancestors, and the other was heavyset and squinty, with a gym teacher's build.

That one I recognized. He was the guy who had led the pursuit yesterday, red with rage and waving his butcher knife, when the tailed woman and I escaped.

"Hang on, El," said Serial Killer Glasses. "This guy's lost. I'm going to walk him down the other stairs."

"Well, don't take too—" The big guy stopped. His attention had moved from his buddy to me. He peered at me for a moment, then his eyes got wide, and I knew he recognized me. At the same time, though, I was having a realization of

26

my own. Serial Killer Glasses had just called him "El," which was the same name that Rick Freeman had given me. The big guy was Eldridge Stamper, the one who put in the order at Fox's Barbecue. If anyone was going to know who the tailed woman was, where she came from, and why she was there, it was him.

Stamper's steps got faster as he got closer. "Who are you?" he asked me.

"You know," I said, "I think I can find my way from here now. Thanks anyway for your help."

I stepped behind Serial Killer Glasses, to put him between me and Stamper, then hustled to the end of the hall, where the other set of stairs was hidden in an alcove. I moved as quickly as I could without breaking into full-on flight. Mentally, I was kicking myself. I should have known someone might recognize me. The worst part was that there was a perfectly serviceable fake mustache in my desk drawer, just waiting for an occasion like this. If only I had remembered.

Behind me, Stamper and the two others were gaining ground. When I looked over my shoulder, Stamper's face was a startling mask of fury. Now, it's not unusual for me to annoy people. Even when you do your best to keep things pleasant, there are occasions where the landlord's henchman is going to get on people's nerves. But I don't think I've ever seen an expression like the one Eldridge Stamper wore as he rumbled down the stairs. His face was an unhealthy beet-red color, and his eyes and mouth were pinched into slits. He was so angry that I could feel it coming off of him like waves of heat. It was the kind of anger that makes people suddenly snap and commit murder over a parking space. That's what seemed to be the end point here: murder. Eldridge Stamper wanted me dead.

At the bottom of the stairs I skidded around the corner and quickly returned to the main hall. From there, I hurried into the ballroom where the card tables had been set up. Obviously, I wasn't going to be playing any clabber tonight, but a public location would give me a chance to extend the distance between my pursuers and me. None of us wanted to start running and attract attention to ourselves, but I gambled I could power-walk through the crowded room faster than the others could. I dodged the card players who were kibitzing before the first round began, and sidestepped the Peregrines who patrolled the floor with carts of drinks and snacks for sale. To my right was a small elevator, which I disregarded as much too sluggish for the present situation. Instead, I threw open the door to the stairs beside it. My shaky mental map suggested it led to the basement. From there I could escape past the kitchen and out the back door of the cinderblock extension. I hurried down these stairs, the soles of my shoes scuffing on the sandpapery anti-slip strips. For a second, there was no sound of pursuit, and I wondered if Stamper had given up the chase or been diverted by his fellow Peregrines.

There was a moment of mirror-image deja vu as I burst into the same room as yesterday, only from the opposite side. I half expected to see myself coming through the other door, leading a stoic, naked, tailed woman by the wrist. No one else was around, and I hurried to the hall that led to the exit. Over the sounds of scraping chairs and general hubbub overhead, I thought I heard a door opening somewhere close by, but I knew I could now outpace any pursuers and make it outside before they caught up. I was just at the bend in the hall when a shape emerged from around the corner, blocking my path. It was Stamper.

"Gotcha," he sneered.

His assistants raced up behind me. One of them grabbed my arms and pinned them behind my back.

"There's a lot of stairs in this place. It's easy to get around in a hurry," Stamper said. Catching me had cooled his white-hot fury a bit. He was somewhere in his fifties, with gray hair cut so short it seemed to merge into the skin. I didn't see a wedding ring or any other jewelry, and he wore an old pair of scuffed loafers with a broken stitch on one corner. Always pay attention to shoes. A pair of shoes will tell you more about someone's character than half an hour of observation.

Stamper nodded to the others, then jerked his head toward the kitchen door. "Take him in there."

The guy with the patchy beard flipped through a massive key ring until he found the one that opened the kitchen door, then they hustled me inside.

"Is this what you do to everyone who can't find the bathroom?" I asked Stamper. "I mean, obviously, it's your club, so you do whatever feels right, but I can't imagine this leads to a lot of new membership applications."

"Shut up." Stamper waved a chunky finger in my face. "Just shut the fuck up."

They backed me farther into the kitchen. Serial Killer Glasses now had me in a hammerlock, while Patchy Beard held onto my free arm. By the time we stopped, Serial Killer Glasses was leaning against the black iron industrial stove. I wondered how hard I would have to shove to get him to bump into the burner knobs and possibly turn some of them on.

"If you don't want that arm broken, you better talk," Stamper said.

"About anything in particular?"

"What's your name, smartass?"

"Samuel van Hoogstraten."

"What are you doing here?"

"I thought it would be fun to play some clabber. I've got to be honest, though, I'm starting to have second thoughts."

Stamper seethed. His mental gears turned for a moment, then he pistoned his arm back and delivered a quick, solid punch to my midsection.

"Still funny?" he asked. "Still want to make jokes?"

"Give me a minute," I gasped. I hadn't expected him to get to the actual violence quite yet, and it had taken me by surprise. The lesson here, I guess, is to start preparing myself as soon as I get dragged out of sight.

Stamper sneered at me while I got my breath back. When I could speak normally again, I said, "All right, you're going to have to help me out here. What do you want from me?"

"What the hell were you doing here yesterday?"

"Dropping off a bunch of stuff from Fox's," I said. "I was trying to do a favor for my buddy. But at this point, I think I probably should have just let his call go to voicemail."

Another punch. That one hurt quite a bit. Stamper may have looked like a square, angry lump, but there was a lot of muscle in there. This is where having been beaten up before comes in handy. You realize that, as unpleasant as this is, you're not actually going to die. Knowing that helps you keep your head. It helps a little, anyway.

"The girl, smartass."

"She wasn't a girl."

"Whatever the fuck she was. The monster. The spirit. Why'd you let her loose?"

"Why'd you have her tied up?"

Another punch.

"Look, if you guys have got something you don't want people to see, maybe you should lock the door next time," I said. "Or even have somebody stand guard. I don't want to be too rude here, but this isn't rocket science."

Patchy Beard shot a pointed look over my shoulder. Based on what I'd heard in the hall upstairs, I suspected this was a wordless rebuke directed at Serial Killer Glasses or Stamper.

"Where is she?" Stamper asked me. "Why'd you take her?"

I cleared my throat. "I think we got off on the wrong foot here. There's no need for any of this. Let me talk to your Head Bird, or whatever you call him, and we'll get it all straightened out. If it's not a problem for him, it's not a problem for me."

Another round of wordless rebukes flashed between the three of them. I could tell what they were trying to communicate. None of them liked the idea of me talking to the Peregrine leadership about yesterday's interrupted lunch. Why was that? Most likely it was because the Peregrine leadership didn't know about it. That meant the whole club wasn't a nest of rampaging semi-cannibals. Instead, Stamper and his assistants were probably using the Peregrine perch as a convenient place to do the things they didn't necessarily want to do in their own homes. They were the only ones who knew about it. And now I did as well. That, unfortunately, was a problem.

It didn't feel like Serial Killer Glasses and Patchy Beard were holding me as securely as they had been a few minutes ago. I wasn't struggling anymore, and they might have gotten distracted. It was just about time to see if I could knock them off balance and make another run for the exit. But even if I did slip loose from them, I was still going to have to get past Stamper. There wasn't much space to work with, but he didn't look too quick. It was probably worth a try. It was definitely better than letting him continue to punch me.

"You just answer my questions," Stamper said to me. "Where'd the girl go?"

"I don't know. I let her out of the car and she disappeared."

"Disappeared for real?" asked Serial Killer Glasses, from behind my left shoulder. His hammerlock had loosened again, to the point where it now felt like he was supporting me rather than restraining me. He could tighten it back up in an instant, but maybe I was fast enough to get free.

"All right. Have it your way," Stamper said. His eyes got even more narrow and piglike. He yanked open a counter drawer, revealing a disordered row of utensils and cutlery. I flexed my knees. It was almost time.

"Give me his hand," Stamper ordered.

"Is everything all right in here?"

We all froze, like rampaging grade-school kids when the teacher returns unexpectedly to the classroom. A man stood in the kitchen doorway with one hand on the knob. He was on the young side of thirty and the short side of average height, with neatly brushed brown hair, a Peregrines polo shirt, and an expression of shocked embarrassment.

Serial Killer Glasses and Patchy Beard immediately let go of me and made awkward efforts to look innocent. Stamper shuffled a step forward to block the newcomer's view of the knife drawer, then cautiously slid it closed with one oversized buttock.

"Just a little discussion," Stamper said to the newcomer. "Nothing to be concerned about."

"Are you sure?" the new guy obviously wasn't certain whether he should be interfering with this or minding his own business. Before he had a chance to change his mind and excuse himself, I decided to pull him into the conversation. "It's no big deal," I said, theatrically straightening my disordered sweater. "The truth is, Egbert here—"

"Eldridge," said Stamper.

"Eldridge was dating my sister. She broke it off, and Eldridge wanted to know if there was anything he could do to get her back. Now, naturally, my sister had a pretty long list of things she didn't like about him. A lot of them aren't correctable without psychological counseling and fairly extensive plastic surgery, but there were a few smaller items on the list. The ones relating to toothpaste and soap, for example, could have been knocked out pretty easily, but I don't think those by themselves would have gotten him back in the running. I told him so, and he took it poorly."

Stamper glared at me. He was wishing he had hit me harder when he'd had the chance, or maybe even gone straight for the knife. Then he backed off, detoured around the new arrival, and left the room. His minions followed, and I heard their footsteps moving away toward the front stairs.

"Well," I said to the remaining Peregrine, "I just stopped by to return my sister's engagement ring, so I suppose I'll be going. Good luck with the clabber tournament."

The Peregrine didn't get out of my way. Instead, he scrutinized me for a long second, as if he couldn't quite believe I was really there. This is a response I've run into more than once, and I knew it would pass sooner or later. I gave it time.

Eventually, he recovered the power of speech. "What in the world just happened?" he asked.

6

I was craving fresh air, so we slipped out the back door and stood under the eaves of the main building, where the mist and the sodium lights made all the parked cars gleam. He handed me a card. It read, "Oliver Helfrich, International Order of Peregrines, Regional Membership Coordinator."

"Call me Ollie." He had an air of clean-cut wholesome authority. I imagined that, aside from working for the Peregrines, he probably coached little-league baseball and served as an assistant scoutmaster somewhere. He had a strong handshake, and he bent a couple of his fingers at an odd angle as he did so. I assumed this was half of some secret Peregrine handshake that I didn't know the response to.

"Can I ask you a question?"

"Ask away." I said.

"That story about your sister? That was bogus, right?"

I nodded. "Well, I suppose the most direct answer is 'yes.' I made it all up. However, if I did have a sister, and if she, through some horrible mischance, had actually dated Eldridge Stamper, I'm sure she would have behaved exactly as I described."

This prompted another stare from him, a mixture of curiosity and fear. He was trying to work out where to place me on the scale stretching from "eccentric" to "insane," and he couldn't make up his mind. I didn't think he lived in a world where he got a lot of practice at this kind of thing.

"It's all right. There's nothing to worry about," I said, taking pity on him.

"What was going on back there? You were having some kind of argument with those guys, weren't you?"

"Just a discussion. I wanted to find something out, and I think they got a little annoyed at my answers."

Ollie thought about this. I could see the wheels turning in his mind as he worked through what this might mean. "Are you a private investigator?" he asked.

"You could say that."

"Are you investigating one of the Peregrines?" he asked.

I hesitated, searching for a polite way to decline to answer.

"Oh, jeez. You *are* investigating a Peregrine, aren't you? It's okay, you can tell me."

"Don't worry about it," I said.

"Seriously, it's all right. I'm investigating, too."

Now it was my turn to look surprised.

"I'm from the Peregrine central perch. I've been doing a bunch of routine meet-and-greets with all the new officers in the region, taking a quick look at the records and the books, but the central perch wanted me to pay special attention to perch 47 here." Ollie gestured toward the building. "They're concerned about some financial irregularities."

For a moment I wondered if Eldridge Stamper might have purchased the tailed woman with the Peregrines' credit card. And if so, from where?

"This happens every once in a while," Ollie explained. "It's almost always bad accounting, not actual fraud. But the central perch wanted me to go over the numbers while I was here." He reached into his pocket and pulled out a package of Doublemint gum. He offered the pack to me, I declined, then he unwrapped a stick and began to chew. "Man, I really hope it's bad accounting. This is my first trip, and I want things to go smoothly. I'd really love not to have any problems this time."

"So when you walked past the kitchen and saw the discussion we were having . . ."

"Yeah, I freaked out a little," Ollie said. "I had just put some papers in my car and was on the way back upstairs when I saw you all in there. I thought about ignoring it, but I couldn't, you know? It's not the Peregrine way. If you see a problem and you walk on by, what kind of a person are you?"

"According to my uncle, a sane person. But I understand what you're saying. Sometimes, you've just got to see what's going on." I paused for a second, then decided to keep talking. "Since we're here for the same reasons, more or less, I might as well let you know that Eldridge Stamper was the one I was interested in."

Ollie made a non-committal grimace. "I don't have a firm grip on all the names and faces yet. He was the big guy, right?"

"Yeah. The one who was going for the knife."

Ollie's eyes got wide. "The what?"

"Forget about it. But if you run across anything about Stamper that seems weird, I'd love to hear it." I gave him one of the cards I keep in my wallet, the cards that only have my name and phone number on them. He wouldn't have been impressed by my "property manager" card, and no one takes you seriously if your card says "occult investigator."

"Okay." Ollie pocketed the card. "I'm staying at the Executive Inn for a few days, meeting with all the committees and looking over the records. If anything comes up, I'll let you know."

"Thanks. And if I hear anything about Stamper skimming money from the Peregrines, I'll do the same."

"It's probably nothing," Ollie said. "Hundred to one chance. I hope."

"Probably so," I said.

It was nice to stand out here in the cool evening air, away from all the hubbub and attempted battery inside. The Peregrines' lot was bordered on three sides by tall rows of shrubbery. They were mature, thick-trunked bushes, probably planted at the same time the perch had been built. There were occasional thin spots where an old bush had died and its replacement hadn't yet formed a firm mesh with the others.

It was in one of these thin spots, near where the corner of the main brick building met the cinderblock extension, that I saw movement. I glanced over at Ollie to see if he had noticed anything, but he was looking up at the roofline. I casually turned my head away, but kept watch out of the corner of my eye. I stretched, then suggested it was time for me to go.

We shook hands and I ambled off into the parking lot. I stopped to tie my shoe, giving Ollie plenty of time to get back inside. Once he was gone, I turned on my heel and walked casually around to the corner of the building. The first thing I discovered was that the grass was damper than I anticipated, and my vintage Jarmans weren't remotely watertight. But I was willing to put up with wet feet to see who was lurking in the shadows around the Peregrine perch. Was it a clabber player, distraught at having been knocked out in the first round? Was it one of Stamper's henchmen, waiting for me to stupidly blunder into danger again? Or was it someone else? Possibly someone with a tail?

I stopped near where I had seen the movement. From here, a thin path snaked between the perch and the yard of the house next door. I made a show of searching my pockets, as if checking for cigarettes or my phone. As I did this, I scanned the darkness one more time. Even though I couldn't see anyone, I knew I wasn't alone. This didn't come from any special psychic training, but rather the ordinary sensitivity that wakes you up when someone's staring at you, or makes you uncomfortable when a person stands right behind you.

It was time to see if I could shake anything loose. I folded my arms and said, "We can do this however you want. Do you want to come out and talk, or do you want me to find you?"

At first, there was nothing but silence. After a few seconds, I heard a rustle. It sounded like someone in a cramped position trying to unwind themselves as silently as possible. I took a step toward the sound and my foot came down on a fallen stick, which split with a sharp crack. Suddenly, there was a burst of motion and a wild flailing of branches, and a shape crashed through the bushes to my left.

It was a person—male, tall and skinny—with a baggy dark coat on. He ran away from me, his feet slipping on fallen leaves and conifer needles until he got some traction. I followed. In addition to waterlogging my shoes, I was going to get plant bits all over one of my best sweaters, but there was no avoiding it now. He broke through the bushes and into the back yard of the house next door, then leaped over the brick retaining wall with his coat flapping behind him like a pair of ragged crow's wings. Luckily, the house was dark and there was no one to raise the alarm as I gave chase.

I followed him down the small alley behind the house, then he turned on Lime Street and headed in the direction of the river. Rather than keeping to the sidewalk, he ran down the center of the street. Lime Street is still paved with its original bricks, which makes it picturesque as hell and the pride of the city's preservation community, but it's also wildly uneven and difficult to run on without stumbling and tripping. I kept expecting the guy to catch the toe of his Chuck Taylors and faceplant onto the bricks, but he was more nimble than I expected. We turned another couple of corners, making a big loop that would lead us back to the Peregrine perch eventually. He wasn't fast enough to outrun me and I wasn't fast enough to catch up to him. However, I was starting to feel the effects of Stamper's punches and was about ready to consider giving up the chase when he stopped short and spun around to face me.

Thanks to the glow of the streetlight overhead, I was finally able to get a good look at him. He was about six feet tall and somewhere in his early twenties, with dark hair and a long beard. It was one of those soft, fluffy beards that paradoxically made its owner look even younger than if he were clean-shaven. The massively bearded early Peregrines from the second-floor photos would have been proud of the attempt, though. He wore a yellow t-shirt under his long coat, with a complex design screen-printed on it in black. With a sudden flash of surprise, like turning down the aisle of a grocery store and unexpectedly seeing someone you know, I recognized the design. It was the Raback Seal.

The Raback Seal is a circle crisscrossed with various lines and symbols. It was found carved into the basement wall of a manor house in Sweden, where a notorious alchemist had lived during the Middle Ages. No one knows exactly who carved it or why, but the seal turns up in a few old books on alchemy and demonology. I'd seen it once or twice while I was doing research, but didn't think it had crossed over far enough into popular culture for someone to make a shirt out of it. He must have noticed me staring, because he shrugged his coat closed while watching me with nervous eyes.

"You don't have to run," I panted. "I just want to talk."

Instead of responding, he threw out his hands, palms upraised, in my direction. This caught me by surprise and I stumbled backward, but nothing happened. From his posture, I could tell he was just as surprised as I was. Clearly, he had been expecting something. He looked down at his hands for an instant, then back over to me, then turned to start running again.

A car horn beeped close behind me and I jumped onto the sidewalk. A dark sedan approached and the window slid down, revealing the driver. It was Mrs. Bates, who lived across the alley from Uncle Willard and me. She and Willard had bonded over shared interest in backyard gardening, and I think she has a slightly maternal concern for the two of us "rattling around in that big house all alone." By the time I assured her I was doing fine, didn't need a ride, and was not (as she probably suspected) staggering into the street under the influence of strong drink, the guy with the Raback shirt had gotten away. I stood there a few more minutes to catch my breath, then walked back to the Peregrine perch to retrieve my car.

7

The next morning, as I buttered an English muffin and waited for the coffee to brew, I shifted from one foot to the other, testing my midsection for signs of soreness. Fortunately, it wasn't too bad at all. In another day or two, it would probably be gone entirely. I felt a little tender in a few spots, but it wasn't nearly enough to keep me from doing what I needed to do today. The first thing on my list was to find out who the bearded man in the bushes had been. It wasn't impossible that he was just some dude who liked to look through windows, but I doubted it was that simple. My mind kept returning to the design on his t-shirt. Last night, while I was at the Peregrine perch trying to learn about a mysterious and supernatural situation, I stumbled across someone staking out the same building, with a mysterious and supernatural design on his shirt. That seemed like an awfully large coincidence. I took a bite of muffin and considered the possibilities. If I spent a week tracking this guy down, only to discover that he was in some obscure local band that had adopted the Raback Seal as their symbol, I could at least buy one of their records and brag to people that I knew about them before everybody else.

I heard heavy steps descending the stairs and Uncle Willard lumbered into the kitchen. He was wearing his plaid pajamas, topped by a purple bathrobe of considerable sentimental value and an equal degree of actual hideousness. His hair stuck up at angles, as if he'd just suffered an electrical accident while wiring one of his little railroad junctions.

"Dean!" he said.

"Good morning. Care for some breakfast?"

Uncle Willard shook his head. "You seemed to be moving around with a purpose this morning, so I wanted to catch you before you left."

"Mission accomplished."

Willard, despite his refusal, was still eyeing the second half of my muffin, so I handed it to him and poured two cups of coffee. He made an effort to straighten his hair before accepting.

"Huldra," he said, after a sip.

"What was that?"

"Huldra. That's what I wanted to tell you. I believe that's the kind of creature you freed on Saturday. It's described in Scandinavian folklore. It often takes the form of a beautiful woman with a tail. They're said to seduce and abduct virtuous woodcutters, which exempts you on several counts. In the literature, they often have backs that show tree bark, or are even completely hollow. Did you happen to get a look at her back?"

"I did. I noticed no flaws of any kind."

Willard frowned. "Well, I still think the identification is sound. This may be some variation on the type."

"Thanks." It was useful to know what kind of creature she was. Calling her a "huldra" wasn't, on the surface, much different than calling her a "woman with a tail," but to name something is the first step toward understanding it.

"How was it bound?" he asked.

"I thought I told you that. She was tied to the table. Regular old nylon cord, I think. The kind of stuff you get at the hardware store."

"That's not what I mean. Mortal rope wouldn't have held it there any more than a net would contain a ghost. Someone must have had power over it, to bind it in place like that." He paused. "Unless it was there willingly. The appearance of helplessness is a powerful weapon."

"Those are some of the things I'm trying to find out," I said. "I'd like to know who brought her here, and why, and what they wanted with her—"

"It," Willard said. "Call it an 'it.' If you keep thinking of it as a 'her,' you're going to put yourself at risk."

I told him I'd take that under advisement. I finished my toast and drained the last of my coffee, then washed the mugs and plates in the sink. Having delivered his information and his warning, Willard rose and returned to his lair. I grabbed my mauve corduroy jacket off the hook and went out to start gathering information.

My first stop was a split-level corner strip mall on the other side of town. It contained an accountant's office, a travel agency, and a number of other small firms, including The Crystal Heart, a new age shop I visited occasionally.

This, however, was not today's destination. The storefront next to The Crystal Heart had a large, multicolored sign reading "Knit Now—Knitting and Crochet Supplies," and that was the door I opened.

The interior of Knit Now was a comfortable jumble of yarn balls in wicker baskets, various textiles hanging from wooden racks, finished pieces for sale on consignment, and pegboards along the walls holding every variety of tool a knitting enthusiast could imagine. The woman at the counter, knitting what looked like an elaborate black cardigan, looked up at me as I entered. She was on the short side, with a lot of dark hair. She wore a scoop-necked white shirt and a motorcycle jacket. Her makeup was striking, though perhaps a bit strong for a yarn shop first thing in the morning.

"Hello," I said as I approached the counter. "Is Dennis around?"

She shook her head. "Sorry. Dennis isn't in this week. Is there something I can help you with?"

"Maybe you can," I said. She was pretty, a few years older than me, with a sort of throwback pin-up model quality. Minus the bulky motorcycle jacket, I imagined she'd be stunning. A quantity of rings armored her fingers, from simple silver bands to thick, chunky handmade copper pieces. One ring held a tiny blue glass eye that floated in its mounting and looked up at me when she set aside her knitting.

"A while ago I saw someone with a design on his shirt that really caught my eye. I'm trying to figure out where I could buy one just like it." I took out a half sheet of paper and unfolded it on the counter. It was a quick sketch I had made of the Raback Seal, copied from one of Uncle Willard's books. I had kept it simple, to make it look like I had drawn it from memory, but it had enough detail for someone in the know to recognize it for what it was.

On the surface, this seems like a strange thing to hope that someone at a yarn shop might recognize, but there was a reason I was here. Knit Now, along with The Crystal Heart next door, were both owned by Dennis Falco. The shops shared a connecting door, as well as access to a shared storage room. That room doubled as a meeting place and library for Dennis's "reading group," a circle of like-minded friends who were all very interested in exploring the hidden corners of the unseen world. For the most part, they were simply people with a genuine curiosity, amateur scholars and researchers, not given to much in the way of practical experimentation. Some of them, if they happened to need a job, would end up at Knit Now, which let them be close to Dennis's impressive library without ever having to deal with the hoi polloi at The Crystal Heart. This was why I started here. I had a feeling that someone in Dennis's reading group might have an idea about who could be skulking around with an obscure alchemical symbol on his shirt.

The woman studied my sketch with a show of attention, moving her hands under the counter as she did so. She did it casually, but she hadn't been quite fast enough. One of the rings on her right hand had held a large enamel disc covered by a clear dome. The disc had displayed a circle crisscrossed with various lines and symbols. I only saw it for a split second, so I couldn't have sworn it was the Raback Seal, but it had been strikingly similar. And she had hidden it from me as soon as I showed her my drawing of the seal, which felt like a confirmation.

"If Dennis doesn't know about this, I bet one of his friends from the reading group probably does," I said. "After all, the Raback Seal isn't something you see every day, and I'd really like to know where that shirt came from. If somebody's made up a batch, I'd be happy to buy one."

She didn't seem impressed that I knew about Dennis's reading group, or that I knew the seal's proper name. "Does Dennis know how to reach you?" she asked.

"He ought to. My name's Dean Sherwood. He knows me."

"Just to be sure, would you mind writing down your number?" Her hands appeared from under the counter again. This time she was holding an index card and a marker, and the ring with the seal was gone.

I took the fat purple marker and dutifully wrote my name and number on the card, then pushed them back across to the woman. She covered the pen with the card and smiled up at me. "I'll let him know when he gets back, but it may not be for a few days. He's in Fort Wayne until Friday."

I made one last attempt. "You're sure you haven't seen anything like this?"

"Sorry."

I tended to habitually take good-looking women at their word, but this time I had my doubts. "Thanks for your help," I said. "I'll ask around with the rest of the reading group. I thought I'd start with Dennis, but if he's out of town I'll take what I can get."

"Hang on." She picked up my sketch again and examined it one more time. She pursed her fire-engine red lips as she turned the paper upside down and cocked her head. "You know, maybe I was wrong. I kind of think I remember this. The old guy has a shirt like this."

"The old guy?"

"Yeah. He's been at the group a couple of times." She made a show of thinking hard. "Yeah, I'm pretty sure that's the same thing."

"This old guy, what did he look like?"

"Gee, I don't know. Just a guy, I guess. It's hard to describe someone."

"Was he tall or short? Heavy or thin? Did he have a beard?"

"Not tall, but not really short, either. About your height, more or less. Kind of stocky. Chunky, you know. Not really fat, but . . ."

"Beefy?" I suggested.

"Yeah, that's it. Beefy."

"And the beard?"

"No beard. His hair was really short, too."

"You said he was old. How old did you have in mind? Are we talking about someone in his fifties, or closer to eighty?"

"Not super old. Fifties, I guess, but I couldn't say for sure."

"You wouldn't happen to know his name, would you?"

She shook her head. "He just shows up at the group every once in a while. Usually he sits in the back and listens when someone else gives a talk. He takes a bunch of notes and that's all."

"But you said he had a shirt with the Raback Seal on it?"

"Yeah, I think so. I'm sure he could tell you where he got it."

I took the paper with the sketch, folded it up again, then returned it to my notebook. "Would you recognize him if I showed you a picture?"

She thought about this for a second. "Yeah, probably so. Do you have one?"

"Not yet, but I'll see if I can dig one up. I might as well make sure we're talking about the same guy before I go bugging him about shirts."

She picked up her knitting again and started working the needles. I thanked her one more time and left the shop. I had parked out of sight of Knit Now's door, so I was able to sit and think for a while without making the woman suspicious. That was good, because I had a lot to think about. Pieces of information were buzzing around in my mind like a swarm of confused and angry bees. I needed to calm the bees down and get them to work for me, taking the raw pollen of facts and producing the sweet honey of knowledge.

First of all, the woman at Knit Now had obviously been lying. She knew about the Raback Seal and she didn't want me to know that she knew. Why was that? Probably because she knew who had been wearing the shirt, but didn't want to tell me. The man she described as "the old guy" was clearly not the person I'd chased through the streets last night. She had described someone nearly the complete opposite of the man in the baggy coat. It was possible she had made up a description at random, just to throw me off, but I didn't think so. It had been a little too specific, like she had someone in mind who she was trying to steer me towards. That possibility made me very curious, because her description of "the old guy" felt like a close match for Eldridge Stamper.

8

I left the strip mall and went back toward the center of town, taking Lincoln Avenue instead of Boheim this time. I never drive to and from a place by the same route if I can help it. This is either a charming quirk or a weird superstition, but I've done it ever since I was old enough to drive. Downtown, I passed the shiny new civic center and the pair of historic hotels that had been fitted with skybridges to connect them to the new structure. The design of the skybridges, with exposed girders and vast sheets of reflective glass, had been an attempt to fuse the aesthetics of the old hotels with the aesthetics of the civic center. In my mind, it wasn't particularly successful. Pecan pie is great on its own, and spaghetti diavolo is great on its own, but if you try to fuse them together the only person you end up making happy is the gastroenterologist.

I parked at a meter and walked the half-block to the Executive Inn's revolving doors. It was the younger of the two hotels, and had reached its final form somewhere in the 1970s. This was where Ollie Helfrich had mentioned he was staying, and Ollie was the person I wanted to talk to. It was now close to eleven o'clock in the morning, and there was no guarantee he was still in the hotel, but I always enjoyed taking a look at the place, so I decided to chance it.

The lobby was all dark carpets and brass and a large array of well-maintained artificial plants. It had its own sort of fusty charm, even though I kept expecting to see leisure suits on the staff and hear Captain & Tennille over the lobby sound system. I nodded hello to the front desk guy and slipped behind a screen of simulated elephant ear plants to make a call.

Ollie picked up before the second ring.

"Hey, it's Dean Sherwood. We met yesterday at the Peregrine perch. Do you mind if I ask you a couple of questions?"

"No problem. Happy to help. You know, I thought that was you. Come on over."

"Pardon me?"

"Oh. You don't see me, do you?" Ollie said. "Look to your left."

One end of the lobby contained a little glassed-in cafe, with a handful of Formica tables and a polished wood counter. Ollie Helfrich was sitting at a table, and he waved when I turned in his direction. He had his laptop open and a plate next to him with a half-eaten club sandwich and a dwindling pile of chips. At his prompting, I sat down.

"Nice to see you again, Dean. Can I get you anything?"

I asked for coffee. Ollie caught the eye of the waitress and made a "two, please" sign with his coffee cup.

"I love this place," Ollie said. "Don't tell anybody I said this, but I'm kind of happy the accounting for perch 47 is all screwed up. I'd be happy to stay here for a month."

As cozy as the Executive Inn was, I couldn't imagine anyone but a historian of patterned carpets finding that much to love about it. I considered myself one of the building's biggest fans, and an occasional five-minute soak in the atmosphere was more than enough for me.

"Look around." Ollie gestured to the rest of the cafe, empty except for the waitress, then out toward the lobby. "No TVs. Nobody's mounted a TV anywhere. I've been on the road for just about a month now, and I can't tell you how nice this is. There's no screen flashing at you, trying to get your attention all the time. It's restful. My room is even nice. It's up on the fourth floor, right at the end of the hall. I can see all the way to the river."

The waitress came with a cup for me and a refill for Ollie. The coffee was fine. It was a change from Planet Caravan, my regular coffee place, where you could taste the bohemianism seeping in from the dishware like residual cinnamon, but there was nothing wrong with it. It was a solid, unadorned cup of well-made coffee. Just right. I stirred cream and sugar into it and asked him how his investigation was going.

"Not too bad at all, really," Ollie said. "The finances are a mess, but they're not *that* much more of a mess than anywhere else. A lot of these perches, they're run by guys without much experience. Money's coming in from different places, money's going out to different places. Sometimes the guys keep records, sometimes they don't. It can be overwhelming if you don't know enough to keep on top of it.

Once people get overwhelmed, they kind of give up and let the money take care of itself, which it hardly ever does. That's when the problems come in."

"Do you get the feeling someone's doing something dishonest here?"

Ollie crunched a chip and considered his answer. "Doubt it. I haven't seen anything to make me super concerned yet, anyway. You can never tell until you get most of the threads unwound, but nothing's jumping out at me, thank goodness." He indicated the spreadsheet on his laptop and the pile of papers on the table. The papers were bank statements and invoices, many of them covered with annotations and arrows in various hands, and a generous dusting of sticky notes.

"The central perch keeps floating the idea of handling the finances for all the perches, to make sure there's an actual accountant watching all the money, not just somebody who couldn't get out of serving on a committee. But it never gets anywhere."

"Why's that?"

He shrugged. "Because it's never been done that way before. Because the perches don't want to give up their independence. Because some of the central board members don't want the responsibility. Same old thing." He shook his head wryly, like an elementary school teacher being patient with a wayward student. "But I don't want to complain. The Peregrines do a great job in their communities, and if their finances cause a few little headaches, that's not the worst thing in the world. Are you a member?"

"Afraid not."

"If you think about it, let me know. I can sponsor you. We're always looking for good people." He moved his papers out of the way. "Now, what can I help you with?"

"Eldridge Stamper," I said. "Do you have a membership file or some kind of directory that has his picture?"

"I think so." Ollie went back to the computer and brought up a page on the main Peregrine web site. He entered a password and we entered some sort of electronic backstage area.

"There's a get-to-know-the-members section on the Peregrine website," Ollie explained. "New members can log in and see who else is enrolled in their perch. It's usually got pictures of everybody. For some reason, the perches are more than happy to let us run a central website for them. Maybe they can see the economies of scale better with this kind of thing. Maybe they're just not interested in becoming web gurus. Anyway, we should be able to take a look in here." He tapped some buttons and the square face of Eldridge Stamper appeared.

I took a picture of the screen with my phone. "Thanks. I didn't have a picture of him, and I don't think he would hold still if I tried to take one."

"Any chance you could tell me what you're investigating?" Ollie asked. "I'm really curious."

I made a thoughtful face for a second, gazing at the distant plants in the lobby. As a man would when considering which secrets to reveal. "I hate to tell you this, but I think he may have been using the Peregrine perch for something . . . Well, something the head office wouldn't have approved of. He and his buddies may have been getting up to some shenanigans with someone who shouldn't have been there."

This was, in broad strokes, true. It was also about as specific as I could be while still staying within the bounds of normal, everyday reality. If I had come out and said, "You know what, Ollie? Stamper and some of his friends captured a mythical creature and were planning to butcher her and eat her with barbecue sauce in the basement of the Peregrine perch," he would have written me off as a lunatic. It takes people a while to wrap their heads around things like unseen creatures, mystical forces, and a whole new set of rules they've never even imagined before. For their sake, and for my sanity, it makes a lot more sense to paraphrase things whenever I can.

Even my vague description, though, made Ollie's eyes get wide and I remembered that paraphrasing had a downside of its own. If you give someone a nebulous answer and say, "I can't tell you any more," your listener is going to fill in all the details with the most lurid things they can think of. It's human nature. If you let your imagination run wild, you're always going to come up with something much more shocking than the actual truth.

"He was doing this *in* the perch?" Ollie gave a quick, resigned sigh, then straightened up and set his jaw. "So this is my problem, too. Or it will be, if anybody finds out. What can I do to help?"

I held up my phone, which had the photo of Stamper. "I'm going to run this picture past someone, just to verify that Stamper's the person I think he is. In the meantime, see what you can find out about him. I don't know what we're going to need yet, so anything you turn up might be useful. Where he works, who his friends are in the Peregrines, what his hobbies are, anything you've got in the files or whatever anyone happens to mention. Don't be too obvious when you ask around, though. We don't want word to get back to him. I'll be in touch soon, and then we can put together what we know. From there, we'll try to take care of this quietly. There's no need to embarrass anybody."

"Thanks for saying that." Ollie sounded relieved. "I was just imagining what would happen when the news people found out about it. People always think the worst these days. I'd hate for this to hurt the Peregrines' reputation."

I stood up. "Reputations aren't the only things that can get hurt. Be careful, Ollie. I'm serious about that."

"Is he really dangerous?"

"That probably depends on who you are and what you're doing. But he's a violent guy. We know that already. Don't take any risks."

Ollie nodded and finished off his chips. He didn't say anything more, but his expression wasn't hard to read. He was shocked to be involved with something like this, but now that he was part of a clandestine investigation, he was also just the tiniest bit excited.

9

I sat on a bench around the corner from the Executive Inn and got out my phone. Behind me, the skinny little maples planted in the decorative border rustled their leaves. They were mostly all yellow and red now, with a few stubborn patches of green leaves still refusing to change over. I found Dennis Falco's contact entry and started to type.

"How's Fort Wayne?" I texted to Dennis.

"Sorry—Who is this?" was the response.

I frowned at the phone. Dennis was given to long stretches of dry sarcasm, and it was difficult to determine his tone over text. "Dean Sherwood. Is this the right number for Dennis Falco?"

"Maybe yes, maybe no. Depends on what you want this time. And what makes you think I'm in Fort Wayne?"

"You're not?"

"Unless I finally gained the ability to bilocate, I most certainly am not."

"I stopped at Knit Now and they said you're in Fort Wayne."

There was a long pause, while I watched the employees of the city-county building stream out onto the sidewalks in search of lunch. Finally, Dennis replied. "I told them to say I was unavailable. I'm at home, taking a few personal days to organize my collection."

"Does that mean I can come over and ask you a question?"

"Can you be brief?"

"I can be positively terse. See you in a few."

On the way to Dennis's house, I took a slight detour along Diamond Avenue and stopped at the Donut Vault. Since I was going to be interrupting his time with his beloved collection, it felt smart to come with an offering of coconut-topped long johns.

While I waited in line, I reconsidered the ethics of asking Ollie to check on Stamper. Ollie had sounded genuinely concerned about maintaining the reputation of the Peregrines, and he felt responsible for whatever Stamper was getting up to at the Peregrine perch, but I was still uneasy about concealing the whole truth from him. If Ollie knew that the situation involved creatures from outside the bounds of reality, he might be more likely to approach Stamper with appropriate caution. Telling him this, however, ran the risk that he would simply stop listening to me.

By the time I picked up my square pastry box with the orange and green Donut Vault lettering, I still hadn't made up my mind if I'd done the right thing or not. I decided to revisit the issue later, once I had a clearer picture of what Stamper was up to.

Dennis Falco lived in a little bungalow in a cozy interwar neighborhood on the east side. Its curving streets were dotted with modest brick houses, almost all of them displaying mature trees in the front yards. Each house had some sort of unique architectural detail to set it apart from its neighbors: a light-and-dark pattern of masonry, a pointed fairytale portico over the front door, or some scrolled ironwork along the top of the chimney. I always got the sense that the architects who put all this together had enjoyed their jobs.

A couple of vintage tin bats hung in Dennis's front windows, a tasteful early Halloween decoration. I pressed the doorbell button and heard the mechanical chiming from somewhere inside the house. A moment later, Dennis opened the door.

"Clever boy! You've brought doughnuts! Come on in."

Dennis Falco was elegantly portly, with black hair brushed straight back and a neat Van Dyke beard. Both hair and beard were tinged with gray, and they probably would have made another man look sinister, but on Dennis they served to soften his essential cherubic nature. If one of the smirking Renaissance *putti* who clustered around the borders of lusty mythological paintings had grown up, eaten a little too well, and dedicated himself to thoroughly enjoying life, he would have looked exactly like Dennis.

"I apologize for the clothes," he said as I followed him through the house to the kitchen. Dennis wore clay-colored painters' pants, a blue cardigan with sagging pockets, and canvas deck shoes that hadn't been white for many years. "I generally don't receive visitors on days when I'm digging around in the collection."

"I won't say a word to anyone."

The interior of Dennis's house had been painted in dark reds, with cream-colored highlights on the molding. Nearly every wall was covered with an endless mosaic of framed images and objects, forming a sort of three-dimensional wallpaper. At a glance, I saw a leaf from a German woodcut missal, several hand-tinted photographs of Mexican pyramids, a lobby card from a Joseph Cotten movie, languid French postcards, and sketches of ancient ruins. Decades ago, Dennis had moved here from Montreal when his wife got a teaching appointment at the University of Garvinville, and he had cast about for something to do. He eventually settled on the role of small-business owner, running The Crystal Heart and Knit Now. Those paid the bills while he pursued his true passion, which was delving into the secret arts of the occult world. When his wife decided she'd had enough of him and left, I think Dennis was relieved.

I'm not sure Dennis knows what to make of me. I'm not part of his reading group, most of whom see me as a killjoy at best and a narc at worst, but Dennis and I have always gotten along. I think it's because I don't treat him as a revered teacher or an unimpeachable expert. With me, he doesn't have the burden of being a sage, and I think he appreciates that. Or, possibly, he just likes having various factions of friends he can play off against each other if he ever wants to. That wouldn't surprise me, either.

"Care for a glass of milk?" he asked when we got to the kitchen. "Doughnuts have to go with milk, I've always thought. I suppose it's a childhood affectation, but it's too late to do anything about it now. Sit wherever you can find space."

The majority of Dennis's kitchen table was covered with tottering stacks of comic books, all carefully protected in plastic bags and hardly any newer than 1980. This was Dennis's other passion, the one he didn't care to broadcast to his reading group. I understood his attitude. We all have things we love that we'd just as soon not have to justify to anyone else.

Dennis shook his head at the stacks. "They just seem to arrive, and then they multiply. If I don't take the time to keep on top of them every once in a while, it all ends up as madness."

The door to the basement was open, revealing some plain wooden stairs and a bare light bulb. Down there, under our feet, was the core of Dennis's comic collection, stored in rows of industrial filing cabinets securely bolted to the floor. When the mood struck him, he would pull out a dozen or so and read them in his easy chair, a glass of whiskey at his elbow, perfectly happy.

I shifted several issues of *Wonder Woman* and accepted a glass of milk, along with a doughnut and a paper napkin on a black ceramic plate.

"So, what's on your mind, Dean?" Dennis asked. "What brought you to my house with a peace offering?"

"I'm afraid I need a little help again."

Dennis pursed his lips in an expression of mock disdain. "Am I wrong, or did those same words lead to my car ending up in a ditch recently?"

"For the record, that was hardly a ditch at all. Barely a slope. And you said it was an adventure."

"I was being generous. The word I wanted to use was 'nightmare.' But that's not important. What's going on today?"

I took out my phone and pulled up the picture of Stamper. "Do you recognize this guy?" I asked.

Dennis studied it. It had that distorted, copy-of-a-copy look you get when you take a picture of a computer screen, but it was legible enough. "I think I do. He's been to the reading group a few times."

"Do you know his name?"

"I'm afraid I do not. Most of my group likes their privacy, so I don't press the people who don't want to talk too much."

That was good enough for me. It was confirmation that Eldridge Stamper wasn't just some square-headed bozo who had tripped over a huldra and thrown her into a sack. If he was hanging around Dennis's reading group, then he might have learned enough to summon the huldra and bind her to his will. It was a possibility, at least. Despite their interest, hardly any of the local demimonde of occultists and dabblers in the black arts could actually "make stuff happen." Just like someone who goes to Grace Abounding

Lutheran Fellowship every Sunday for thirty years isn't necessarily going to experience the Beatific Vision, most of the warlocks and moon-priestesses running around can't necessarily bend reality to their own will. But some of them, if they're sufficiently motivated and diligent, can achieve surprising results. Occasionally those results will surprise even themselves. That's when things often end up causing problems for people like Uncle Willard and me.

"To be honest with you, I always assumed he was a plainclothes detective," Dennis said. "He has that cop look, don't you think? And he took a lot of notes. I noticed that. We do get the police occasionally, you know. There's nothing we do that's *illegal*—we read and we talk. I'm sure it's all very boring to the rest of the world, but every once in a while somebody gets a bee in their bonnet about *sacrifices* or *black masses* or some nonsense, and an undercover officer eventually finds his way into the group. We treat him politely, and eventually he gives up and goes away. I can only imagine what they put in their various police reports about us."

"How did this guy dress?

"Like he had taken off his tie and sport coat in the car just before coming in to the meeting."

"He never wore a t-shirt?"

"Why are you asking this?"

"I was at Knit Now earlier, and the woman I talked to said she'd seen this guy wearing a t-shirt with the Raback Seal on it." I retrieved my notebook from my jacket pocket, unfolded the sketch I'd made, and showed it to Dennis.

He shook his head. "Never. Wasn't the type. Not the seal and not the t-shirt. Who told you this?"

I described the woman. "Little bit on the short side. Black hair. Sort of a rockabilly vampire look."

Dennis nodded sagely. "That's Lenora. Lenora Scanlon."

"Any idea why she'd want to send me off on the wrong track?"

"Nothing specific, but I can't say I'm wholly surprised. It's possible she was refusing to cooperate on general principles. Not everyone in the reading group likes you. They seem to feel you're some sort of goon."

I decided not to engage with the "goon" comment. "So you don't think Lenora might be protecting this guy for some reason? Are she and him . . . together?"

"Good heavens, no," Dennis said. "They may have exchanged a few words, but nothing like what you're implying. Lenora's a natural teacher. If someone has a problem, a concept they can't figure out, Lenora's always the one who tries to help. She's very good at it. In fact, that's why I'm sure she isn't getting up to any funny business with the fellow you're so interested in. To the best of my knowledge, she's already involved with her current student."

I didn't say anything, and Dennis kept talking.

"Teacher and student. Tale as old as time. Lingering glances over the textbooks. Stolen kisses in the library stacks." He shook his head. "Nothing good ever comes of it. When I realized what was going on, I said a discreet word to her, but she didn't listen. No one ever does, then everyone's shocked when it all ends in tears."

"Do you know her student, too?"

"Oh, certainly. He comes to the group with her, though they haven't been around as much as usual. I think Lenora took offense at my advice and is sulking. Perhaps she wants to start a group of her own. I could imagine her wanting to try."

"What does her student look like?"

"Why are you so concerned about all these people, Dean?"

"Right now, I'm just trying to put a bunch of pieces together. Humor me. What does this guy—"

"Tim. Timothy Grimes."

"What does he look like?"

Dennis thought about this for a second. "Tall. Slender. Sort of haunted-looking. One of those horrible beards that the young people like right now, the ones that make them look like Nantucket harpooners."

That certainly sounded like the guy in the baggy coat from last night. So Lenora knew him—was involved with him, apparently—and she had sent me off in Stamper's direction rather than tell me the truth. That was interesting. It didn't clear up many questions, but it was certainly interesting.

"So these two, Tim and Lenora, were they working on any projects? Any special research interests?"

Dennis glanced over to where the doughnut box sat open. After a moment of internal discussion, he came to a decision. "Half of one more. Anything for you?"

I accepted another glass of milk and the other half. No point in letting it go to waste.

"I don't think they were doing anything in particular," he said. "Lenora's not the type to see how far she can push things, thank goodness. But I haven't seen them at the group in a while, so who knows?"

We talked for a few minutes longer about general, non-occult subjects, like the civic opera's new season and whether I would take Dennis's niece out to dinner when she came for a visit next month. The pauses got longer as he became increasingly distracted by the comic books on the table, and I decided it was time to go.

"Thanks again," I said as I stood up.

Dennis put the remaining doughnuts in a plastic container and flattened the pastry box. "I'd really love to know what this is all about," he said.

"Somebody summoned something, and now it's running loose. I don't know how, I don't know why, and I don't even have a good grasp on who did it. But I want to find out."

"Is it the man in your picture?"

"I think it might be. But there's half a chance that Lenora's friend Tim is involved somehow, too."

"Really?"

"It's starting to look that way."

Dennis pointed a stubby finger at me. "When you find out, I want to hear all about it. Especially if it ends up being one of my group."

"I'll keep you in mind," I said.

10

On the way back from Dennis's house, I tried to decide what I ought to do next. Should I return to Knit Now and try to find out why Lenora's student Tim had been skulking around the Peregrine perch? Or should I ignore those two for the moment and stick with Eldridge Stamper and the huldra? Maybe the information that Ollie was digging up would give me more insight into Stamper's plans. As I weighed these questions, I was driving more or less on autopilot and didn't start paying attention until I saw people standing in the intersection in front of me. At first I thought there had been an accident, but as I got closer I realized they were all wearing identical shirts under their reflective yellow vests, and carrying metal cans and bags of candy. It was some charitable organization—not the Peregrines, I hoped—raising money from drivers as they stopped at the intersection, and handing out candy to anyone who donated.

There were a few cars in line ahead of me, so I had time to fish through the change compartment in the center console. I always feel like a jackass if I have to shrug and say, "No cash, sorry!" in situations like this. By the time I reached the intersection, I had scraped up a small handful of coins. The power window stuttered a little bit when I pressed the button, then slid down. The guy working this side was big, with a pot belly and a mop of graying hair. A couple of quarters slipped from my grip and landed by my feet. I hunched down to retrieve them, since without those quarters all I had to donate was a couple of nickels and a large number of the pennies I habitually pick up from the sidewalk.

I didn't want to hold up traffic any more than I had to, so I tried to hurry. From my peripheral vision, I could see the guy standing next to my window. I heard the clatter of coins in his can and the rustle of his candy bag over the sounds of the traffic. I snared my quarters with two fingers, managing not to drop the rest of the change, and straightened up. That was when the man leaned in through the window.

This would have been startling enough on its own, but the face suddenly inches from my own was not a normal face at all. It was made of stone, the pitted cold marble of an ancient statue. The tumbling gray curls were, horribly, still human hair, but beneath them hung a pair of blank, hollow, statue's eyes. My vision darkened, narrowing down to nothing but the expressionless face before me. I tried to speak, but all I could do was make a choking sound. The thing reached through the window, then opened its hand to show me what it held. In the center of the marble palm was a red smear and a lump of something yellowish-white and glistening. For an instant I thought it was a chunk of flesh, with pieces of bone and gristle still attached, but then my eyes refocused and I saw it was a piece of honeycomb, but one saturated with blood rather than honey. The statue withdrew its hand and its lips parted, as if preparing to speak, but all that came out was a cold, hollow sigh.

Somehow, I managed to get through the intersection without hitting anyone. From there, I swerved into the Royal Chicken parking lot and sat there for a long time with my foot jammed on the brake. Eventually, it occurred to me that I ought to shift into park. My eyes watered and I rested my head groggily against the steering wheel, which must have been a concerning sight to the other Royal Chicken customers.

I felt hollow, as if the purpose had gone out of my life and would never return. All I wanted to do was to curl into a ball and never do anything again. I knew this was the result of my vision at the intersection, and that someone was trying to make me feel this way, but knowing wasn't enough to repair the damage. It took several minutes of concentrated happy thoughts (including vintage shoes, playing chess at the Planet Caravan coffee house, an antique briefcase I'd been debating buying, and chicken with broccoli from the Red Panda) before I started to feel any better. I put the car in gear and experienced a quick moment of confusion when it refused to move. Somehow, I'd engaged the emergency brake during my fugue state. Once that was sorted out, I decided not to risk defeat at the hands of the

Jag's CD player and played the T. Rex disc that was already loaded.

On the way, home, listening to "Buick Mackane" for the third time in a row, my head started to throb. It felt like the beginning of a fever, though I doubted I was really sick. It was only a side effect, a physiological reaction to what had just happened. But what *had* just happened? Someone had made an attempt to get me to stop investigating. Where sorcery was concerned, it was much easier to frighten a person or sap their will than it was to kill them, and it still achieved the desired effect. After all, I certainly wasn't going to keep asking questions while overcome by existential despair. But who had been responsible? Who was unhappy with me nosing around? I doubted it was Dennis. If he'd wanted to do something to me, he would have done it inside his house, his sanctum, where his powers would have been at their strongest. In addition, if Dennis had wanted me to quit bothering him, he could have summoned up a much stronger messenger. The vision of the living statue and the wave of despair that followed it were viscerally unpleasant, but didn't have much staying power. Dennis could have flattened me if he'd been really trying.

I passed a park and saw a dozen kids dressed as wizards and goblins playing a live-action role-playing game. One of the wizards threw a handful of ping-pong balls at her opponent, and I assumed that was supposed to represent some type of magic spell. Her gesture as she threw the props was weirdly familiar, and it took a few seconds for me to realize why. Last night, when I had been chasing the guy with the baggy coat and the beard—the guy I now knew was Tim Grimes—he had turned and made a similar gesture at me. Nothing had happened, and he had run away, but what had he been trying to do? Could he have been attempting to produce a magical effect? It's not an easy thing to do, especially when you're rushed and you only have a few seconds before someone tackles you, so it wasn't too surprising that he hadn't succeeded. But had he tried again today?

No, I thought. It hadn't been him. It had been Lenora, the one who had tried to divert me away from Tim and back toward Stamper. I recalled writing my number down for her, and Lenora covering up the pen I had used. She may have tried calling down unpleasant forces against me, using the pen as a focal point. I had only held it for a few seconds, so it wouldn't have been as effective as an actual possession of mine, and it certainly wouldn't have been as good as hair or fingernails, but it was better than nothing. I wondered if the lack of a good focus had been why the effect was so easy to shake off. This was a decent theory, but I preferred to credit my natural, iron-like resilience.

My head continued to pound, and I decided further cogitation could wait until later. At least until after I took a nap. At home, I let myself in through the side door, then down the hall lined with Uncle Willard's favorite paintings, and into my little office off the foyer. I took my blanket from the couch and wrapped it around my shoulders. It wasn't cold, but I was still slightly feverish and a blanket always makes you feel better. On a whim, I opened the wooden box on my desk and took out the blue plastic bear the huldra had given me. Its impassive little features didn't have any message for me, but I liked the look of the thing. I let it sit on the desk and watch me as I dropped onto the couch and fell asleep.

When I woke up an hour later, the bear was still there. After I stood up, folded the blanket, and straightened my clothes, I put the thing in my pocket. I detected the sounds of a large figure lumbering about in the kitchen, and picked up the scent of eggplant Florentine.

Uncle Willard had obviously given up hope that I would cook tonight, and had begun to make dinner on his own. Neither of us mind cooking, but both of us understand that food always tastes better when someone else does all the work. The smart thing to do, of course, would be to make a schedule, or at least keep track of who cooked last, but neither of us liked the idea of chaining ourselves to a routine. Who could say what would happen tomorrow to prevent us from fulfilling our scheduled obligations? Willard might disappear down the rabbit hole of replacing all his rolling stock connectors and not leave his attic for a week, or I might get eaten by a monster. The future was always uncertain.

I retrieved some plates and a bottle of wine, and Willard put some twelfth-century Spanish court songs on the record player, and we ate in the dining room like civilized people.

"Mrs. Bates told me to say hello to you," I said. This was answered by a noncommittal grunt.

"She nearly ran over me last night, by the Peregrine perch. I found somebody lurking outside the building and chased him. We ended up in the middle of the street, and that's when Mrs. Bates drove past." When this didn't get a response, I added, "Do I look like a goon to you?"

Willard put his fork down. "Right now, or in general?"

"Dennis Falco said some of his people think I'm a goon."

He ripped a roll in half and thought about this. "If and when one of Dennis's dilettantes takes an experiment too far, you're the one most likely to clean up the mess, so there may be a degree of resentment there. No dilettante likes to be rescued. It injures the pride. It's only natural that some of them might see you as a . . . ."

"Goon."

"An enforcer of conventionality. If it bothers you, let them fend for themselves. What were you doing talking to Dennis?"

"I think one or two of his reading group might be mixed up in the business at the Peregrine perch. I don't know for certain. I've got hold of the tail of something, so to speak, and I'm not sure where it's going to lead me."

Willard exhaled in a pointed manner. "Am I still right in assuming no one is paying you?"

"There's more to life than money."

"There's more to a house than its foundation, but I wouldn't want to try living without one."

I knew enough to realize I wasn't going to get anything helpful out of him tonight, so I turned the conversation to model trains. I was largely ignorant of the technical details, though I did enjoy watching his trains glide through their serene miniature landscapes. I did my best to ask intelligent questions as he described in detail the strengths and weaknesses of various digital control systems. His deeply-reasoned monologues on the subject kept my mind off all the things I still didn't understand about the huldra, the Peregrines, and Dennis's reading group. When you deal with things that are defined by their inability to make logical sense, which is to say, "magic," it's hard to find an underlying pattern and learn from your experiences. It can drive you nuts. If any of this stuff made sense, you could deal with it using the rules of biology or physics or anything else that belonged to the regular, everyday world. Without that, all you can do is work on intuition, searching for a path to follow that feels right. Then, when you're on that path, you have to hope nothing starts chasing you.

11

The next morning I was at Planet Caravan, my treasured neighborhood coffee place, sipping a dark roast and watching the street. Ollie had texted me last night, asking if we could meet, and this was the location I suggested. In addition to my view of the street, I could also see Sophie, the owner, leaning on the counter and totaling up the previous day's sales in a ragged spiral notebook. Every so often, an auburn lock of her hair would slip and she'd absently tuck it behind one ear with a gesture that I found hypnotic. When she noticed me, she smiled and made a face as I tried to pretend I hadn't been staring.

On the table in front of me, between the coffee mug and a plate with the crumbs of a pumpkin muffin, sat a tarnished brass box, barely two inches long, with an incised pattern along one side. It was a match safe, the kind of thing people used to carry around to keep their matches secure and dry. I'd found it in a junk store when I was a kid and always had a fond feeling for it. I opened the lid for the third time this morning and took another peek inside. The blue bear stared up at me. The bear had been on my mind ever since last night, and I liked the idea of having it with me. The match safe kept it from getting scratched, and made me more likely to notice if it fell out of my pocket. It also kept me from staring at the bear obsessively. Every time I looked at it, I recalled the moment when the huldra gave it to me, and I didn't want that feeling to fade, the way a dried flower eventually loses its scent.

I still had no idea what the little thing might possibly signify, or whether it had some hidden power of its own. I had tried a few experiments with it after dinner, reading some formulas from Willard's books over it and watching to see if it would react. So far, I had come up with nothing.

"This is nice," said a voice from over my shoulder. Ollie Helfrich had managed to sneak up on me, and I quickly returned the match safe to my pocket while he took in the interior of Planet Caravan.

"So much character," Ollie added. "And perch 47 is only a couple of blocks away. I wonder why they didn't tell me about this place."

"So, were you able to find out anything?" I asked him, once he had ordered his coffee from Sophie and rejoined me at the table.

"That was why I wanted to meet with you." Ollie's tone of voice suggested he was about to break some bad news. "You're sure you need to know this stuff?"

"Yeah, I think so. At this point, I don't know what's going to be helpful or not, so I'm looking for everything."

"Okay." Ollie paused when Sophie approached with his coffee. She has that effect.

"Large mocha, there you go," she said, setting it down.

I jumped in with the introductions. "Ollie Helfrich, this is Sophie Wolfe. She runs the place."

"It's really beautiful," Ollie said. "How long have you been here?"

"Three years, I think. Isn't that right, Dean?"

"More or less."

She put a hand on my shoulder. "I can't tell you how surprised I was when I first came to check out the space and it was Dean waiting to show me around. We were in high school together, but hadn't seen each other for years."

"My uncle owns the building," I explained to Ollie. "He's retired, which means I'm the one who handles all the management."

"He's our Mr. Fix-It," Sophie said.

"More like Mr. Call-a-Professional-and-Write-a-Check," I said modestly.

"Even better. You guys need anything else?"

I shook my head. "We're good here. Thanks, Sophie."

"I thought you were a private investigator," Ollie said when we were alone again.

"I am. But it's not the kind of thing that can pay the bills every month. My uncle Willard has a couple of buildings that he doesn't want to deal with, so I take care of things for him. The salary is borderline criminal, but I get room and board to go along with it. There are worse ways to spend a day. Usually."

"I see." Ollie chewed on his lip, as if trying to come to a decision. "About that information you asked for—I'm a little worried. The Peregrines have a lot of confidentiality rules related to the membership files. I could get in trouble with the central perch for letting you see any of that stuff."

It was apparent I had made a tactical error in telling Ollie that I worked for my uncle. For some reason, "nepotistic property manager" didn't have the same cachet as "roguish private investigator."

"I understand," I said. "If it would make you feel better, I can show you why I need to know this stuff. I'd have to break a few rules of my own, but I think it's worth it. Would that help?"

Ollie thought about this. "Yeah, maybe so."

Damn. I was hoping he would tell me not to worry about it. Instead, he had called my bluff and now I was going to have to turn Ollie's world upside down. But it had to be done. My questions were piling up faster than my answers, and I was looking for any leads I could get.

"All right," I said. "I can show you why I'm so concerned about this. But I can't do it here."

"Why not?"

"It's only going to make sense if you see it for yourself. You don't have any place you have to be right away, do you?"

Ollie was free until the late afternoon, so there was no rush. While we finished our coffees, I told a few stories about the odd things that happen when you're in charge of a handful of old buildings, and Ollie told me about his life as an itinerant Peregrine, traveling around the country and meeting with the local perches, many of whom greet him with a mixture of suspicion and resentment. It was a good conversation. On the outside, Ollie and I didn't seem to have much in common. He was one of those straightforward, cheerful people who tended to end up working for college admissions departments, insurance companies, or fraternal service organizations. I, in all frankness, was not. But Ollie had a secret weapon: He was a good listener. Nothing makes Person A disposed to like Person B more than Person B's willingness to let Person A talk about the collection of hand-painted hula girl ties he'd once found in the attic of an old office building. Pretty soon, I was getting to like Ollie quite a bit, which made me feel even worse about what I was about to do to him. We got up, I left a tip on the table and waved to Sophie, and we went out to my car.

"I grew up here," I told Ollie as we drove across town, zigzagging a bit to get down to Covert Avenue. "All these neighborhoods, they all have a story attached to them. I dated a girl over there. Or my dad used to live there when he was growing up. Or I worked there when I was in high school."

"That must be nice. I come from an Army family," Ollie said. "We moved around every year and a half. I'd finally get to know the kids in my class, and all of a sudden we'd be off to somewhere else. Okinawa, once, and then to Egypt for a while. Wyoming, even. I didn't like it back then, but I appreciate it now. It taught me how to make friends fast. But I always missed having a hometown, you know what I mean? Some place that was *yours*. A place where you fit in."

I continued down Covert for a while, then pulled into the parking lot of Pleasureland Adult Boutique. I very deliberately avoided looking in Ollie's direction until I had guided the Jag into the most distant parking spot and shut off the engine.

"So," Ollie said, trying hard to find the correct words, "what are we doing here?"

Instead of responding, I led him around to the alley behind Pleasureland, which did not make him any less apprehensive. We stopped halfway down the alley, next to a trash bin containing neatly folded cardboard boxes from various sex toy wholesalers, and opposite the emergency exit for Pit Crew Auto Parts.

"A hundred years ago, this place was out in the middle of the country." I held up the small plastic bag, tied with a yellow length of yarn, that I had extracted from the glove compartment. Inside was a stubby piece of misshapen, homemade chalk. "There was only one house out here. And a guy who really valued his privacy. He had a reason for that."

Ollie didn't say anything, so I got down to work. The goal here was to keep Ollie from running away before I showed him what I had to show him, so I didn't want to waste time.

I drew a circle on the ground, following the rain-blurred contours of earlier circles, then added thinner lines on the inside and the outside.

"What's that?" Ollie asked.

"Just chalk. Plus some other stuff."

"What I meant was, what are you doing?"

Along the outer edge of the circle, I wrote an alternating series of alchemical symbols and Greek words. As I did this, I hummed to myself a fifteenth-century melody by Josquin Des Pres.

"This is going to make sense in a minute," I said, "but right now, I need quiet for a bit. Okay?"

Ollie nodded and I spoke the words that needed to be said, to the meter of the Josquin melody. Within the space of a few heartbeats, the sky got darker, that shade of unnerving indigo that happens during a solar eclipse. The sounds of traffic faded away into a distant whispering sound. I glanced over to Ollie, who was immobilized with surprise, and gave him a thumbs-up to let him know everything was going to be all right. I thought about preparing him for what was going to happen next, but then he caught sight of something over my shoulder and his eyes got huge. Eleazar had appeared.

In the center of the circle stood the apparition of a man. He was dressed in a black coat and string tie, and faded to an indistinct vapor somewhere below the knees. His white hair and angular face made him look like a daguerreotype of a humorless revivalist preacher, but the lack of eyes spoiled the effect.

Eleazar opened his cracked lips. "Release me."

"You know I can't," I said. I moved sideways a few feet to keep Ollie in my peripheral vision. I didn't want him to run, but it wasn't safe to break eye contact with Eleazar. Although, technically, I suppose it was eye-socket contact.

"What do you want, popinjay?"

"I have to make a point, Eleazar. What's your name?"

"Eleazar Dunmore."

"When were you born?"

"The year seventeen hundred and eighty-nine."

"How did you die?"

"Murdered at the hands of George Franklin, the reprobate and swine."

"How much longer do you have to stay where you are?"

Eleazar's voice was papery and soft, and probably would have been inaudible except for the unnatural silence that engulfed the alley. But the seething malevolence in the words was unmistakable. "Until the line of George Franklin has died out completely, Satan rot them all."

"Thank you, Eleazar."

"Or until a sorcerer of rank contrives to break the chains that hold me to this place." Eleazar's lifeless breath rasped. "You could do it, popinjay. Put off your jester's finery and put your mind to the working, and you could destroy the curse that binds me. Even in my current state, I could reward greatly the man who frees me."

If Eleazar ever got free, I'm certain that "reward greatly the idiot who let him loose" was nowhere near the top of his to-do list, but there was no point in saying that out loud. Instead, I thanked him formally and spoke the words that sent him down again, leaving only the fading sound of a groan and a dust-devil of vapor, which quickly dissipated in the renewed breeze.

I carefully rubbed out the symbols around the circle with the toe of my shoe, then knelt down and erased the words with my thumb and a little spit. When I stood back up, Ollie was staring at me.

12

"You're not going to freak out, are you?" I asked him.

Ollie opened and closed his mouth a couple of times, like a fish suddenly yanked from its pond. He finally managed to say, "I . . . I can't guarantee that."

That was an answer I could live with. "Look, Ollie, I didn't mean to scare you—"

"Pretty sure you succeeded anyway. Who was that?"

"You heard him," I said. "Eleazar Dunmore. Or what was Eleazar Dunmore in life."

"'In life?' I think I need to sit down."

The employee door to Pleasureland opened next to us, and a young man with frosted hair and a silver nose ring stepped halfway out, noticed us, and discreetly withdrew. I led Ollie back to the parking lot, where we leaned against the Jag's trunk and watched the traffic go by.

"Just watch the cars and keep breathing," I said. "The more normal stuff you look at, the quicker this is all going to seem like a bad dream. You'll feel better in a minute, I promise."

"What just happened?"

"Here's the truth, Ollie: I said I was an investigator, and I meant it. But the kind of investigations I do aren't about divorces or insurance investigations or missing persons. Well, okay, sometimes missing persons. But not persons who are missing for the usual reasons."

"Was that a real ghost?" Ollie asked. "Did we just see a real ghost? That wasn't a trick?"

"That was not a trick. I raised him up, I talked to him, and then I put him back down again."

"So you, you're . . ." Ollie groped for a word he never expected to use in an adult conversation. ". . . a wizard?"

"Nope. Just a guy. A guy with an unusual side job. Some people sell scarves on the internet. I do this."

Ollie rubbed his eyes. Across the street, people were going in and out of Schenk's grocery store. It was the biggest, best-stocked grocery store in the city, and Uncle Willard sometimes sent me there for fresh produce.

"Why did you show me this?" Ollie asked.

"This is the kind of stuff Stamper's involved with," I said. "It's what he's dragged the Peregrines into. If I had told you Stamper was dealing with creatures from the unseen world, would you have taken my word for it?"

"Okay, fair enough. Probably not."

"I'm sorry I had to shock you like that, but people generally don't believe these things until they see them. You needed to know I wasn't making stuff up. Introducing you to Eleazar was about the mildest way I could think of to make my point."

"You couldn't have just made a rabbit disappear or something?"

I shook my head. "Sorry. Rabbit phobia. I got bit by one when I was little."

We climbed into the car, and I looped around the auto parts store and then onto Jefferson Avenue.

"I thought people usually sat around a table or something when they wanted to talk to ghosts," Ollie said. "Why did we have to go into an alley next to a strip mall?"

"That's the thing about an unmarked grave: People forget it's there, and they eventually build over it. Just be glad we were talking to Eleazar. To raise up his brother Zenas, we would have had to be in Pleasureland's bathroom."

"How do you know all this?"

"You've had a busy day already. Let's not worry about that too much."

I drove on for a few more minutes with no specific destination in mind.

"Eldridge Stamper really does stuff like that?" Ollie said at last.

"That's what it looks like. When I first saw him, he and some of the other Peregrines had captured something called a huldra."

"A what?"

"Huldra. You hear about them mostly in northern Europe. Beautiful woman with a tail."

"You're kidding me," Ollie began, then added, "No, I guess you probably aren't. What were they doing with a huldra?"

"I think they were going to eat her. In the basement of the Peregrine perch. With barbecue sauce."

Ollie sighed, the sigh of a man whose day keeps refusing to get any better.

"I'm the one who found her and let her go, and that's why Stamper was ticked off at me. But there's a lot I don't understand about what happened. For example, they had her tied up, and I have no idea how they were able to do it. Binding a creature like the huldra takes a lot of skill, and if Stamper's capable of that, I'd like to know what he's planning to do next."

We stopped at a light near a cluster of rickety, Charles-Addams-style mansions. Ollie stared out the window for a second, then unlocked his phone and loaded up a document. "Eldridge Stamper," he read. "Peregrine for twenty years in the Garvinville perch. He's been a vice president, a sergeant at arms, and a charity committee member. Right now, it looks like he's the chair of the catering committee."

"They may want to look into electing somebody else."

Ollie didn't answer me. Instead, he kept reading. "Industrial technology teacher, assistant football coach, West Central High School."

"Do you have a home address?"

"Hang on." Ollie rapidly scrolled in all directions on his phone. "This wasn't really made for little screens. Let me see . . . 710 Deffler Lane."

I made a turn at the next intersection. The map of Garvinville in my head is embarrassingly good. If I ever got tired of working for Willard, I could become the city's most thorough tour guide. We passed the enormous Jonn-Meade vitamin factory, then Reiter High School on its hill, looming over the neighborhood like Dracula's castle. A few more twists and turns, and we were in a sprawl of housing developments on what used to be a floodplain. Streets of two-story apartment buildings alternated with streets of single-family houses, all just a little bit too similar for comfort.

Ollie read off the house numbers. "Okay, we're getting close. 706. 708. There it is. That's it." Stamper's house was a gray split-level with a dark blue front door and window trim. I took my foot off the gas to give myself an extra second to study it, but continued on down the block.

"Where are you going?" Ollie asked.

"Look around," I said. The house next to Stamper's had a contractor's truck in the driveway, and two guys in baseball caps were installing a new garage door. On the other side of the street, a car sat in the driveway with its hood up and a teenager leaning into the engine compartment, while a pair of legs protruded from underneath the chassis.

"What's the matter?"

I hesitated at a stop sign and turned to go around the block. "Lots of witnesses. If we pulled into his driveway and peeked in all the windows and checked to see if the door was locked, Stamper would know about it all ten minutes after he got home."

"You think?"

"It's human nature. I live in a neighborhood where people take pride in minding their own business, and every time I have to drag a wrapped bundle into the carriage house in the middle of the night I hear about it for a week. I can't imagine the people around here are any different."

"Well, what should we do, then?" Ollie sounded disappointed.

"I can drop you off at your hotel," I said. "There's no reason for you to be following along, and I don't want to put you in any danger."

"Are you kidding? Stamper's my responsibility, too. If you're going, then I'm going."

"Okay." I checked the car clock. It was already close to three. Where would a high-school teacher and coach be at three o'clock on a Tuesday? "Let's go see if he's still at work. Maybe we can check his car."

I navigated through the subdivisions and back into the city proper, eventually reaching West Central High School. Due to the campus's odd layout, the first thing a visitor sees is the Brutalist concrete football stadium, and then, if you're really paying attention, the complex of school buildings behind that, hidden by a slope. A number of cars were still in the parking lot when we got there, and the sounds of whistles and yelling, all magnified and distorted by the empty stadium walls, told us that football practice was still going on.

"Your secret Peregrine file didn't happen to mention what kind of car Stamper drives, did it?" I asked as we got out and walked toward the stadium.

"Afraid not," Ollie said.

Ollie kept glancing over his shoulder and flinching at every strange sound, doing his best to make it obvious that he wasn't supposed to be there. Despite his excessive caution, though, he didn't seem particularly scared. In fact, I think he was excited to be doing something a little bit forbidden. He had gotten over his encounter with Eleazar's ghost, which I was glad to see. Some people have a hard time with that, and will chew on an unexplainable encounter like a dog worrying at a sore paw, until you have to put the psychic equivalent of those satellite-dish collars on them for the sake of their own sanity. Ollie, on the other hand, had taken it in stride. The most "normal" ones usually do, accepting the experience and moving on with their lives. It probably helped in this instance that he had a new adventure to occupy his mind.

We made our way through the stadium gate and between two blocks of risers, keeping to the shadows as much as we could. A hundred high school kids in yellow practice jerseys and football helmets were running drills on the field. In the center, just to one side of the over-muscled bee mascot painted at the fifty-yard line, half a dozen coaches in baseball caps, polo shirts, and Russel shorts were watching the practice and making observations to each other.

"Do you see him anywhere?" I asked Ollie.

"I'm not sure if I could recognize—Wait, is that him?" Ollie pointed to the opposite sideline, where a tank-shaped man was demonstrating how a running back was supposed to receive a handoff. Over and over again, a rangy high-school kid slammed a football into the man's midsection while a semi-circle of other players watched. I kicked myself for not keeping a pair of binoculars—not even pocket-sized opera glasses—in my car, but I was pretty sure Ollie's identification was right. The coach taking the handoff looked a lot like Stamper to me.

"He's going to be busy for a while," Ollie said. "They're breaking up into position groups now, so I think the practice is just starting." He noticed my surprised expression and added, "I was a volunteer assistant at my old high school last year, before I got promoted to this job and started traveling all the time. My wife still helps out with the girls' volleyball team. So what should we do now? How do we find out what kind of car Stamper drives?"

"Well, if we've got plenty of time, maybe we can do better than just looking for his car. I wonder if he has an office or something. Do coaches have offices?"

"If he's an assistant coach, he probably doesn't have one of his own," Ollie said. "But he's a teacher, too, so he's got to have a classroom. It might be worth checking out his desk."

"That's a good idea. Remind me again what he teaches."

"Industrial technology," Ollie said.

"Is that computers or welders?"

"Probably more welders than computers," Ollie said. "People think 'industrial technology' sounds nicer than 'metal shop.' But now that I think about it, they probably work with computerized welders, too."

We left the stadium and let ourselves into the school building through a pair of smoked glass double doors with the same angry bee mascot painted on them.

"What should we be looking for?" Ollie asked as our footsteps echoed in the locker-lined corridor.

"Anything out of the ordinary," I said. "I know that's not much to go on, but it's one of those things you'll know when you see. Usually when people are messing around with . . ." I groped for the right word.

"Black magic?" Ollie volunteered.

"Well, yeah. More or less. When people are involved with this kind of thing, it tends to leak out into the rest of their life. It's hard to keep that compartmentalized, though they usually try."

"What about you? I mean, it's pretty obvious you're hip-deep in this stuff," Ollie said. "Does it come out in other areas of your life, too?"

"Yes. Continuously. But it helps that I don't try to hide it too much."

"I noticed."

"I'm also not trying to get anything out of it. I'm not out for power or money or love. Don't get me wrong—I wouldn't say no to power, or money, or love, but I'm not trying to use sorcery to get them."

"Why not?"

I shrugged. "Trying to get a specific result from this work is like trying to get a cat to walk on a leash. Generally, the cat's going to go where it wants to go anyway, and you're going to end up with a bunch of infected claw marks. It's not worth it."

"Then why do people do it?"

"Because every once in a while, it really, really does work."

As we talked, a woman in a blue sweater and glasses appeared out of an intersecting hallway, noticed us, and stopped. "Excuse me," she said. "Can I help you?"

13

The woman gave off very strong "suspicious teacher" vibes, as if she'd just discovered us without a hall pass and was determined to find out the reason why. Before I could say anything, Ollie chimed in.

"Hi, Ollie Helfrich. Nice to meet you." He stepped in front of me and shook her hand. "We're here to see the football coaches. We need to get a student's name for the Peregrine athlete of the month award."

"Oh."

The woman shook my hand as well. "Samuel van Hoogstraten. Nice to meet you," I said.

She directed us to the football offices down the hall, then left us to go about our business.

"Nice job," I said to Ollie. "How'd you come up with that?"

"I don't know. It just sort of jumped into my head. A lot of the Peregrine perches sponsor high school athletic awards, so I figured they might do that here. Who's Samuel van Hoogstraten?"

"An old Dutch painter," I said. "If you decide to keep doing stuff like this, which I don't recommend, by the way, you ought to think up a fake name or two to keep handy. Real names are easy to remember, but they have a way of coming around and biting you in the ass."

Since we now knew where the football offices were, we decided to make a quick check inside, just in case there was something interesting. Past the main door were a handful of smaller rooms, all opening into a central area with whiteboards and computer projectors. A big door on one end was marked as the exit to the field, and a short passageway led to the locker rooms. Only one room looked like a real office, and that had a nameplate with "Head Coach" on it. A number of briefcases and backpacks sat on the floor inside, suggesting that this was where the other coaches stashed their things during practice. I gave the other rooms a cursory check, but all I found were medical supplies and weightlifting equipment. We gave up and went to locate Stamper's classroom.

It took us a couple of minutes, creeping up and down school corridors that felt like a combination of Soviet post office and set from *Logan's Run*, but we got there eventually. The industrial technology room was a high-ceilinged, metal-walled space filled with hulking machines that seemed purposefully designed to tear limbs off, as well as cars in several states of disrepair and a number of scarred metal tables. Ollie pointed. A nameplate reading "Mr. Stamper" sat on the green, wood-topped desk at the front of the room. The desk was cluttered with papers and grade books, and a computer whose frame had been taken apart and resealed with duct tape. I was about to start rifling the drawers, but the heavy door behind the desk, stenciled with the name "Supply Room," caught my eye.

"I wonder what's in there," I said, half to myself.

Naturally, the door was locked. I was about to return to the desk when Ollie held up a ring of keys.

"While you were looking around in the football rooms, I went into the head coach's office," he said, jingling the keys. "One of the briefcases had Stamper's name on it, and these were in the outside pocket."

"Ollie, I think I underestimated you."

Ollie tried to hide his appreciation as he went through the keys on the ring. He found a match on the third try. The door unlocked with a heavy 'clunk' and whined on its hinges as we pulled it open. It revealed a narrow room crowded with rows of metal shelves, all holding wire baskets full of various car parts and power tools.

Ollie made a disappointed grunt. "Well, it was worth a shot, I guess."

I stepped inside. Something didn't feel right here. I stood still for a second, trying to figure out where the feeling was coming from. This wasn't a very big place, and it didn't extend far enough to meet the wall of the hallway we'd just come from. Was it a sense of improper geometry that had stopped me, or was it something else?

"What's the matter?" Ollie asked.

I muttered something about not being sure as I scrutinized the wall behind the shelves on our right. Most of the wall was cinderblock, painted prison-camp green, but there was also a large metal panel. It was painted in the same shade and mostly obscured by the ends of two shelving units. I took a step back.

"What do you see?" Ollie asked.

I pointed to the floor. The sealed concrete in front of the panel was scratched and scuffed, as if heavy shelving units had been dragged across it repeatedly.

I don't want to get too mystical about this, but at that point I was sure I was on the track of something important. It was more than just a hunch or a suspicion. It was that little voice you sometimes hear, the voice that says, "Yes." It's never very loud, and it's easily drowned out, not only by the outside world but by your own thoughts as well. More often than not, though, this is the voice that leads you in the direction you're supposed to go.

We moved the shelves out of the way and took a good look at the painted panel behind them. It was, sure enough, a door, with sliding bolts at the top and bottom to keep it closed. I glanced at Ollie, who seemed uncertain whether apprehension or glee was the appropriate response for this situation. With what I hoped was a convincing display of bravado, I undid the bolts and opened the door.

Neither of us said anything for a moment.

"Well, I'm pretty sure this is the place," I said eventually.

"Yeah," Ollie echoed.

Even before I recovered my senses and started feeling around for the light switch, it was obvious we had entered the private domain of a person with some pretty weird interests. In a way, it reminded me of Uncle Willard's attic. Willard's sprawling landscape of toy trains and model buildings was a lot different than what lay before us here, but it gave the same impression of a space completely defined and filled by one singular personality.

Naturally, there was a mannequin. I don't want to imply that mannequin ownership is an obvious clue to derangement, since there are three mannequins in the basement at home, but at least our mannequins are wearing clothes, and none of them have been marked up with dotted orange paint lines, depicting what looked very much like butcher's cuts.

Canvas banners, chopped roughly from paste-colored painters' dropcloths, hung from brackets in the ceiling. The images on them, done in what I desperately hoped was red paint, all had a sort of cryptic unity. Giant stick-figures with square heads held up squirming smaller figures and stuffed them into their impossibly wide mouths. Several crouching figures offered disembodied limbs to another giant, one who was drawn as if curled in a fetal position.

A number of pictures were taped to the walls. Most of them were photocopies or printouts, but a few had been hacked out of books with a knife. They all tended to depict people in the act of butchering meat or consuming it, and sometimes that meat was the two-legged kind. One of the hacked-out pictures showed an engraving from what looked like the sixteenth century, a hut in a jungle somewhere, with a man standing at a table chopping at a corpse, and a growing pile of arms and legs at his feet. There was a Latin caption, but without a dictionary I couldn't make heads or tails of it.

"This . . . This is not normal, right?" Ollie's voice, up until now as cheerful and bracing as a firm handshake, sounded thready. "Even for whatever it is you do, this isn't normal."

"Yes," I assured him. "This is definitely out of the ordinary. But, on the bright side, I think we've got our confirmation that Stamper's involved with something strange. No more uncertainty about that."

"What's he doing here?"

"That's a good question," I said. "At the moment, I'm not really sure what any of this means. All the cannibals I've known—relax, it really hasn't been that many—they all treated their dietary practice as something ultimately misunderstood by the public at large. Like nudists. They considered themselves perfectly normal people, and maybe just a smidge better than average because they were doing something the rest of the world hated because it didn't understand."

"Please, please, tell me you're joking."

"I am," I lied. "But my point remains: This is more than just a guy who wants to eat people. This is on another level. He's in this for a different reason."

Ollie retreated a step and sagged against the doorframe. I momentarily worried about him fainting, but then he seemed to rally, so I began studying the place in earnest. There was a work table in the center of the room, just like the ones in the classroom outside. I was surprised to see that it held a series of small metal-working machines and a plastic rack with delicate tools that wouldn't have been out of place in a watchmaker's studio. A flexible gas pipe attached to a Bunsen burner, and beside it several pans contained ashes of varying hues and consistencies. The contrast between this tidy workspace and the rest of the room was stark, but I couldn't understand what Stamper had been using it for. Eventually, I went back to studying the decorations.

All the dropcloth paintings had the same cave-drawing feeling. It gave me the sense that the artist was trying to get across a very big idea with limited tools and technique. The largest banner showed more of the square-headed people, the ones who ate the smaller people in the other pictures. In this image, however, they were following another, much larger figure. This central being was all angles and slashing lines, with a triangular head and a mask-like face. Above the eyes were a pair of marks that could have been ears, but I was certain they were horns. Something in the square-headed people's attitude showed they weren't following the larger figure in order to eat it. They were following it because they wanted to connect with it.

I stared hard at these images, probably giving Ollie a very good impression of a self-important art critic at a gallery opening. This all meant something. If I could just get my mind around the symbolism and the intent, I knew it would explain what Stamper was trying to do, and it might even explain how a huldra—a very dangerous creature in her own right—ended up under his power.

Just as I was about to get out my phone and take some reference photos, the noise of muffled conversation and footsteps penetrated through the wall. Ollie and I froze like prairie dogs when the shadow of a falcon glides across the ground. The sounds grew louder, as if the speakers had stopped in front of the industrial technology classroom for a moment, then they faded away. We took the hint. It was time to go. I closed the door of the secret room and we slid the shelves back in place in front of it. After that, we locked the supply room door, made sure the coast was clear, and returned to the hallway.

"Mission accomplished," I said as we walked. Noticing Ollie's incredulous expression, I added, "If you keep your missions small enough, you can accomplish them all day long. We learned what we came here to learn. Now we've just got to figure out what to do about it. The first thing after this is—"

I stopped when it was obvious Ollie wasn't paying attention to me anymore. Instead, he stared down a connecting hall with a growing look of concern. All I saw when I followed his gaze was a sweaty kid outside, walking slowly past one of the plate glass windows. He was in a yellow and black football uniform, and carried a set of shoulder pads in one hand and a helmet in the other.

"Practice is over," Ollie said.

"I thought you said they were just starting."

Ollie made a helpless gesture. "Coaches don't always structure their practices the same way."

"That's fine. We're leaving anyway."

Ollie held up the ring of Stamper's keys. "We've still got these."

My eyebrows went up like a cartoon character's. I wanted to keep Stamper from realizing we were on his trail, and the disappearance of his keys was not going to help that. Before I could ask Ollie for suggestions, he was already race-walking down the hall in the direction of the football rooms.

"The whole team doesn't always get done at the same time," he explained as we hurried. "Maybe there's time to put them back."

When we got there, a dozen football players were sitting on the benches, leaning back with their legs stretched out in the posture of the physically exhausted. As soon as we stepped in, all heads swiveled in our direction. I wondered if, even after all these years, they could smell the scent of a drama-club kid invading their territory. To deal with this insecurity, I turned my adulthood up to the maximum.

"Anybody lose a set of keys?" I barked, and Ollie held up the ring. "I found these on the floor in the hall."

When there was no response, Ollie stepped forward. "I'm going to put them on your coach's desk," he said to the players. "Tell him they're there, okay?" Ollie deposited Stamper's keys and we took off.

14

As we drove, I kept sneaking glances at Ollie. He had the window down and was tilting his face into the breeze. I worried that a delayed-reaction freakout was eminent, due to our discovery of Stamper's hidden room so soon after his introduction to Eleazar. I shouldn't have been concerned. In fact, it became increasingly clear that Ollie was enjoying himself.

"Is this what you do all the time?" he asked.

"Not exactly. It's usually a bit quieter than this. I'd be lying if I said I never did anything reckless, but I spend most of my time in libraries and archives. Graveyards, too, now that I think about it."

"I hope I did okay back there," Ollie said.

"You did great. If you ever get tired of the Peregrines and want something else to do, let me know." I was only half kidding. I couldn't envision myself working with a partner, but there was no denying Ollie had a knack. He was the kind of person others instinctively trusted. In other circumstances, he could have been a natural con artist.

We passed the Donut Vault and a waft of maple-sugar scented air drifted in through the window.

"I've got a question," Ollie said. "Why in the world would Stamper set up that . . . room right there in the school where anybody could find it?"

I thought about this for a second while we drove under the covered walkway connecting two sections of a furniture factory on either side of First Avenue. "Could be a number of reasons. It's possible that's the only place with the right kind of energy. It's like what I told you with Eleazar. I couldn't have raised him up anywhere else but where he was buried. It's possible that Stamper has a connection to something that's under the spot where the school is now."

"Like an ancient Indian burial ground?"

"Possibly. But it could be anything, really. A meteor, an underground stream, some gizmo that somebody else buried a hundred years ago. There's no telling." We passed Familias Felices Mexican restaurant and the rickety old Priory

Hospital. Opposite, keeping watch over the neighborhood, was St. Roch's church and the Corbusier-inspired building behind it which housed a small colony of nuns.

"There could also be a completely different reason," I added. "He may have set up that stuff in the school precisely because it was dangerous. Maybe he wanted to prove to himself that he wasn't afraid of getting discovered. Or maybe the chance of getting caught makes it more exciting. That happens to people."

A row of Second Empire houses sat on high banks above the sidewalk. Several of them had been converted to offices, though the presence of swing sets and toys in some of the front yards indicated there were still a few holdout families.

"Do you think he's dangerous?"

"I do," I said. "He's either flirting with the idea of being a killer, or he's a full-on killer already. On top of that, he's messing around with forces he might not understand and probably can't control. Things could get out of hand and cause problems for a lot more people than just himself and his buddies."

"But what if he *can* control what he's doing?" Ollie asked. "I know he looks like kind of a blockhead, but if he's able to handle all these magic powers, what then?"

"If he was better at this, we wouldn't know who he was, and we wouldn't know what he was doing," I said. "For a serious student, the first thing you learn to do with your power is conceal it."

"Does that include you?" Ollie asked. "Are you a serious student?"

"I am not." I turned left into the maze of odd-angled one-way streets that led to Ollie's hotel. "On top of that, I don't have any power."

"Didn't you just raise the dead a couple hours ago?"

"There's power and then there's *power.* That was just a party trick. But don't tell Eleazar I said so."

I parked in front of the Executive Inn. Ollie sat in the passenger seat for a second, as if trying to re-acclimate himself to the idea of the safe, mundane, normal world.

"What should I do now?" he asked.

"Nothing yet. I need to think about what we found today and figure out what to do next. With any luck, I should have some ideas by tomorrow."

Ollie took this in stride. He got out of the car, then turned and gave me a little two-fingered salute right before he hit the revolving door. He was going to be all right. Ollie had seen a lot today, but I could tell he was a fairly well-adjusted guy, and it was going to take more than a couple of shocks to knock him off his foundations. He would go up to his room, order some room service and watch TV. Eleazar's ghost and the contents of Stamper's supply room would start to lose their edge. Sooner or later, they would seem more like dreams than memories.

That evening, I struggled with the idea of cooking dinner. For the millionth time, I made a mental note to look up employment agencies and see how much it would cost to hire a real cook. I had a pretty fair idea of the household's financial state, barring whatever secret accounts and bundles of cash Willard had hidden, and I suspected we could afford it, at least for a few times a week. It might be a nice addition. After all, having Mrs. Robinson in to clean the place had worked out great, once we established which rooms she was better off leaving alone.

But right now I wanted to make sure Willard was in a good mood, so I put away the plans for the future and got down to cooking. I pulled out the rabbit we'd gotten recently—one of Willard's associates is an actual falconer, so we have access to an endless supply of fresh rabbit—and started chopping up rosemary and onions. While the pan was warming, I prepared a tray of biscuits and pretty soon the smell of cooking drew him down from his lair.

I waited until halfway through dinner before I sprung on him the details of what I'd found today. His first response was a pained look. I sympathized. Both of us like to think we have fairly strong stomachs, but it's an unsettling experience to be talking about cannibalism over a plate of rabbit cacciatore. However, meal times are just about the only times during the day when our paths cross, so this was my best chance to get answers out of him. Fortunately, basketball season hadn't started yet, so my window of opportunity was larger. When the University of Garvinville's season starts, Willard is glued to the TV from the first minute of the pregame coverage to the final postgame analysis, and woe betide anyone who interrupts.

I wrapped up my description of Eldridge Stamper's secret room. "If I'd been thinking faster, I would have gotten a couple of pictures as soon as we turned on the lights. While I was still poking around, though, we heard someone in the hallway and decided to cover our tracks and escape."

Willard slumped in his Korean lacquer chair. "If we talk about this now, are you going to let me eat dessert in peace?"

"Absolutely. Tell you what, I'll even go get the good ice cream." There was a half gallon of hand-made peach ice cream, from a dairy out in Fort Haub, hidden in the chest freezer under foil-wrapped rib roasts. I figured that now was as good a time as any to play that card.

It worked. "Tell me again what you saw," Willard said.

I went over the details one more time. "Lots of drawings—like cave paintings, really—of big people eating little people. Sometimes tearing them apart and handing out the pieces. There's one figure with horns, who all the rest of the big people seemed to be in awe of."

"Did that suggest anything to you?"

"One or two ideas," I said. "It suggested Stamper maybe shouldn't have a teaching career, surrounded by any number of young, naive, and potentially delicious teenagers. It also suggested I should practice drawing more, since Stamper can do better with finger paints and dropcloths than I can do with fancy art supplies."

"Have you done any research?"

"What do you think I'm doing right now?"

Willard shook his head ponderously, while buttering a biscuit and drizzling it with honey. "Dean, you can't use me as a crutch. You have to build up your own body of knowledge."

He continued in this vein for a minute or two. I let him talk. This is a speech I've heard once or twice before. If I'm going to become a competent, independent investigator, he says, I have to do my own research, not just rely on someone else's expertise. It's not terrible advice, but I can't help noticing how self-serving it is on Willard's part. After all, if I never needed anything beyond my own experience and ability, then Willard would be left alone to build his railroad and watch basketball in peace.

Eventually, he wound down his diatribe with a single word that brought my attention back to the present: "Wendigo."

"Could you repeat that?"

"You've heard the term, surely. A man eats the flesh of another man, and he takes in not only nourishment, but a part of the other man's spirit, too. The man who eats gets stronger, more powerful. He grows. 'Wendigo' is a First Nations word, but you see the same behavior throughout the world."

"Sounds like the same principle as blood doping," I said. "Add in more of what you've already got to make yourself better at whatever you're doing."

"That's a clever way of putting it."

"Thank you." I reached for the pot of honey. "So you think Stamper might be a wendigo?"

"That's hard to say. The literature is unfocused, and I've never had a personal experience with this kind of thing."

"I'm not sure I believe you."

Willard did not accept the invitation to tell me more of his life story. "The term 'wendigo' itself is equally hard to pin down. It may be more accurate to say it describes a state of being, rather than a particular individual."

"Whether he's 'a' wendigo, or he's got 'wendigo-ishness,' it doesn't really matter," I said. "What he's trying to do is eat people and draw their power into himself. Correct?"

"Does it sound correct to you?"

"I'll take that as a 'yes'." I hated the Socratic method, and he knew it. "But his intended victim wasn't just some hapless high school kid or some idiot from the Peregrines who didn't know enough to get away from him. It was the huldra. The woman with the tail. She's not even human."

"I imagine if someone had been expecting a fast-food hamburger, a cut of Kobe beef would be a very welcome surprise. You eat a man, you gain some of a man's power. You eat something more than a man . . ." Willard shrugged his heavy shoulders.

"That still doesn't explain how he ended up with a hul-dra in the first place," I said.

"It does not." Willard stood up. "That was delicious, Dean. Thank you."

I retrieved the gourmet ice cream while he loaded the dishes into the dishwasher. By the time I filled a couple of red stoneware bowls, Willard had moved to the couch and changed the subject. He was in the planning stages for a new rail bridge to connect two of his tiny towns, and he had recently learned that someone else in the Garvinville Model Railroad Hobby Society was working on a very similar design. We discussed whether he'd be better off choosing a different project or continuing forward and braving any possible copycat allegations.

As far as Stamper and the huldra went, I couldn't tell if I had made progress or not. I had a few answers, and I had some of my hunches confirmed, but there was still a lot to learn. Parts of the jigsaw puzzle fit together, but I still couldn't make out what the picture was supposed to be. On top of that, I had the nagging feeling that a number of the most important pieces, the corners and the edges, had fallen off the table without me noticing.

The thing to do now, I knew, was to think about something else. My subconscious mind had an excellent track record of coming up with good ideas, but I had to leave it alone for a while and let it do its thing. To the uninitiated, this process looked very much like ignoring the problem, but Uncle Willard both understood and endorsed this technique, so he wasn't about to give me grief as I made some green tea and sat down in the armchair to cogitate. He had picked up his tablet from the occasional table and was scrolling through his sites.

"Did you hear about the dog?" he asked, apropos of nothing.

"What dog?"

"Someone's dog was killed over on Judson Street. It came up on my neighborhood news page. According to the article, no one saw the attack, but it looks like it was killed by some other animal. They don't go into details, but reading between the lines suggests it was particularly unpleasant."

"You don't think it's our friend with the tail, do you?"

He shook his head. "Unlikely. And it's not your friend." Willard pondered the account of the event for a moment, then dropped the matter and switched over to one of his online model railroad catalogs. "Dean, take a look at this."

He pointed to the screen. "I suspect this warehouse kit could pass for a maintenance shed, but I'd like a second opinion."

Fortunately, my phone chose that moment to ring. I excused myself and stepped into the kitchen. "Dean Sherwood speaking," I said.

"Dean, are you free?" It was Dennis Falco.

I edged toward the patio door, just in case I felt the need to step outside for more privacy. "Yeah, mostly free, I suppose. What's up?"

"How would you like to do me a favor?" When I wasn't quick enough with a polite refusal, Dennis continued. "There are some people with a problem, and one of them called me asking for help. I don't want to get involved, but I thought you might be interested."

"What makes you think that?" I asked.

"First of all, you can't resist a challenge, and coming to anyone's rescue makes your little heart grow two sizes. But more importantly, these people are friends with the couple you're interested in."

"The couple from your reading group?"

"Precisely. Lenora Scanlon and Tim Grimes. If you make these folks happy, they might introduce you to Lenora and Tim."

My keys were hanging from a brass hook next to the door. I reached for them. "Who am I looking for?" I asked.

"His name is Roland Apfel. I've never met him, so I have no idea where he got my number from."

"Where is he?"

"The McCallum Library. He said he'd be playing there until it closed tonight, whatever that means."

15

Naturally, the McCallum Library was way the hell on the other side of town, but a lead was a lead. Even if it turned out to be a wild goose chase, it sounded like a more interesting use of my evening than listening to Uncle Willard evaluate various kitbashing possibilities. I told him I had to go follow up on something and let myself out the patio door. I drove south through a patchwork of little neighborhoods until the houses thinned out an I reached the edge of Park Prospect Cemetery. The McCallum Library was a few blocks beyond that, a chunky, International-style shoebox at the outer edge of the Jefferson Square Mall's vast parking lot.

When I stepped out of the Jag, the first thing I noticed was a feeling of tension. That wasn't completely unusual. The library was right on the borderland where the long expanse of commercial lots along Green River Road switched over to residential neighborhoods, and there's always something uncanny about liminal areas. At the moment, though, the feeling was stronger than usual. I made a slow circuit of the building. The library was bounded by Jefferson Avenue to the north, the mall's parking lot to the west, and a vine-tangled hedge obscuring a chain-link fence on the east. Past the fence was the expansive yard of a trim, steep-roofed bungalow. I tried to look inconspicuous as I ambled around, still attempting to identify my sense of foreboding. Floor-to-ceiling windows along the front of the library showed a few people reading in the big chairs or working at the computer stations. At the circular main desk, a woman with indigo hair was filling out electronic records. I love looking in through windows at night and seeing people doing things. I don't know what that says about me, but I can't deny I enjoy it.

The sensation wasn't so strong around the back, where the air handlers and other machinery were enclosed by a tall fence. A cluster of three six-story apartment buildings stood a little to the south, probably built at about the same time the library went up, since they were the only things in sight that looked like they belonged together. Small jungles of potted plants still sat out on a few balconies, enjoying the last weeks before the nights got frosty. A set of five-colored Tibetan prayer flags hung from another balcony, illuminated with strings of white fairy lights.

As I completed my circuit, I found a bank of windows looking into the conference rooms. In one of them, half a dozen people were packing away notebooks, dice, and thick hardcover rulebooks into their bags. At the head of the table, a skinny guy in an Avantasia t-shirt folded up a cardboard screen and set miniature figures back into a padded carrying case. It was just about the library's closing time, so I figured these were the guys Dennis had told me about. My first impulse was to press my nose against the glass and try to figure out which one was Roland Apfel, but I didn't want to get caught doing it. Besides, the game was clearly breaking up for the night, so all I had to do was wait. I took up a position in the shadows by the overgrown hedge. It gave me a good view of the parking lot, so I planned to lurk there until some of the players came out, then get one of them to direct me to Roland. As I waited, it struck me how much fun it might be to have a "game night." I loved playing chess with Sophie at Planet Caravan, using the green and white set I'd gotten her for Christmas a while back. Maybe I should try to make those games more of a regular thing. I considered this pleasant scenario for a few seconds, then something in the air abruptly changed and I knew, with absolute certainty, that someone was behind me.

It wasn't just the sense that somebody was spying on me, but rather the almost tangible presence of another person mere inches behind me. There was no way they could have sneaked through the bushes without me noticing, but nevertheless, I was no longer alone. The air was still. I smelled something earthy and damp, the kind of scent that belongs in the middle of a forest, not a hedge next to a library parking lot.

I knew who was there.

"It's you," I said out loud. I didn't try to spin around, or defend myself, or even run like mad. She had me where she wanted me. She could do whatever was on her mind before I could shift my weight from one foot to the other. The only option I had was to accept the situation and see what she was thinking. After all, if she had been angry enough to kill me, I would have been dead already.

At the same time, though, I dearly wanted to turn and see her again. The huldra was, quite literally, an unnatural beauty, and the chance of getting another look into those fathomless eyes was very tempting.

"What do you want?" I asked.

No response. Was it getting colder, or was it just my own fear? I couldn't tell, and I couldn't trust my perceptions. Suddenly, there was a hand on my shoulder. A delicate hand, soft but deliberate, as if we were dance partners. Logically, I should have tensed up in anticipation of whatever was coming next, but the opposite happened. I felt myself relaxing. The sensation of dancing, of being in intimate but formal contact, continued to grow. I reached up to put my hand over hers.

Without warning, the bushes behind me rustled violently, as if someone had grabbed the stems and shaken them back and forth. The hand disappeared from my shoulder and I got the impression of something heavy and large moving at great speed very close by. It was the same kind of feeling you get when you're walking along the edge of a busy street with no sidewalk, a foot and a half from the cars racing past.

Then I was alone again. I turned around, but there was nothing to see besides the lights of the bungalow, just visible through the gaps in the bushes. My heart was hammering, and there was an ache in the back of my throat, an intense disappointment that the huldra was gone. But something else had been there, too. Were there two creatures running loose now? Were they working together?

I rubbed my eyes with the heels of my hands and tried to focus. The huldra was gone, the other presence was gone, and so there was no reason to get agitated. I was here for a reason, and a little spookiness in the shrubbery wasn't enough to call it off.

The doors of the library creaked and a handful of people emerged. They all had bags and satchels, and I recognized the guy in the Avantasia shirt, whom I had seen while peeping through the window. This was the role-playing game group. One of them peeled off from the rest and headed in my direction, toward his car. He looked young, but he was one of those people who were going to seem baby-faced until he was sixty. He wore an orange sweater and a plaid jacket with the collar frayed and disheveled. His hair was dark and cut close, and his glasses had heavy frames and square lenses. He looked like some singer-songwriter's anxious little brother.

I reached him just as he got to his car. "Hi, are you Roland Apfel?" I asked.

"Yeah?" He seemed startled, as anyone would be when accosted in a library parking lot by a handsome stranger.

I was pleased with myself for having picked correctly on the first try. "My name's Dean Sherwood. Dennis Falco told me you were here."

"Dennis?" He was still trying to catch up.

"Do you mind if I ask you a couple of questions?"

"Sure," Roland said, clearly not meaning it. He had edged close to his driver's-side door, most likely so he could throw it open and dive inside if the need arose. I hardly blamed him. He hesitated for a second, and the expression of uncertainty on his face resolved itself into recognition. "Wait, you're that guy, aren't you?"

"It's possible," I admitted. "Which guy are you talking about?"

"Dennis told me he couldn't be here, but he said he knew somebody else who could help us. He must have been talking about you." Roland straightened up. Most of his wariness had drained away and he waved at two of his fellow players as they drove past. He regarded me for a moment. "You don't look at all like what he described."

"Dennis has a way of describing things that don't necessarily match any reality except his own," I said ruefully. It sounded like Dennis had already promised my help before he'd even called me. I debated bringing this up with Dennis the next time I saw him, but decided it wasn't worth the effort. Besides, I owed him for the information he'd given me.

"I'm sorry," Roland said. "What did you say your name was again?"

"Dean Sherwood. Listen, I didn't get many details from Dennis. Could you fill me in?"

"Well, it was the thing with Lenora and Tim. What they did. You can help, right?"

"I'll see what I can do." This was my go-to answer, and it rarely let me down.

"Okay. You probably want to go and look at where it happened, don't you?"

I attempted a confident smile. "As a matter of fact, I do."

"It's over on Franklin Street."

"I'll follow you."

Roland's red Honda led me past the plastics factory and over the Pigeon Creek bridge, and I began to get a surprising feeling of *deja vu*. I had been on this section of Franklin Street a couple of days ago. I had driven here, possibly of my own volition and possibly not, right after freeing the huldra from Stamper and his Peregrines. Roland's car flashed its turn signal, and suddenly it was clear we were stopping in the very same parking lot where I had dropped her off.

16

Roland got out. His canvas satchel of rulebooks and papers remained in his car, so I assumed this was not where he actually lived. He looked up at the back side of the building. It had seen plenty of use over the decades. The walls were seamed with old repairs and renovations, with windows bricked up in one place and cut fresh in another, and metal conduits running along the outside like anemic vines.

"That's Tim's apartment." Roland pointed to a window on the second floor.

"Is Tim there?" I asked, and Roland shook his head.

"No. He hasn't been back since . . . Well, I should probably just show you, right?"

He unlocked the vestibule door, the same door that the huldra had slipped through, and we went inside. I followed Roland up the narrow stairway.

"Just to be clear," I said, "what did Dennis say I could do for you, exactly?"

Roland gave me a quick look over his shoulder, the kind of look you might give a plumber who comes to check a leaky faucet and asks if he can borrow a wrench.

"He said you knew all about this. That you'd worked with magic before. He said you'd understand what happened."

Roland led the way down a short hall with pale gray walls and speckled blue carpet covering the floor. I was reminded very strongly of the decor in a nursing home. There were four apartment doors on this floor. Roland stopped at the last one, unlocked it, and we went inside.

The front door opened onto a snug living room, with a kitchen and a bedroom beyond. This was a pretty normal layout for a small apartment, but that was where the normality stopped. The living room furniture had been pushed against the wall, and I saw the scuffed remnants of a magic circle chalked on the floor. The couch was shredded like someone had taken a lawnmower to it, and the walls were peppered with fresh divots and chunks knocked out of the drywall. A card table and a laptop computer had been smashed, and there were deep gouges in the tile floor half-covered by snowdrifts made from ripped-up books.

The kitchen was in no better shape. Like the living room, it looked like a wild animal had been turned loose. Some of the cabinet doors hung pathetically by a single hinge, while others had been torn off completely. The refrigerator was open and dark, and the characteristic smell of rotten food hung in the air. Parts of chairs and an old Formica table, bent nearly in half, littered the floor. In the bedroom, a foam mattress and several blankets had been shredded just like the couch in the living room. The dresser was tipped over on its side, and something about its position made me stop for a moment.

"This had been blocking the door," I said, with my hand still on the leg of the dresser. "Someone barricaded themselves in here."

Roland nodded. "Yeah. It didn't work."

By my toe, I saw a Doctor Strange action figure, formerly a part of someone's collection, possibly taking pride of place on a dresser or shelf. It had been snapped in half, which seemed to me inexpressibly poignant. All of a sudden, I felt tired. I righted the wooden desk chair and sat down.

"All right," I said, "why don't you tell me what happened?"

Roland gave me a hesitant look. Despite getting this far, into the apartment and through the debris, he was now clamming up. I resisted the urge to sigh.

"Think of me as a doctor," I said. "I can only help if you tell me what's going on."

"Lenora has a circle," Roland said. "People who practice ritual magic." He paused again, checking my reaction. When it was clear I wasn't going to clutch my pearls or sneer, he continued. I didn't blame him too much. When you talked to an outsider about this kind of thing, there was no way of knowing what the reaction was going to be. That's why I always call myself an "investigator" or a "researcher" rather than an "occult detective" or something similar, even though it's much closer to the truth. It's just too weird for everyday conversation.

"Lenora was the leader. We called her the *princepa*."

I got distracted for a second trying to work out if this was a reasonable feminization for the Latin noun, but I knew what he meant: the first. The leader.

"She decided what we would study, and how our rituals would go. She was the teacher, and we were the students. Tim was her assistant."

"Were they together? Romantically?"

"I couldn't say. I mean, maybe, but I never knew for sure," Roland said. "We all assumed they were at least partners in sex magic workings, but I don't know about the romance part. If they were together, they kept it quiet when the circle was meeting."

"I'm sorry I interrupted. Go ahead."

Roland was getting warmed up now. He sat down on the surviving corner of the bed. His hands, which had been locked together tightly behind him, now began to flutter and punctuate what he was saying. "Last week—I think it was last week—Tim asked us to get together here, at his apartment. He told us Lenora needed us for some kind of powerful working, and the more of us who were here, the stronger it was going to be."

"How many were there?"

"Just the main group: Lenora and Tim, me, Jerry Morgan, Patty Embry, and Jenny Swift and Tony Swift."

"Seven of you."

"Yeah, I guess so." Roland ran through the guest list in his head again. "Is that important?"

"You never know. Just trying to get all the facts."

"When we got here, Tim had his furniture pushed back, like he always does when we get together for a working. We liked doing the rituals here. It's an old building with thick walls, so it's really quiet. Besides, the rest of the building's full of old ladies, and they all love Tim. For some reason. Anyway, while Lenora was getting ready, Tim handed out sheets with the text of the ritual on it."

I asked if he still had a copy, but he shook his head.

"It all started out like normal. We were going to do the thing and get some pizza, the way we usually did. Tim got the candles arranged and pulled all the curtains, then Lenora drew the circle and said the words to seal it."

"Did she use salt?" I asked. When you were calling up something that you wanted to keep in place, salt was a common ingredient.

"Lots of it. I didn't ever remember Lenora using that before, so I was kind of curious about what she was thinking. But I figured she knew what she was doing, so I didn't worry too much. I didn't worry right then, anyway." Roland adjusted his glasses and ran a hand over his mouth. For a second, I felt bad about making him relive all of this, but it sounded like he was glad to be able to tell the story.

"We all stood around at the points of the circle. It wasn't anything we hadn't done a dozen times before. Then Lenora began. She'd say a section of the ritual, and we'd all say the response. A lot of it was in a language I didn't recognize, but she was always doing stuff like that. The parts that weren't in English were written out phonetically, so it wasn't hard to say. I do remember that she kept looking at Tim. That wasn't normal. Lenora, when she's on, she's in charge. I'd never seen her check with anyone during a working. But this time she did. It was a long ritual, and we were about halfway through the pages when I started to notice something different."

"What was it?"

"I'd never seen anything like it before. Usually when we get together, we set up our equipment and go through our ritual, and that's the end of it, right? The rituals are how we make changes in our own lives—to attract something or to protect ourselves from something. The effects are subtle. You don't actually *see* anything. Nothing pushes itself up from the floor. This time, though . . ."

I understood what he meant, and I thought I could visualize what had happened. Suddenly and unexpectedly, they had gone from the theoretical to the practical. The effect must have been like driving your safe, modest hatchback down the street at a sensible speed, then making a left turn and suddenly finding yourself in the middle of the Indianapolis 500. Or sitting down with your friends to play an entertaining fantasy adventure game in the library conference room, and suddenly the door is kicked open by a horde of actual trolls.

"I don't even know how to describe it," Roland admitted. "It just came up from the middle of the circle. Like it was rising out of a lake or something."

"What did it look like?"

"Big. Dark." Roland sounded frustrated, like his vocabulary couldn't give shape to the memory. "Tangled."

"Tangled?"

"Yeah. Something about it made me think of a plant. Like one of those weed patches where everything is all grown up and jumbled together and you can't tell where one thing ends and something else begins. Just a big mass of plants. A thicket."

"Then what happened?"

"None of us ever expected to see anything like this. I'm sure I didn't. The others—Jerry and Patty and the Swifts— I don't think they did, either." Roland paused, working out what he wanted to say. "I guess I never thought for sure that all this was real. I always kind of imagined it was maybe more of a symbolic thing, a sort of way to take control of your life. But now . . ."

"It's a surprise, sometimes," I said.

"Anyway, I was just terrified. I couldn't take my eyes off the thing. I kept thinking to myself, it can't cross the circle. It can't cross the circle. Then I realized somebody was saying that out loud. It was Lenora. She was saying it. She was telling all of us not to be afraid because it couldn't cross the circle."

"And then it did?" I asked.

"Not at first. There were a few seconds where it just sat there, sort of bunched-up. Like it was in a cage that was too small. But then it reached out a paw—"

"It had paws?"

"That's what it looked like. Or maybe it didn't look like that, and it just seemed like that's what it was supposed to be. I can't really remember the details. I don't know."

"Don't worry about it," I said. "You're doing fine. This isn't easy, but you're really helping."

"It reached out its paw, and it stopped where the circle was. Like there was a wall of glass going up from where we drew the circle on the floor. It touched that, then it pulled itself back. I remember Lenora saying, 'See?' to us. And then it got free."

17

What Roland was telling me right now did not sound like good news. A protective circle, if constructed correctly, can keep you safe from quite a bit. Even when hacked together by a couple of hobbyists, it would take a creature of unusual power to push its way through.

"I don't remember a lot after that," Roland said. "Screaming. Running. The thing took up half the room. It was flopping around, like it wasn't able to get its legs steady and walk. Everything was breaking—the couch, the TV, Tim's desk. We ran back into the bedroom."

"Why didn't you run outside?"

"I wish I knew. That would have been the smart thing to do, but at the time it never crossed anybody's mind. We just wanted to get away from the thing. We ran in here and threw that in front of the door." He gestured toward the dresser.

"What were Lenora and Tim doing?"

"Nothing that I can remember. They were as scared as we were. I think Tim was digging through his books over there, looking for something to try."

The wreckage of a simple wooden bookcase slouched against the other side of the bed, and I got up to have a look at what remained inside it. This was a prime opportunity to get a picture of Tim Grimes's personality. We can present ourselves however we like to the rest of the world, but three things always betray who we really are: our music collection, our porn collection, and the books by the side of our bed.

Just like the rest of the room, a lot of the books had been pulverized, ripped apart in long, ragged gouges by something with sharp claws and a grudge. Here and there I could make out a few surviving covers: *The Sword of Shannara. The Weirdstone of Brisingamen. The Dungeons & Dragons Players Handbook. Moby-Dick. The Complete Tales of Winnie-The-Pooh.* Some others caught my eye for professional reasons: *The Book of the Arcadians. The Veils of Life and Death,* by Gertrude Jensen. *The Magicians Speak.* I was familiar with these from Uncle Willard's library, but they weren't exactly the books that came up when you browsed in the "occult" section of your local bookstore or read a "getting started with the secret arts" website. Maybe Tim and Lenora knew a little more than I was giving them credit for.

"After a minute, it broke open the door," Roland said, interrupting my thoughts. He seemed to want to finish his story. "I swear, I thought I was going to die right here. At first, it just stood in the doorway. I don't know for how long. I couldn't turn away from it. Those eyes."

He pinched the bridge of his nose, as if trying to control a headache. "Then it jumped at us. I think it was going for Lenora. Or maybe Tim. I don't know for sure. After that, it was just a frenzy."

I didn't doubt that. There were claw marks all over the walls, with a few of them even reaching the ceiling. In a little space like this, the chaos must have been exceptional. But still, they all managed to survive. That was significant. I asked him what happened next.

"People were screaming and crying. I guess I was, too. Lenora and Tim were chanting something. I don't know if they were trying to get the thing to leave us alone, or just to divert it away from them and towards the rest of us. Eventually, it just threw itself out the window and got away."

Roland indicated the old-fashioned hinged window, a couple of feet tall and set into the wall at about chest height. It opened and closed with a crank built into the frame.

"I know what you're thinking," Roland said, as he watched me examining the window. "I don't know how it got through, and I don't know why the glass didn't break, but that's what happened."

A small crack snaked across the central pane from top to bottom. I ran my finger along the fissure and felt where a chip had come out, leaving a pea-sized hole.

"Things don't always need a particularly large opening to get from one place to another," I said. "Especially the kinds of things that get called up inside a magic circle."

"Oh."

"The normal rules don't always apply," I said. "That's why the neighbors didn't hear anything and call the cops. You were the ones who brought it up, so you were the only ones it showed itself to. To anybody else, the whole episode would have been less than a quiet breeze. Unless it wanted them to notice."

"So is it still out there? Can you tell?"

"Is this why you called Dennis for help?" I asked. "Are you worried about that thing running around?"

Roland nodded. "Yeah. Every time I hear about something on the news, a weird break-in or somebody getting hurt in some strange way, I wonder if that's because of what we did, and if it's partially my fault. I've been having nightmares about it. Eventually I remembered that Lenora said she knew Dennis, so I decided to call him. Just so I can sleep a little better."

"What do Lenora and Tim have to say about this?"

"I haven't heard from them. None of us have."

My first thought was that they were either dodging responsibility or working frantically to undo the situation. But it was also possible that the thing had already eaten them.

"Do you even know what it is?" Roland asked.

"No clue." Seeing Roland's nakedly distressed expression, I continued. "I wish I had a better answer than that, but it's the truth. Yes, that thing's probably still out there, and it may not want to be found right now. It's going to take me a while to figure out what it is and what to do about it."

Suddenly, Roland looked even more nervous than before.

"I appreciate you showing me all this," I said, "but I'll need to talk to Lenora and Tim, too. Do you have a way to reach them?"

I was prepared to convince Roland that I didn't harbor any ill-will toward them, and only wanted to help put right what had gone badly out of control. In groups like this, loyalty can run strong, even in the worst of circumstances. I could see where a disciple wouldn't want to potentially rat out his *princepa*. But before I could articulate a reason for him to trust me, he was scrolling through the contacts on his phone.

"This is Lenora's number," he said as he texted me the information. It included a business name, "Garden Witchery," and a phone number. "You don't know the address?" I asked Roland.

"I don't know for sure where she lives. Somewhere over on the east side, I think. All our meetings and rituals were always over here, at Tim's apartment. Maybe Lenora didn't want the rest of us to know where she lived. That would kind of make sense. She's private."

"What about Tim? Do you know where he is?"

"I imagine he's been staying with Lenora." Roland looked around the wreckage with grim distaste. "Tim hasn't been back here since it happened, obviously."

We closed up the apartment and went back down the stairs. As we descended, we passed a gray-haired woman walking a Yorkshire terrier. We smiled and nodded at each other. Roland had mentioned that Tim got along with his fellow tenants. I hoped none of them would get worried and ask the super to open Tim's door, revealing the hellscape inside.

In the parking lot, Roland asked, "You're going to be able to help, aren't you?"

"That's the plan." Roland's repeated need for reassurance was starting to get on my nerves, but I tried not to show it. If the situation were reversed, I'd probably act the exact same way. "I'll try to figure out what that thing was and how to get it under control," I said.

"Is there anything else you need me to do?"

"Not that I can think of," I said. "Just go about your life. You haven't seen it anywhere else, have you?"

"No. Not since that night. Once was enough."

I nodded. "Maybe try to go easy on the rituals for a while. Once you tear open a hole big enough for monsters to get through, more of them tend to keep trying."

Roland got in his car and drove away. I stood there thinking for a minute or two. I recalled the sensation of the unknown presence moving behind me in the bushes next to the library. It had seemed large, dangerous, and malevolent. Was it the creature Lenora and Tim had summoned?

On the way home, I called Ollie's number and got voicemail. "Ollie, it's Dean. Give me a call. I've got some new leads already. I'm not a hundred percent sure they're all connected to what's going on at the Peregrine perch, but at this point I'd be surprised if they weren't. Anyway, call me when you can, and let me know when you're free tomorrow."

A few heavy drops of rain hit the windshield, and by the time I got back home it was raining hard enough to knock the leaves off the tree in the front yard. I hit the button for the garage door and pulled inside. I sat there in the darkness, listening to the rain patter on the tile roof. I stared at the jumble of garden trellises and coiled hoses in the corner of the garage and wondered if the shape they made in the darkness was the same as yesterday. Sometimes the mind can play tricks, but sometimes other things can play tricks, too. I tried to shake off the uneasiness. If there really was something lurking in the garage, I had already given it plenty of time to jump out and get me. Therefore, it was probably nothing. I resisted the urge to switch on my phone's flashlight and illuminate the dark corners. Instead, I called the number Roland had given me.

Voicemail. Nobody was picking up their phone tonight. "Hi, Lenora, this is Dean Sherwood. We met at Knit Now. I wrote down something for you to give to Dennis Falco and you were very careful about the pen I used, remember? Anyway, Roland Apfel gave me your number, and he showed me around Tim's apartment. I think I can help with what's going on. Get in touch, and we'll meet someplace."

While I walked to the kitchen door, keeping to the narrow dry patch under the awning, I pondered the odds that my message would actually lead Lenora to contact me. My professional estimate was only about one chance in four, but I had to start somewhere. If this didn't produce a fruitful conversation with her, then my next step would be showing up unannounced at Knit Now again.

Uncle Willard had vacated the living room and was nowhere to be seen on the ground floor. He was most likely back in the attic, or in his study on the second floor, a former bedroom that he'd converted into a combination of "gentleman's private library" and "Dr. Jekyll's chemistry lab." The memo pad on the kitchen counter, next to the wooden statue of St. Genesius that we use as a message depot, had a new list of things he wanted me to pick up, including 18-gauge wire, a replacement airbrush nozzle, and multiple formulas of specialist glue. He must have finally settled on plans for his latest model building. I hoped it would keep him in a good mood for a few days.

18

The next morning, I spent more time than I'm prepared to admit deciding which of my old Viyella flannel shirts to wear before heading downstairs to fix a bowl of oatmeal with blueberries. I put on the coffee maker for Uncle Willard and checked my phone again. Lenora hadn't called and she hadn't texted, which was not much of a surprise. Ollie hadn't either, and that struck me as unusual. Given his enthusiasm, and everything he'd seen yesterday, I would have expected to hear from him right away. I wondered if he'd gotten cold feet, or if his mind had simply short-circuited and declared that it had all been a hallucination, never to be thought of again. Ollie didn't strike me as the type, but it certainly happened sometimes.

My watch said eight-thirty. Was that too early to call someone? It had been a long time since I'd had a job with regular hours, so I was unclear on the etiquette on this point. Instead, I settled for texting Ollie: "How's it going? We've got things to check into today, so let me know when you're up."

For the length of time it took to finish the oatmeal and eat a banana, I waited. This was a real achievement. I am not a person who is comfortable waiting. Once it became clear that staring at the phone wasn't going to make a reply arrive any faster, I slipped on some shoes and ambled the two blocks over to Planet Caravan. A few of the houses along the way had gotten out their Halloween decorations already, displaying antique blow-mold jack-o-lanterns in the windows and decorative cobwebs on the porches. I rarely paid much attention to the Halloween season, probably because my whole year is liberally populated with ghosts, ghouls, and things that—at the very least—go bump in the night. For me, the best part of Halloween is watching Uncle Willard hand out candy all evening dressed as John Carradine's Dracula.

After I said hello to Sophie and ordered my dark roast, I noticed the green and white chessboard folded up on the shelf behind a glass jar of biscotti. It reminded me of what

I'd been thinking about last night while waiting to ambush Roland.

"Hey," I said to Sophie. "Got time for a game?"

She pursed her lips. "I don't know, Dean. I'd hate to crush your confidence so early in the day."

She handed over counter duties to Kharma, one of her lieutenant baristas, and we sat down at a corner table and set up the pieces. She wore an oversized paisley silk shirt knotted at one hip and, as usual, a couple of necklaces and more rings than I could count.

"I like your nails," I said.

"Thanks." She studied them for a second. "You don't think they're too dark?"

"No. They go with your hair."

We played quickly, moving the pieces without a huge amount of calculation. Eventually, though, my moves got slower and slower.

"You okay?" she asked, brazenly thrusting forward a rook.

"Sorry. I'm waiting for a couple of calls. I don't like waiting for stuff."

"Really? I never knew that about you. You never complain when it's busy here and you have to wait for your coffee."

"That's different." I moved a bishop to a position of safety. "I like it here. The more excuses I have to stay here, the better."

"Does this have to do with your other job? The private investigator stuff?"

"Yeah. In my capacity as Uncle Willard's lackey, waiting doesn't matter so much. Right now, it could matter quite a bit."

"Is there anything I can help with?" she asked.

"No, I'm just tracking a few things down." Sophie had a decent idea of what my "private investigator" work really meant, but I still tried to keep the details vague. I wasn't sure if this was because I didn't want to risk upsetting her, or because I wanted to present myself as a largely normal person. "The people I need to talk to won't return my messages."

"That's a shame," she said. "Maybe they just need to get to know you better."

"Exactly."

"Tell them to call me. I'll vouch for you."

"I appreciate that." I took another sip of coffee and studied the board. "This is really fun. We should do this more often. Make it a weekly thing. You're here on Thursday afternoons, right?"

"Ooh, sorry. I just started a metalwork class with Carl on Thursday afternoons."

Carl was Sophie's boyfriend. By all accounts, and to any reasonable person, Carl was a perfectly nice guy. Possibly even above average. I, however, couldn't help thinking the worst of him. "No problem," I said with nonchalance. "Some other time."

In short order, I was down two knights and a bishop, and the future wasn't looking bright. Then half a dozen middle-aged women came in with books under their arms and the unmistakable aspect of a book club, which gave me the opportunity to resign gracefully and let Sophie get back to work. I finished my coffee and waited for the phone to ring.

It did not ring. I sent Ollie another text, since I wasn't concerned about spooking him by being too aggressive. Lenora was going to require more patience. As I stood up to get a refill, I happened to notice what the book club ladies were reading. It was a thick, lurid, true-crime book with the title *Brotherhood of Death* in two-inch letters. This, combined with my growing sense of unease, sent my thoughts in a new direction. I hadn't known Ollie long, but he didn't seem like the kind of person who would ignore a message. What if he hadn't responded because he *couldn't* respond? Of course, there were still plenty of other innocuous explanations: He might have had an early morning meeting with the Peregrines. He might have dropped his phone in the sink. He might have decided not to have anything to do with me anymore. All of those were perfectly valid and reasonable possibilities. But now a small flicker of concern was glowing in my mind. I said goodbye to Sophie, then walked home to get my car.

Ollie had said his room was on the fourth floor of the Executive Inn, at the end of the hall with a view of the river. Fortunately, the way the rooms were laid out left me no doubt that room 412 had to be his. I stood on the olive carpet and knocked repeatedly. There was no response. Calling his number didn't produce the sound of a ringing phone from inside. At the front desk, they couldn't tell me if he'd gone out this morning, making them noticeably less helpful than hotel clerks in the movies. But I wasn't going to give up. Finding Ollie had become a priority, a nagging mental itch. Something wasn't right, and I was going to have to keep searching until I knew where he was.

My next stop was the Peregrine perch. Several cars were in the parking lot, and that gave me hope that Ollie might have been drawn into some Peregrine business this morning. I let myself in through the back door, past the kitchen where Stamper and his friends had threatened me, then up the stairs into the main building. It was quiet, and I could hear the hum of a fan in the distance, moving the musty air around. When I reached the atrium, sounds of conversation led me upstairs. In one of the smaller rooms, a handful of people sat around an old round table with foliate legs. They had papers spread out on the polished surface, and one of them had a laptop open. None of them were Ollie, and none of them were Stamper or his associates, which was good because they noticed me before I had a chance to step away from the door.

"Hello, can I help you?" said one of the Peregrines, a rangy guy with half-size reading glasses and a gray beard.

"Sorry to bother you, but I was looking for Ollie Helfrich." There were no expressions of alarm or guilt when I mentioned that name, which suggested that these were either the normal, run-of-the-mill Peregrines or exceptionally good actors. "Ollie and I were supposed to meet this morning, but I haven't been able to find him. Has he been here today?"

"Are you a Peregrine?" asked another one.

I didn't know what degree of equivocation was necessary at this point, and before I could come up with a convincing story, the bearded guy helped me out. "He was supposed to meet with us, too," the guy said, and held up a sheaf of what looked like invoices. "We got started without him, but he was supposed to be here half an hour ago."

"Maybe El knows something," suggested someone from the other side of the table.

"Eldridge? Stamper?" I asked.

"Yeah. They were talking about something in the parking lot after the meeting broke up last night." He asked the other Peregrines, "Did anybody else see that? That's who was talking to El last night, right? Little guy, short hair? Red Peregrine jacket?"

The others nodded noncommittally and agreed that, as far as anyone could recall, the last time they'd seen Ollie was last night, in the company of Stamper.

"Ollie's been here for days, and this is the first time he's ever been late for something," added the bearded guy.

"Odd," said another. The rest of them agreed to that, too.

"Well, I'll keep looking. Thanks for your time." I backed into the hall. Their mention of the name "Stamper" had given me a cold feeling. After all the prying we did into Stamper's life yesterday, this felt like anything but a coincidence.

19

My intuition took me halfway to West Central High School before I realized that pushing my way into the building and interrogating Stamper in front of a class of metal shop students was not likely to lead to a productive outcome. But this thought led me immediately to something better, an idea that made me cut across two lanes of traffic and onto Diamond Avenue. If Stamper was teaching, then his house was going to be empty. If Stamper's house was empty, then I would be free to look around inside. Who knew what kinds of clues I might find there?

A section of road construction stymied my attempt at a shortcut, so I had to painstakingly backtrack through an adjoining development before I reached Stamper's house. His street was empty this time, so there was nobody to see me sneak around the house and into his back yard, nonchalantly carrying the pry bar from my trunk. A short deck connected to his second-floor back door, and I didn't hesitate to jam the pry bar into the doorframe right above the knob. I threw myself against it a couple of times and felt something start to give. I tried to work quickly. Breaking into a house in the middle of the day was unquestionably a risk, and there was no telling how long I would have to look around before a patrol car showed up.

Stamper's kitchen was plain and utilitarian, with a sort of bachelor minimalism that signifies a fundamentally orderly person. I stood still and smelled the air. Every house smells different, and you can learn a lot about a place in those few minutes before your nose gets acclimated to the ambient scents. I detected cleaning products, lots of them, which made me uneasy. There were plenty of reasons why an industrial arts teacher would need heavy-duty detergents and solvents, but there were plenty of reasons why a cannibal would need them, too. Under the cleaning products was another scent, something metallic that I couldn't place right away. I continued my exploration. The living room had a big TV in the picture window, and a couple of recliners and a small sofa opposite. Instead of pictures on the mantel, there stood a number of items that looked like old stone age artifacts: flint knives and a round stone with worn grooves that may once have been the head of a mallet. A hall led off to a couple of bedrooms and a bathroom, but I went down the stairs to examine the lower floor of the split-level.

It was darker here, with the only light coming in from a couple of curtained windows near the ceiling, just above ground level. A pool table stood in the center of the room, and an old pinball machine glowed in a corner. It was a chrome-laden antique from the 1970s, with the painted backboard showing the band Kiss in concert. Part of me really wanted to see if it was rigged for free play, but I kept my mind on the task at hand. The metallic smell was stronger down here, and for a moment I wondered if it was some auto-maintenance product from the garage, the entrance to which was down a short access corridor. Two other doors connected to the little corridor as well. One was open, showing a laundry room with plank shelves holding tools and various household goods.

The other door was padlocked.

I didn't bother knocking or trying any other time-wasting effort to confirm my suspicions. Instead, I went right to work with the pry bar. Within a couple of minutes, I had pulled the screws loose enough that I could rip the hasp, the plate, and the lock itself, all still connected together, free from the door.

Inside, it was pretty much what I had expected. The metallic scent was blood, which had been splashed on the concrete floor and on the walls. Ollie Helfrich, the source of this blood, was manacled to the back wall in his boxer shorts.

He'd been thoroughly beaten up. His face was swollen with bruises and partly obscured with caked blood. When I entered, he looked up at me with one bleary, half-closed eye. The other one was swollen shut. My stomach lurched, but I forced myself to concentrate.

"Ollie," I said as I crouched next to him. "I'm going to get you out of here. Just hang on for a second." There was a faint groan from behind his split lips, and I got to work. The chains on the manacles were run through a heavy eye bolt drilled into the concrete foundation, and after a brief struggle I decided I was never going to get that bolt loose without a pickaxe. Instead, I switched my attention to the chain itself. After looping a few links together to give myself a sufficient fulcrum, I was eventually able to exert enough force to separate the ends of one link and unhook it from the next one in line. Ollie would still have a length of chain attached to each wrist, but at least he could move.

Or, he could move in theory. Once the chain was detached from the wall, Ollie made a manful effort to stand, but it was clear he wasn't up to the job.

"It's okay. I've got you." I put his arm over my shoulder and transferred as much of his weight as I could onto my back. It was ungainly, but we were able to scuttle like a paralytic crab in the direction of the garage.

I didn't make any effort to cover my tracks or hide what I had done. I figured that Stamper would check on Ollie as soon as he got home, so there wasn't much point in concealment. I also didn't bother picking up the stacks of household junk that we knocked over, or putting the garage door back down after our exit. It wasn't until later that it occurred to me I was leaving a mess on purpose. I wanted Stamper to know, as soon as he got in sight of his house, that someone had been here.

I dropped Ollie into the passenger seat of the Jag and pulled out of Stamper's driveway. A few blocks later, I saw a police car driving rapidly in the opposite direction. If they'd been called out to investigate a break-in at Stamper's house, they were going to find something very surprising if they looked in the garage and followed the trail of blood-spatters back into the house. But, to be honest, I hoped the police were on their way somewhere else. I wanted to find Stamper before they did. I didn't care about his occult activities anymore, and I didn't even care about how he'd managed to subdue the huldra. Now all I wanted was revenge for trying to eat my friend.

I hit a pothole and Ollie shifted in his seat. He mumbled something inarticulate, then lifted his head slightly. "Hi, Dean," he said.

"Don't try to say anything. Just hang on for a few more minutes. Can you do that?"

To my relief, I was rewarded with a shaky thumbs-up. I coasted into the University Liquors parking lot and grabbed my phone. I hated to stop, but wasn't certain I could trust myself to drive and talk at the moment, so I sat there and waited an excruciating number of rings until the call picked up.

"Uncle Willard, can you call Dr. Helmbach?" I asked. "Get him over to the house as soon as you can. Make sure he brings his medical bag. I'm on the way. I'll explain when I get there. Just make sure Dr. Helmbach is there. No, it's not me. It's . . . Forget it. I'll be there in a few minutes."

I disconnected the call and got on the expressway. Ollie was a mess. Every time I saw him shifting restlessly in the seat, I was relieved he was still alive. To my eyes, he looked like a car crash victim, someone who'd been hurled through a windshield and bounced across a dozen yards of blacktop. I tried not to think about whose fault it was that he had ended up this way. The obvious answer, of course, was Stamper, but I couldn't let myself completely off the hook. On Sunday night at the Peregrine perch, if I'd just thanked Ollie politely for rescuing me and gone about my business, he wouldn't be in the state he's in now. I had a moment of sympathy for Roland Apfel, and his guilt about the part he played in Lenora and Tim's creature getting loose. But then I reminded myself to quit ruminating and focus on the job at hand. I was driving quickly and aggressively in an effort to get Ollie back to the house, and didn't want to end up rear-ending another car because I wasn't paying attention.

Dr. Helmbach's white Cadillac, most likely the last one in the world, was parked in the driveway when I got home. I stopped at the curb, honked the horn to see if I could summon any assistance, then began to carry Ollie up the slope using the same half-drag, half-carry technique as before.

"Dean, what happened?" Willard asked as I got to the front door.

"Hang on. Let me put him down first." I looked over Willard's elbow to where Dr. Helmbach stood in the hall with a somber expression on his face. "Where do you want him?" I asked.

"Over there." Dr. Helmbach pointed to the couch in my office. Once Ollie was down, Dr. Helmbach took over. Willard and I served as orderlies, running for towels and water as needed, and stuffing the blood-soaked cast-offs into trash bags. It was a testament to the seriousness of the situation that I didn't even worry about Ollie's blood soaking into the upholstery of my couch. Not a whole lot, anyway.

Dr. Mitchell Helmbach had been Willard's personal physician for years, and Willard had helped untangle some unpleasant circumstances regarding one of the doctor's ex-wives. Ever since then, he'd been more than willing to answer the call when a medical emergency like this arose. It's very reassuring to know a doctor who isn't going to run away or call the police whenever he sees something the tiniest bit weird.

While Willard and I stood outside my office, waiting for instructions, I explained where I had found Ollie, what I suspected had happened to him, and what would have happened next if I hadn't shown up.

"This Stamper person was planning to eat him?" Willard asked.

"That's certainly the impression I got."

Willard nodded, as if in confirmation of a theory. "Wendigo madness. The more a man eats, the more he wants to eat. Fortunately, you've stopped him before things could get any worse."

"I haven't stopped him at all," I said. "Not yet, anyway. That's next on the list, though, right after . . ." I gestured to Dr. Helmbach as he knelt beside my couch.

"Be careful," Willard said. "Obviously, this man is violent, and most likely insane. Do you want the pistol?"

"No, I don't want the pistol," I said after a second's hesitation. Willard had a lovingly maintained Luger in his desk drawer upstairs, but guns made me squeamish. I always felt I was likely to accidentally shoot Willard—or even worse, myself—with the thing, so I tended to keep it out of my arsenal of problem-solving tools. Still, though, not everybody was as civilized as I was, and I might be quickly reaching a point where the Luger was going to be necessary.

Dr. Helmbach, looking disconcertingly like a Civil War field surgeon, stepped into the hall, peeling off his blue rubber gloves.

"He's stable now. I gave him something to help him sleep, but I'm going to have to admit him. He needs a CAT scan, and I'm worried about internal bleeding. What in the world happened to him?"

"He got beat up," I volunteered.

"Good God."

"He may not look it, but Ollie actually got off easy."

Dr. Helmbach clearly wanted to ask me for details, but he also knew he would have to live with the knowledge of whatever I told him. On top of that, if he didn't get the details now, he wouldn't have to lie about them later. He glanced over at Willard, who nodded agreement.

"We should take him to Priory," Dr. Helmbach said. "I know people on the staff. We can play fast and loose with the paperwork for a while if you need to keep things quiet. I won't be able to hold off the questions forever, especially if there are more serious injuries, but I think I can do a good job." He took a plaid handkerchief from his pocket and dabbed at his forehead. "Ideally, he should go in an ambulance, but a car will work."

We maneuvered the cars around and I got the Jag under the porte-cochere at the side of the house. There, sheltered by the overhang, Dr. Helmbach and I carried Ollie down the three steps and into the back seat. I couldn't help glancing around to see if anyone had stopped on the street to stare at us. Willard and I have a slight reputation in the neighborhood for being eccentric—a reputation that he instigated and nurtured far before I arrived, I might add—and it probably wouldn't help to be seen lugging an unconscious figure into the back of my car.

Ollie, heavily sedated now, shifted slightly and mumbled something I couldn't understand. He smelled like disinfectant and new bandages. His bruises, formerly crimson and raw, were beginning to darken and turn black.

I put a hand on his ankle before I stepped back to close the door. "I'm sorry, Ollie," I said. "I should have known."

I followed Dr. Helfrich to the emergency entrance at Priory Hospital. He motioned for me to wait, then went in alone. He was gone for five or ten minutes, which felt much closer to sixty. When he returned he was accompanied by a gray-haired nurse wearing a grim expression and pushing a wheelchair. Together, he and the nurse transferred Ollie into the chair. Then the nurse pushed Ollie through the automatic doors and disappeared into the shadows.

"It's going to be easier if he's alone," Dr. Helmbach said to me. "I'll give Willard a call and keep him updated on the man's condition. Is there anything else you can tell me?"

"Not at the moment," I said. "But maybe soon." While waiting for Dr. Helmbach to re-appear, in between checks to make sure Ollie was still breathing, I had looked up a few things on my phone. One of them was the online calendar for the Garvinville Peregrine perch. They had a general chapter meeting scheduled for tonight. If I didn't have any more information now, I was definitely going to have some after that.

20

The Peregrines' meeting didn't start for a couple of hours, which gave me enough time to clean the blood out of my car. This wasn't my first attempt at mopping up unpleasant fluids, so I knew what steps to take. After using two different cleaners, a spray, a gentle scrub-brush, and two rolls of paper towels, the interior was as good as it ever had been. I, however, was a pink-tinted mess. I threw my clothes in the washing machine, turned the knob to the "cold" setting, and draped myself in a bedsheet before going upstairs to take a shower. When I was done, I found Willard in the recliner, reading a biography of Jack Parsons with a plate of sandwiches and a glass of wine by his elbow.

"Are you going out?" he asked.

"I am."

"Does this have to do with the Peregrines?"

"It does. I'm guessing that Stamper is going to be at the Peregrines' meeting tonight. Whether he knows Ollie is gone or not, he's not going to want to vary his routine. It's possible he may even go straight to the Peregrine perch from football practice."

"The man plays football?"

"He's a coach. High school."

Willard snorted. He disapproves of authority figures, from presidents and executives all the way down to cops and, apparently, high school football coaches.

I took my old Czech army jacket from the coat tree in the hall. It wasn't particularly warm, but it fit the tone I was trying to project better than the unraveling mustard-yellow pullover I put on when I got out of the shower.

"I'm planning to hide outside the building, wait until he's alone and unsuspecting, then get the truth out of him," I said.

"How do you propose to make that happen?"

"I'm going to trust to inspiration when the time comes," I said. "I'd get the law involved, but I want to know how he got control of the huldra, and no one besides me is going to interrogate him too closely on that point."

In my office, I grabbed a few other things I thought might be useful, including a notebook, a tarnished old set of brass knuckles, and my match safe. I liked having a few things in my pockets in situations like these. It made me feel prepared.

"Be careful," Willard said when I returned to the living room. "This man's already shown himself to be quite capable of violence. I'd just as soon you not end up as someone's entree."

"That makes two of us," I admitted. "I don't know how late I'm going to be. While I'm gone, do you think you could see about getting the blood stains off my couch?"

Willard reacted as if I'd just asked him to change his own oil.

"Or at the very least, think up an excuse for Mrs. Robinson when she comes in." I pointed at him meaningfully. "This time, see if you can find one that doesn't make me sound like a monster. She's still suspicious about what happened with the sink."

Willard gave an exasperated snort. "The woman surprised me. It was the best I could achieve in the heat of the moment."

Declining to dignify that with a response, I let myself out the side door and into the garage. I parked on the street, close to the Peregrine perch but not too close, and approached the building on foot. The meeting wasn't supposed to start for another half hour, but all the lights were on and there were already cars in the lot. The autumn mist in the air made the street lights glow, and gave the nearby Queen Anne and Italianate houses a sheen. In different circumstances, I would have been happy to stroll around the neighborhood and take in the air. Tonight, though, I was busy, so I filed the impression away for later, when I had a little more time to appreciate it.

Instead of climbing the front steps or going around to the parking lot, I walked purposefully through the gap between the shrubs on the opposite side. The "purposeful" part was the most important element. If you act like you're afraid of getting caught, it's obvious to anyone who might be watching you. If you carry yourself like you've got every right to be where you're going, people assume it's true.

There wasn't much light back here, and my boots squished into the muddy track as I walked. I stopped when I could see through a pair of stone-framed windows into the meeting room on the ground floor. A few people had already gathered there and more were arriving. None of them looked like Stamper or his cronies, but I still felt certain he'd show up. If it turned out that I was wrong, I planned to corner the head of the perch, tell him everything I knew, and keep repeating it until he believed me.

Somewhere close by, an owl hooted. The sound of an owl in the city is always unnerving. I stood and waited. It was colder than I expected, and I rubbed my arms to ward off shivering. My righteous fury had faded a bit by this point, so it was hard to keep myself alert while I stood in the dark under a dripping pine tree, watching a bunch of people sitting on folding chairs. The hedges rustled. They seemed much thicker at night. Another owl hooted from a different direction. More and more Peregrines arrived. I couldn't hear anything from my vantage point, but I saw a lot of informal conversation, talking and laughing in small groups. None of the faces were somber or upset, as if they'd just learned that one of their number had been arrested for kidnapping, or that the visitor from the national Peregrine office had been savagely beaten and was now in the hospital under an assumed name.

I took a step closer, so I could see both of the room's doors and keep better track of who was coming and going. Then I saw him. Eldridge Stamper was pushing a catering trolley laden with sandwiches and chips, and flanked by his two associates, Serial Killer Glasses and Patchy Beard. I'm not a particularly vengeful person, but for an instant I regretted not taking Willard up on the offer of his gun.

The Peregrines gathered around the sandwich cart, and Patchy Beard disappeared into the hall and returned with a wheeled cooler. Pretty soon, everyone had a paper plate on his lap and a can of light beer or soda in his hand. I kept watching Stamper. He didn't act like a man with a secret worry. Did he know that Ollie had been freed? Was he just putting on an act? I doubted it. The more I watched Stamper, the more I thought he wore the expression of a man with something to look forward to. It was the same expression I'd have if I were running errands for Willard and knew there was a key lime pie in the fridge and a movie queued up that I'd been wanting to see for months.

However, it was also possible that I was completely misreading Stamper's expression. He was frustratingly far away, and I wished I'd brought some binoculars instead of those ridiculous brass knuckles. I also wished I had brought a hat, as the normal night sounds of a quiet neighborhood gave way to the increasing pitter-patter of rain on leaves. I turned up my collar. At least my army jacket was waterproof.

The Peregrines oriented their chairs to face a long table, where several officers had taken their seats. Everyone stood up together and gave some sort of pledge, then sat back down and settled in, with the characteristic pose of people listening to a report of the last meeting's minutes.

It continued to rain, and I felt like the decreasing air pressure was doing something to my ears. Everything sounded far away, like I was listening to it through a sea shell. For a second I wondered if I was getting ill, but wrote it off as simply one of those weird things that happens when the weather changes. Inside the perch, Stamper must have felt the change in the air, too. He squinted momentarily at the window with a troubled look on his face. I tried to wriggle deeper into the bushes, then realized there was no possible way he could have seen me.

Somewhere nearby, I felt the bushes shake slightly, like a dog or a raccoon was nosing about. Before I could determine the source, Stamper stood up and went into the hall. He didn't return right away and I began to get anxious. I wanted a better idea of what was happening inside, and I also wanted to make sure Stamper wasn't going to escape. On top of all that, I was tired of standing in the rain. I emerged from the bushes and headed toward the front door.

Inside the building, I picked up on a familiar sensation, a feeling that had nothing to do with the onset of the rain. I had encountered the same impression more than once in Uncle Willard's office, but my last experience of it had been in Tim Grimes's apartment. It felt like someone had recently been monkeying with the veil between this world and some other, and I wondered what other resources Stamper might have besides his wendigo mania.

An alcove by the front door led to a coatroom, heavily screened by several tall potted plants. I hid there, peering through a decorative ficus and leaning at an odd angle so I could still keep an eye on the hall. From inside the meeting room, someone was reporting on the new procedures for reserving softball diamonds from the city parks department. It sounded like the Peregrine officer I'd met here earlier in the day. I wondered if he'd mentioned to the group that Ollie Helfrich was missing.

Stamper returned to view, carrying two twelve-packs of light beer. He stopped abruptly in the hall and stared toward the front door with a furrowed brow and an expression of confused belligerence on his lumpy face. For a moment, I thought he'd seen me, but then he shrugged it off and went back to join the others.

It wasn't a good idea to rush in and accost Stamper, no matter how satisfying it might feel. Aside from Patchy Beard and Serial Killer Glasses, I had no idea how many other allies he had, and I doubted many of the unaligned Peregrines would believe my claims without benefit of evidence. Instead, I would wait until the meeting broke up, then engage Stamper in conversation while the others were in earshot. I would casually mention what I knew about Ollie and try to provoke a reaction from him. If I was lucky, he would fly at me in a rage and expose himself as a dangerous lunatic. If not, I would shadow him until he was alone and play the "dangerous lunatic" role myself.

Then, while I was mentally refining my plans, a number of things happened one after the other, with lightning rapidity. First, I felt the air change again, and a cold, salty breeze rolled over me. The leaves of the ficus, which I had been absently stroking, suddenly ripped themselves out of my hands. An enormous crash reverberated from down the hall, like a massive object being hurled through a window, immediately followed by shouts of confusion and alarm.

When I got to the meeting room, it was in chaos. Dozens of stunned Peregrines stood in a litter of upended card tables and mangled chairs. One of the windows was smashed, and the spray of glass showed it had been broken from the outside. But no one was paying attention to the broken glass. Everyone's attention, including my own, was focused on the center of the room, where a naked woman was rising from a crouch into a standing posture. A naked woman with a tawny, lashing tail.

21

What I remember most about that moment is her expression. I would have expected a look of cold fury, similar to what I had been feeling toward Stamper for the past few hours. But there was nothing like that, no trace of anger, bloodlust, or any kind of strong emotion at all. The huldra had the same disinterested, mildly curious demeanor as when I first saw her tied to the table in the basement of this same building.

She looked into the eyes of the shocked Peregrines surrounding her. It was more than a casual glance. She went from face to face, never spending much time on any particular person, but definitely not skipping over anyone. There wasn't any overt malice involved, just the inscrutable professionalism of a predatory animal.

Someone at the officers' table found the presence of mind to ask, "Are you all right?" in a choked voice, but his words gave out when the huldra turned to him. No one else said anything. We were speechless. The shock of her arrival and her alien mannerisms were part of the reason, but not all of it. She was also the most beautiful woman any of us had ever seen. She had the kind of beauty where the only sane response was awed silence. Speaking personally, it was all I could do to keep myself from kneeling.

My fingers tingled as I opened my match safe and extracted the blue plastic bear. If there was a connection between the huldra, the blue bear, and me, I could perhaps use this strange little toy to distract her and let the rest of the Peregrines escape. There was no guarantee it would work, but it was a better alternative than simply standing there in dumb shock. I entered the room, but before I could get the huldra's attention I saw her perfect back stiffen. She had completed her survey of the Peregrines and found someone who interested her.

A frightened voice, low and shaky, croaked out "Wait!" It was Stamper's.

The huldra drew closer to him. "I'm sorry," Stamper said to her. "I didn't mean to. Look, I'm sorry. I'm sorry!"

I wondered why Stamper didn't run. Anyone, let alone a person who had been tampering in the dark arts, could see this was a bad situation and was rapidly getting worse. Why didn't he make a break for it? That was when I realized Stamper *couldn't* run. He could beg for mercy, and he could babble, but he couldn't run. He had been pinned to the spot by the huldra's deep-blue eyes, like a mouse hypnotized by a cobra.

"You can't!" Stamper's face was florid, and there were beads of sweat on his temples. As he struggled against the huldra's magnetism, unable to move his feet, he dug one hand into the back pocket of his gray slacks. For a brief instant, I imagined he was reaching for his wallet to offer the huldra a bribe.

Stamper stopped fumbling with his pocket and turned to Serial Killer Glasses, who stood beside him, equally frozen with shock.

"Take him! Take Jerry!" Stamper begged of the huldra. His face was now an unhealthy crimson, glistening with sweat and tears.

The huldra was only inches away from him, close enough for him to breathe in her scent. I felt a quick and nauseating pang of jealousy. The huldra reached out. She took Eldridge Stamper's face in her hands, then leaned in and kissed him.

To the rest of us, it seemed like a perfectly normal kiss, as normal as anything could be in these circumstances. But then, after an eternity, the huldra stepped away and Stamper fell to the floor. He hit the threadbare Persian carpet with a boneless thud. He had changed. His florid skin was grayer now, and he seemed to have shrunken in on himself, like a dried-out cut of meat. His unfocused eyes pointed to the ceiling. At first I thought he was dead, but then he gave a convulsive shudder, and his chest began to rise and fall.

The huldra examined the crowd of onlookers again. Her tail twitched. Despite her inhuman manner, I thought I recognized something familiar in her posture. She seemed for all the world like Willard when there are cookies in the house and he's trying to decide if he has room for one more Milano.

The huldra's eyes finally met mine and, damn it all, my heart leaped in my chest. It leaped just like it had in the ninth grade when I danced with Jenny Osborn at the Christmas formal, just like it had when I opened the door of Planet Caravan for the first time and found Sophie waiting there. All I wanted to do was stare back and hope she would smile at me. The huldra's head tilted a fraction of an inch. I couldn't tell if her unreadable face was now showing recognition, curiosity, or simple hunger. A small part of me retained the knowledge that I was in danger, and these few moments, no matter how breathtaking, might just be my last if I didn't take action soon.

The huldra broke off her eye contact with me. My sense of heartbreak was overwhelming. Before I could recover myself, she turned away, balled her fists, and opened her mouth, crying out with a shriek like a dissonant violin. It was a terrible sound, the first I had ever heard her make. Many of the Peregrines reflexively covered their ears. She rocked back on her heels, then raced past me, out of the meeting room and into the hallway. I was too startled to notice where she went, and a few seconds later something new drove all thoughts of the huldra from my mind.

A great creaking sound came from the direction of the broken window. It was the noise of wood ripping from nails, plaster and lath cracked by incredible physical power. A massive shape, large and indistinct, had reached a limb through the window frame and was working to enlarge the opening. A second later, it was inside, with wrong-kneed legs propelling a long body low to the ground. Despite never having seen it before, I knew exactly what it was. I had undeniably *felt* it before. This was the presence that had loomed behind me while I waited at McCallum Library. This was the creature Roland Apfel had described, the thing that had come through the magic circle at Tim Grimes's apartment.

It was made from thousands of thorny dark vines, all continuously twining around each other, forming muscles and claws as needed, and then returning to the churning mass that had spawned them. Its size varied wildly from moment to moment. Sometimes it was as small as a horse, and other times it nearly stretched from one side of the room to the other. Its head was low and pointed, and as it pushed its way toward us, it reminded me of a massive, unearthly weasel.

This was where the Peregrines finally lost their collective nerve and routed. The huldra had been one thing. Most guys, myself included, are more than willing to put up with a little danger when the perpetrator is not only hauntingly beautiful but completely nude. But an enormous weasel, composed entirely of thorns and malevolence? Well, that was something different. Their primal and eminently reasonable instincts for self-preservation kicked in hard, and within milliseconds there was a stampede for the exit. Judging by the sounds of running feet behind me, the Peregrines scattered in all directions. Up the stairs, out the front door, down into the annex, it made no difference as long as it was away from what just crawled through the window.

After the exodus, the only remaining occupants of the room were the thorn weasel, Stamper, and me. The weasel's massive shoulders heaved, and its undulating body stretched out warily, mere inches above the carpet. Then, quick as a scorpion strike, its jaws closed over Stamper's head. Stamper twitched for a second as the writhing, barbed vines that made up the creature flowed over him. There was a wet tearing sound and the room filled with the smell of rottenness. When the thorn weasel withdrew, all that was left of Eldridge Stamper's head was a tangle of crushed, red-streaked bone.

If I had been thinking more clearly, I might have tried reciting an incantation to protect myself. I had a few of them memorized, and some of them were quite useful. Or I might have tried simply running for my life. That had worked for the huldra, and it had worked for the Peregrines. But, acting on instinct, I decided to confront an unknown magical monster with some unknown magic of my own. I stepped toward the weasel and raised my right hand, holding the tiny blue bear in front of me like a Hammer Studios vampire hunter brandishing a crucifix. The thorn weasel stopped moving, though I didn't know if this was due to any power inherent in the bear, or to simple surprise. The monster gathered itself into a solid mass, preparing to either spring forward or escape through the window. I tensed, anticipating the worst. Then the dark vines exploded, lashing out in all directions at once.

I leaped backwards, naturally enough, and managed to immediately tumble over a card table, tangling one arm in the slats of a folding chair for good measure. By the time I thrashed free, the thorn weasel was gone. A wet breeze that smelled of old leaves blew in from the smashed window. I stood there for half a minute, breathing hard and waiting to see what was going to happen next.

The ravaged remains of Eldridge Stamper lay on the carpet six feet away from me. His entire body, what was left of it, continued to dry and wither before my eyes, taking on a sepia color as the desiccation advanced. I nudged his midsection, previously solid and barrel-shaped, with the toe of my boot. It crackled, and I thought of a gigantic cicada shell. His hands were flaking away from the cuffs of his long-sleeved sweater. It wouldn't take much rough handling for the rest of him to crumble into powder. My burning desire for revenge against Stamper, my righteous fury and my determination to make him pay for what he did to Ollie, all seemed very far away now. Stamper had gotten what was coming to him, Ollie was in the hospital, and here I stood. Wherever Stamper was now, he had taken his secrets with him, and that sort of felt like he'd gotten the last laugh.

"What in the goddamn hell was that?"

I awoke from my musings. Several Peregrines had returned, crowding the doorways and regarding the destruction, and me, with horrified confusion. I recognized one of them, the lanky guy with the gray beard whom I'd spoken to earlier when I was here looking for Ollie.

"Are you in charge?" I asked.

"Gord Mattingly. Chief of the perch," he said, nodding. "Who the hell are you?"

"Dean Sherwood. We met earlier, remember?" This would have been the ideal point to produce a badge, or any kind of explanatory paperwork. I, however, had to get by on personality. Glancing down one more time, I saw that much of Stamper's body had already fallen apart. The rest of it—clothes and all—was going as well. Soon there would be

nothing left but dust. "Can we talk somewhere in private?"
I asked.

22

Gord ordered a couple of Peregrines to close off the meeting room and keep everyone out, then he led me into a sitting room across the hall. A band of mosaic tile decorated the walls, depicting vaguely Roman characters cavorting. He motioned me to a wing chair next to the marble fireplace while he and two other senior Peregrines sat on the couches to either side. None of them, I noticed with relief, had been part of Stamper's group.

"First of all, should we call the police?" Gord asked me.

"There's really not much point," I said. "This isn't a situation they're equipped to handle."

"And you are?"

"As a matter of fact, I am."

"What, is this your job or something?"

"Part-time," I said modestly.

"Well then, Mr. Sherwood—"

"Dean is fine." No point in getting all formal now.

"Do you want to tell us what's going on? What *was* that thing?"

"Which one?" I asked.

"Whichever."

"The woman—sort of a woman—is called a huldra. I'm not going to insult your intelligence by trying to convince you that things like this really do exist. You were there. You've got eyes. Let's just assume what we all saw five minutes ago actually happened. Sound good?"

There were no objections to this, so I continued. "One of your Peregrines, Eldridge Stamper, captured the huldra a few days ago—I don't know how—and he was going to eat her."

To give him credit, Gord Mattingly wasn't passively letting this craziness wash over him. As soon as he had a question, he spoke right up. "Hang on. Say it again? El Stamper was going to eat that?"

"Yes. But then she got loose." No need to complicate the issue by mentioning how she got loose in the first place.

"And Stamper wasn't the only one involved. Some of his friends, too."

"For God's sake, why?" was the perfectly reasonable follow-up question.

"They'd gotten the idea that if they ate people, they would absorb the people's strength and power. Now the huldra definitely wasn't 'people,' but she had plenty of strength and power. Unfortunately, she could also fight back."

Gord Mattingly was clearly not happy to be dealing with this, but I admired his poise. He hadn't gone into denial and he hadn't gone into shock. Most people need a lot more complaining and hysterics before they get their equilibrium back.

"Okay. You said this involved more people than just El. Who were the others?" Gord asked.

I described Serial Killer Glasses and Patchy Beard as well as I could. Gord was pretty sure he knew who I was talking about.

"All three of them. The whole damn catering committee," Gord said.

"Well, that's kind of appropriate." Gord rightly ignored my comment. "There were some others, but those are the only three whose faces I remember," I added.

Gord asked an associate to check on all the members who hadn't fled. When he returned, neither of us were surprised that the surviving catering committee members had declined to stick around.

"After they saw what happened to Stamper, they probably figured they were next on the huldra's list," I said.

"Are they in any danger?" asked Gord.

"Possibly. The huldra may decide there are more scores to settle. But I'm going to do my best to send her back where she came from."

"Can you do that?"

"Yes." I was getting sick of saying "I can try" to people, so I decided to be more positive. Besides, I thought the Peregrines could use some reassurance right now. "I'll have to find her again, but I can do that." Again, I refused to add "I think" or "I hope."

Another of the senior Peregrines, a pear-shaped guy whose tightly cinched belt made him bulge out in both hemispheres, asked, "What about the other thing? The big monster thing? What was that?"

Someone else arrived with an insulated pot of coffee and half a dozen paper cups with fold-out handles. While those were being passed around, I used the delay to think about my answer.

"I'm not certain," I said, taking a sip. "I've never seen anything like it before. Whatever it was, though, I think the huldra was afraid of it. Let's go take a look and see if it left anything behind."

We returned to the meeting room, where Gord and the other officers watched as I examined the place in greater detail. To my annoyance, I didn't find any clues—such as stray vines or broken tendrils—that I could have used to help identify what the thorn weasel actually was. As for Stamper, there was nothing left of him but a pile of oily, cockroach-colored flakes.

"El, what did you get yourself into?" Gord said quietly.

I sighed. "There's something else you ought to know about him." I explained to Gord and the other officers why Ollie Helfrich had gone missing. In as few words as possible, I described how Stamper had abducted him, beaten him senseless, and locked him away as a future snack.

When I had finished, Gord took off his glasses and carefully cleaned them with a handkerchief. "You know," he said at last, "the lady with the tail was bad enough. That would have been plenty. It really would."

"What are we supposed to do now?" asked an officer.

I frowned at Stamper's remains. "If you want my advice, just sweep up the mess and tell the rest of the Peregrines that Stamper got away. Tell them you're looking for him and his friends. You can even call the police and report them missing. I doubt they're going to show up here again."

"What about the, you know, monsters?" Gord pointed at the smashed window, through which the creatures in question had entered. "What are we supposed to tell people when they ask?"

"Tell them you don't know. Tell them you're trying to find out. As long as they think somebody's looking into it, they're not going to worry too much. Halloween's getting close, so you can say it might have been some kind of prank. People in makeup and costumes.”

“Do you really think they’ll believe that?”

“I’d be very surprised if they didn’t,” I said. “People do it all the time.”

Gord frowned, digesting this advice. “What’s the next step after that?”

“That’s all. You take care of the Peregrines the best you can, and I’ll take care of—” I gestured toward the window. “—all of the other stuff.”

The pear-shaped guy, whose name I learned was Dan, left the room abruptly. A few seconds later, he returned holding a tan windbreaker and deliberately not looking in the direction of Stamper’s remains.

“This is El Stamper’s jacket,” Dan said, holding it out toward Gord and me. “It was in the coat room and, I don’t know, I thought you might need it.”

It was only natural that a member of a fraternal service organization, and an officer, no less, would feel a deep need to be useful in a crisis. I took the coat from him with a word of thanks.

Gord went off to address the membership. Dan and the other officers went to fetch a broom, a dustpan and, if they had any sense, some liquid courage. I raked through Stamper’s jacket. The haul wasn’t particularly large. A folding pocket schedule for West Central High School Hornet sports, with advertising spots from Lloyd’s Ice Cream and Tip-Top Burgers. A set of car keys on an electronic fob. A golf pencil and two crumpled dollar bills. At the bottom of the inside pocket I found a miniature package, smaller than a bottle cap, wrapped in a shred of tan canvas and tied with twine. After a moment’s hesitation, I pulled at the twine until I could get the cloth free and unwrap the contents.

It was a tiny chain, thirty or forty links of bright silver glittering in the light of the chandelier. I studied it in the palm of my hand. The links were slightly irregular, with an unmistakable hand-made appearance and marks along the outer edges, just barely big enough to notice. I couldn’t be sure without a magnifying glass, but it looked an awful lot like someone had inscribed a series of miniscule runic letters on each link. I thought about this for a second, remembering Stamper’s day job as an industrial arts teacher, and the delicate metalworking tools he'd set up in his hidden room. A chain like this, made in the proper way and fortified with the proper words, could probably bind a creature like the huldra. Apparently, Eldridge Stamper had picked up some useful information during his time at Dennis's reading group, and then put it into practice. But it hadn't quite been enough to protect him.

I wrapped the chain back up and dropped it into the pocket of my own jacket, hanging Stamper's over the armrest of a couch next to the smashed window. The smell of wet plants was very strong here. To my surprise, bright green tendrils of new growth were already expanding across the cracked frame. I was about to pluck a few strands when, outside in the darkness, an unexpected motion caught my eye. A person, hidden in the bushes, had frozen into immobility just half a second too late. I had seen him, and I knew he was out there. On top of that, I knew who he was. I put a hand on the wobbling remains of the window frame and leaned out into the night.

"Tim," I called.

Tim bolted, crashing through the foliage with no further attempts at subtlety. I hesitated for the span of a heartbeat, then convinced myself that Gord and the rest of the Peregrines had things well in hand and didn't need me around anymore. I jumped out the window, landed heavily on the damp ground, and pursued Tim Grimes.

He tried to take the corner around the cinderblock extension too quickly and tumbled into the mud. That gave me a few seconds to close the distance, but he was back up and running before I could reach him. A small, detached voice in my mind pointed out that this was the second time Tim and I had chased each other around the Peregrine perch, but I was in no mood to appreciate the irony. As he ran across the gravel parking lot, his oversized coat flapping, a pair of headlights snapped on across the street. Tim jumped the post-and-chain divider at the edge of the lot and took off at an angle toward the car. He threw himself in the passenger door as it pulled away from the curb.

It passed near the streetlight and I saw the silhouette of the driver. A woman. Straight hair down to the shoulders. Severe bangs. It had to be Lenora. From where I stood, the

Jag was only half a block away, so I turned, skidded wildly
for a second, and raced for it.

23

It didn't take me long to catch up with them. Fortunately, their car had a dent in the bumper—and several stickers besides—which made it easy to keep track of it. I stayed a few car-lengths back to keep them from getting suspicious, even though I knew most cars looked the same through a rear-view mirror on a rainy night. I was hardly an expert at tailing anyone, but I got the impression they weren't too familiar with being tailed, either. Maybe the head start they'd gotten when they escaped from the Peregrine perch had made them stop thinking about pursuers, or maybe the idea of being pursued never even entered their minds. Either way, I didn't want to press my luck.

My mind wandered as I followed them. The huldra had been enough of a problem on her own, but now there was the thorn weasel, that gigantic vine monstrosity, as well. Lenora had conjured it up at Tim's apartment, where it had broken free of its confinement, trashed the place, and disappeared into the night. What did it want? Everything wants something. The concept of a mindless rampage is much rarer than most people think. Whatever the thorn weasel was doing, it was most likely doing it for a reason.

Lenora's car flashed its turn signal. This was another good indication they didn't know they were being followed. I got off at the same exit and traveled south down Green River Road. We passed the big chain bookstore at the top of the hill, then Captain Davey's a little bit farther on. It's a hole-in-the-wall seafood place I inexplicably feel drawn to whenever I crave fried fish and hush puppies, and I made a mental note to stop there on the way home if the next hour or so went well.

They turned left just before Jefferson Square Mall, passing the McCallum Library and entering the residential neighborhood behind it. I pushed my luck and followed Lenora's car from the next street over, keeping them in sight at intersections as they got deeper into the tangle of odd-shaped blocks and cul-de-sacs. I considered this a wise precaution, since even the most oblivious driver will eventually notice when the car behind them makes all the same turns as they do. In addition, it made me feel like a skilled and resourceful investigator, and that's always fun.

Their car slowed down, made another turn, and suddenly their destination was clear: the Medieval apartment complex. Its official name is Nottingham Court Gardens, but in my mind, it's always been "the Medieval apartment complex." It's an oval-shaped cluster of two-story apartment buildings, not a particularly unusual thing to see in the border between a neighborhood of single-family houses and a light-industrial area, but this one sported some unique and frankly delightful features. A crenelated wall of imitation stone stucco surrounded it, and each of the units displayed half-timbered facades in the Tudor style, gothically pointed entrance doors, and spire-capped towers on each end. It had been built in the early 1980s, when the popularity of *Dungeons & Dragons* and the endless *Conan* knockoff movies led to a brief resurgence of fantastical and Olde Fashionede design and art. Naturally, I loved the place. It was a bit run down, but to me that only added to the charm. Back when I was a delivery driver for my aunt's restaurant, I would come out here occasionally, and I always half expected to see a dwarf in a jester's costume gesture meaningfully and then disappear into the shadows, or a unicorn study me from behind the stacked plastic trash cans.

Right now, though, I didn't have time to indulge in fantasies. I was on the trail of two rogue wizards whose implacable monster was now terrorizing the villagers. As I parked the Jag in front of the turreted recreation center in the middle of the complex, I couldn't suppress a momentary grin. I had to admit to myself that there were times when, despite everything, I really loved my job.

Lenora and Tim passed under the groined arch that led to the doors for building three. I scampered along behind them, still keeping my distance. I planned to wait to announce my presence until after they'd gone inside, thereby minimizing the chance for additional escape attempts. They were out of sight for a few seconds, and I heard the sounds of a door closing somewhere down the short hall to my left. There were only two choices. The door to 3-A was a plain rectangle of yellow ocher, but 3-B was decorated with a painted clay plaque depicting a mermaid and a kraken. I knocked on 3-B.

There was no answer at first. I imagined the scene behind the door, with Tim and Lenora staring at each other in alarm, wondering if this was a coincidence or something more sinister. After the past few days, and the debacle at Tim's apartment, they were probably jumping at their own shadows. They might even be frightened enough to actually talk to me.

I tried again, attempting to imbue the knock with a firm but friendly tone. It's harder than you might think.

"Lenora, this is Dean Sherwood," I said to the peephole. "I don't want anything, but I'd like to talk with you for a minute, if I can."

The silence continued, and I began to wonder if they'd chosen a strategic withdrawal and let themselves out the back door. I was about to go check on their car in the parking lot when I heard the bolt unlatching. The door, still on its chain, opened a few inches. A pair of dark eyes under jet black bangs looked up at me. I turned on the charm.

"Hi. Do you remember me? We met at Knit Now. I know you're dealing with a problem right now, and I want to help you with it. Do you think we could talk for a few minutes?"

"What do you want?" Lenora asked.

"I don't want anything," I said, then changed my mind. "No, I take that back. What I want is to stop the thing that smashed a hole in the Peregrine perch this evening. Isn't that what you want, too? Isn't that why Tim was out scouting the building?"

Lenora was impassive, neither confirming nor denying.

"Look, this thing is big, it's powerful, and it's obviously in a bad mood. You know that more than I do. There's a better chance of getting it under control if we work together."

Lenora considered this, and I added, "Dennis Falco will vouch for me. Go ahead and call him. Or Roland Apfel. He knows me, too. Talk to both of them. I don't mind waiting."

Lenora closed the door with a sigh, and I heard the chain being unhooked. A second later, the door opened again.

Lenora Scanlon's apartment was probably the same size as Tim's, but it seemed smaller. It was on the ground floor, so the bushes and fencing outside the window made it feel more hemmed-in, but the place was also crowded with substantially more stuff. Plants were everywhere, standing in racks, hanging from hooks, or simply sitting in pots and covering half of the available horizontal space. Many of them were in bloom, and I could smell the flowers from the door. The profusion of plants made me recall the "Garden Witchery" business name I had seen when Roland sent me Lenora's contact information. I briefly wondered how they had started from something so innocuous and ended up raising a monster.

On the walls and shelves, I noticed Edward Burne-Jones postcards, collages of milagro figurines, original paintings, movie posters, and framed bits of brightly colored candy packaging and miscellaneous ephemera. Then there were the books. Tim had kept a number of occult books in his apartment, but his collection was miniscule compared to the library in Lenora's living room. A glass-fronted lawyer's bookcase, actually a fairly nice antique, sat against one wall, and opposite that was a husky set of white shelves from Ikea. All of them were full of books. I couldn't read all the titles from where I stood, but I had no doubt that someone like Jimmy Page or Helena Blavatsky, or even Uncle Willard, would have found plenty to read. Contraptions of boards and milk crates held more books wherever space allowed. A pair of lumpy love seats draped with blankets sat in the middle of the living room, and the flower-scented air contained an undertone of incense.

Tim Grimes hesitated next to one of the love seats, resting a hand on the corner and leaning awkwardly, as if unsure whether to appear casual or menacing. Lenora stood in front of me with her arms folded, and blocked my path into the rest of the apartment. She had on a black vinyl raincoat that ended at her hips, and a pair of tights under that. Her shoes were shiny red low-rise Doc Martens. Given the decor, the outfits, and the general inability to keep out of trouble, I had the feeling that I probably could have been friends with both of them. Currently, though, neither of them seemed in the mood to be sociable.

When no one said anything, I began. "All right, let's start at the beginning. What happened?"

"I don't know what you're talking about," Lenora said.

"We're a little bit past the point of playing dumb." I tried not to sound like an irritated grown-up chewing out a couple of mischievous kids, but I may not have succeeded. It had been a tiring day. I took a deep breath and adjusted my tone before continuing. "You were both there at the Peregrine perch, just like me. Tim, you saw what happened, just like I did. So let's all be honest with each other and figure out how to stop this thing."

"It's nothing," Lenora said willfully.

"It is most definitely not nothing," I replied.

"We're taking care of it," Tim said.

"That's great. Let me help you," I said. "I've done things like this before. Whatever's going on, I can help."

I meant it, too. I truly did not care at all who sent the thorn weasel back to where it came from, and who took the credit for it. All I wanted was to make it go away. The thorn weasel was probably responsible for the dead dog that Willard heard about, and it was definitely responsible for eating Stamper's head. What the weasel did next was anybody's guess, but it was actively dangerous to the population at large, and that moved it to the head of the problem list. The huldra, by contrast, appeared primarily focused on her own revenge. To my mind, the weasel was where we needed to focus our attention now.

The response to my offer was Lenora scoffing, "We don't need your help."

"We can handle it," Tim added. "Just go back to your big house in your rich neighborhood and let us do the real work."

I refused to take the bait, despite really, really wanting to. "Okay, here's what I think," I said. "If you two could control this thing, then you would have done it already. You wouldn't be skulking around in the rain waiting to see what it was going to do next. It looks to me like you need *some* kind of help. Does it even have a name?" I asked. "I've just been calling it a 'thorn weasel' because that's what it looks like to me."

No response.

"Be that as it may, how did you figure out it was going to show up at the Peregrine perch? The DuClasse pendulum ritual? The Long Whisper? Or did you just get lucky? There's nothing wrong with getting lucky."

Tim, I could tell, was thrown by my casual mention of two common ways to get information from the unseen powers. Lenora had a better poker face.

"It's under control," she said. "It'll be gone before the moon is full."

"That's three days from now. What are you going to do?"

"Everything will all be fine if you stay out of our way. We're in the middle of fixing it. The last thing we need right now is some amateur fooling around and making things worse."

That was exactly the same thing I was thinking, but it wouldn't have done any good to say it. Lenora glared at me from under scowling, sculpted brows, and Tim was taking his cues from her. Every so often, he'd glance in Lenora's direction, and his posture would subtly adjust itself to match hers. I could tell Tim was worried, and he was looking to Lenora for reassurance. Lenora might have been worried, too, but she didn't show a bit of it. She had the expression of someone who had been doubted and dismissed for so long that her reflexive response to any friction was to dig in obstinately and not give an inch. Still, I hoped she was worried. If she wasn't worried, then the two of them were even more out of their depth than I thought they were.

I began to realize I wasn't going to get any cooperation out of them tonight. It wasn't too surprising. I had hoped they would talk to me, but it just wasn't going to happen. Instead of attempting to argue further, I gave each of them a card with my name and number. I made a point of giving one to Lenora and one to Tim. I had a feeling that Lenora might shred hers out of pure irritation, but Tim might hang on to his.

"I can't make you do anything you don't want to do," I said. "But if you change your mind, I can help. And I do want to help. Call me. Please."

I let myself out. When Lenora closed the door behind me, I thought about listening to see if I could hear them debating their next steps, but I imagined they'd check the hall in a minute to see if I had really left. So I did.

24

Despite the unsatisfying interview with Lenora and Tim, I stopped at Captain Davey's anyway. A fillet and hush puppies to go sounded infinitely more appealing than ransacking the kitchen for something easy to prepare when I got back. I put shoe trees in my wet boots and set them by the heating register to dry, then ate at my desk while I made notes in an old loose-leaf memo book. I was exhausted, but I had also developed an idea about what to do next, and I wanted to get my thoughts down on paper before I fell asleep.

The next morning, after a good rest, a shower, and a splash of citrus aftershave, I felt like a new man. I checked my notes from last night and was pleased to confirm that they hardly seemed crazy in the least, and the plan I had sketched out was well worth pursuing.

As a preliminary step, I cooked up a batch of waffles, along with a few strips of bacon, a couple of eggs, and the half-cantaloupe we had left in the fridge. I'm not an exceptional cook, but I like to think I have a firm command of the basic breakfast elements. As with anything, it helps to have all the necessary equipment. Our waffle maker, for example, was a superb piece, a Krampouz commercial model that Willard had picked up second-hand in Europe years ago, and it could produce angelic Belgian waffles with a supremely low level of effort. I loved that waffle maker. Most days, it came in right under the Jag—assuming the Jag was running—on the list of inanimate objects that I cared for more than the majority of my own family. When the magnificent smells of all this had produced sounds of movement from the upstairs bedroom, I poured boiling water from the kettle into a pot of Willard's favorite lapsang souchong tea. By the time he lumbered downstairs, wrapped in his crimson bathrobe with the gold trim, breakfast was ready to be served.

"Well, this is impressive," Willard grunted as he lowered himself into a chair. "Do I assume you're celebrating some occasion?"

"Why would I need an occasion to make a nice breakfast for my favorite uncle?"

"So there's going to be a request after this."

"Of course there is. Do you want syrup or marmalade? Both?" I set a fully loaded plate in front of him, then sat down with two waffles of my own, Cup Creek maple syrup, and a mug of coffee.

"I got a message from Dr. Helmbach this morning," Willard said. "Your friend is in stable condition. They want to keep him for another couple of days to monitor for internal bleeding, but the prognosis is good. Equally good is that no one's grown suspicious about the cover story. Dr. Helmbach didn't go into detail, but I believe he settled on a catastrophic home-repair accident."

"That's not bad at all," I said. "It's a much better idea than a hit-and-run, which is what I would have used. No call for a police investigation if you fall down some stairs carrying a load of tools. I think Dr. Helmbach could have a second career in crime if medicine gets too boring for him."

"I'm sure he's aware of that. Incidentally, I wouldn't go visiting your friend if I were you. There's no telling how many hospital functionaries might ambush you with awkward questions."

Willard was right. Even though I felt bad about it, staying away from the hospital made sense. We talked on various topics for a while, including the upcoming basketball season for the University of Garvinville and whether I ought to buy myself a houndstooth suit. Opinions were mixed, trending to negative, on both issues. Eventually, Willard paused in slicing his cantaloupe and said, "All right, Dean. This is as good of a mood as I'm going to be in. What do you need?"

"I need some help in the lab."

He sighed theatrically. Despite that, I could tell he'd been expecting something much more onerous than a small amount of alchemy. "If you keep having me do these things for you, you're never going to learn," he said.

"I'm all in favor of learning by doing, but if I get this wrong the first time, there's a decent chance I won't get a second try. Therefore, in this case I'd like to defer to the expert instead of getting myself killed."

Willard arched a bushy eyebrow. "Killed?"

"Yes. The thing I'm looking for has already killed someone, and will probably try to do the same with me if I keep
getting in its way."

"May I have the details, please?"

I described to Willard what I had seen at the Peregrines'
meeting last night, including the appearance of the huldra,
her singling out of Stamper, and the appearance of the second creature, which quickly overshadowed everything else
and ended with fragments of Eldridge Stamper all over the
carpet.

"Before you ask, I don't know what it was," I said. "Imagine a weasel the size of a cargo van, all made up from
thrashing vines and branches."

He frowned. "I see. Continue."

"The only thing I know about it is who summoned it in
the first place."

"You do? Let them deal with it."

"Don't think I haven't considered that. The problem is,
I'm pretty sure they're in over their heads." I gave him a
quick description of Roland Apfel's request, my visit to Tim's
apartment, and what I learned there. "The two of them, Lenora and Tim, were there at the Peregrine perch last night,
watching from the shadows. I followed them back to Lenora's apartment and offered to help—"

"Nicely?"

"I was a model of restraint and civility. As always. Despite that, they weren't interested. I guess I shouldn't be
surprised. Like anyone who gets in over their heads, their
first impulse was to refuse to admit how bad the situation
is. I couldn't convince them otherwise."

Willard drank his tea with an expression of prim disap-
proval that seemed out of place on someone his size. I knew
what he was thinking. There was one basic rule of thumb
for people whose lives tended to include a lot of magic circles and crumbling demonology manuals, people like Uncle
Willard and, I suppose, me. That rule was: "Do not call up
what you cannot put down." Failing to follow this was almost unthinkably reckless.

"If those two aren't going to help, I'll have to work on my
own," I said.

Willard reached for the last piece of bacon and crunched
it meaningfully. "What about the huldra?" he asked.

"I'll deal with the huldra when the thorn weasel isn't running amok. My gut tells me she's the lesser of two evils right now."

"I hope you're right. And don't call it a 'she'."

"Before I can send the weasel away, or keep it from murdering me, I have to learn more about it."

"Agreed," Willard said.

"I want to prepare a bottle of *aqua sapientis*, and I need some help. But don't worry," I said. "All I really want from you is to watch me while I make it myself. Just tell me if you see me doing anything wrong."

That did it. To Willard's mind, supervision and critique were vastly more congenial options than actually doing anything himself. He went to get dressed, and I quickly loaded the dishwasher and got his lab ready.

The lab occupied one-third of what had originally been a master bedroom on the second floor, and was now Uncle Willard's lair. That section of the room looked like a combination of herbal pharmacy and chemistry lab, with a steel-topped table, various glass tubes, and an industrial sink. The rest of the space was more conventional, consisting of shelves with his favorite and most potent books, a row of binders containing decades of occult research notes, an exceptionally comfortable chair, small tables and reading lamps, and a slate fireplace.

I pulled jars off the shelves and set out the mixing equipment, then retrieved the binder that held Willard's notes for the *aqua sapientis* formula. By the time he arrived, I had already measured and laid out all the components we needed, and got the gas burner going. I could also have started on the simple preliminary mixing steps but, as I said, I was very concerned about getting this right. With Willard at my elbow, I slowly worked my way down the water-spotted paper that contained his formula. I asked his opinion at every step, from combining the substances, to placing the brass bowl over the heat, to chalking the protective sigils on each corner of the table. The continuous checking got old quickly, but it was a good way to keep his attention focused on the task.

Eventually, the reagents coalesced to form salts, solid chunks the size and color of crystallized ginger, which I ground back down into a powder, all the while reciting the archaic Greek chants that infused the salts with their potency. About halfway through the process, I got the same goosebump-inducing sensation that often happens when I have occasion to resort to "applied" magic. The same thing happened when I raised the ghost of Eleazar for Ollie, but at the time I was so focused on keeping Ollie from running that I hadn't noticed it much. Here, though, standing in the flickering light of the burner and chanting words that hadn't been uttered by normal people in centuries, it was hard to escape the feeling. We were toying with the nature of reality, and being aware of that does something strange to your mind.

Several hours later, after an elaborate sequence of distillation, crystallization, pulverization, filtration, heating and cooling, hydrating and waiting, all punctuated with various types of incantations and ritual gestures, and seasoned with commentary from my uncle, I was finally done. My throat was sore and my clothes smelled deeply of ammonia and incense, but I also had an old-fashioned cologne atomizer full of topaz-yellow liquid that reflected the light with unexpected shimmers. This was the *aqua sapientis*, the water of understanding. Properly applied, the liquid would allow me to see the true nature of any creature. If I could see the thorn weasel for what it truly was, not what it appeared to be, I could probably figure out where it came from and how to send it back. I dried my hands carefully and checked again to make sure the atomizer's cap was tight. *Aqua sapientis* was a dangerous substance. I had no desire to accidentally see Willard's true nature, and I was sure he felt the same about me.

With the lab-work over, my clothes in the laundry, and a fresh cup of coffee, there was only one other preliminary task to take care of. I cleared off my desk and unfolded the large map of Garvinville I'd bought at a gas station. Then I opened an old Luden's Cough Drops tin and took out a bent, rust-spotted nail attached to a length of waxed cotton thread. In order to use the *aqua sapientis* on the thorn weasel, I first needed to find it again.

I held up the thread so that the bent nail dangled, pendulum-like over the outspread map. I took a deep breath and tried to exhale all the stray thoughts out of my mind. This process only worked, when it worked, if the querent—

a fancy way of referring to the dope asking the question—was focused and undistracted. Historically, those mental conditions have been difficult for me to produce, though I did have the "dope" part down pretty well.

Speaking in a whisper, I said the words that would encourage the pendulum to show me what I needed to know. The words themselves wouldn't do much without the proper mental focus. At the same time, however, mental focus isn't going to get you anywhere unless the correct rituals are observed.

Magic. It's kind of a pain.

I closed my eyes and kept my mind blank until I could feel a connection between myself and the nail, a sort of miniature gravity indicating that the two of us, the inanimate object and the dope, were now part of one connected system.

"Direct me," I thought, bringing an image of the thorn weasel to my mind.

Slowly, the pendulum began to move on its own, no longer bound by the laws of normal physics. It rotated and circled as I moved my string-holding hand slowly over the map and it pointed itself toward the strongest concentrations of mystical energy.

Like dowsing, consulting the nail was as much of an art as it was a science, and the process required a degree of interpretation. I wasn't just looking for any old mystical energy that happened to turn up. I was looking for the *right* one. On any given day, there were going to be numerous other centers of esoteric power that might catch the nail's attention. This house, for example. I also had to tug the thing away from St. Brigid's church, due to what I knew Father Byrne kept locked in a battered silver reliquary in the basement. The shopping center on the east side of Weinbach Avenue attracted the nail for some reason, but it didn't feel like what had invaded the Peregrine perch last night.

My circles got wider and wider, moving out from the center of the map. Suddenly, the string tightened, sticking out at an angle as if the nail had gotten caught in a strong magnetic field. Which I suppose it had, so to speak. I waited a moment to make sure the connection was steady, then carefully stood up and leaned over the map while trying not to move the hand holding the string. I wanted to get the best overhead view I could, without any parallax distortions that might send me into the wrong neighborhood.

I sighed. The nail wasn't moving, and the direction it pointed was unmistakable. Once I saw what I needed to see, the nail dropped out of its state of alertness and became a regular old piece of metal on a regular old string, swaying lazily in the still air. The message had been delivered.

"The zoo," I said out loud to no one.

25

Naturally, it was the zoo. It couldn't have been a junkyard, or some parking lot behind an office building, or some other place that would have been simple to sneak into. It had to be Melton Zoo. I thought about checking again tomorrow to see if the thorn weasel had moved to anywhere more accessible, but waiting that long sounded like agony. Besides, I'd gotten into more difficult areas than this. I was just disappointed that it hadn't been someplace easy. I put the nail back into its box and folded up the map again.

I dug around in the closet and found my old rucksack with the stitched-up reinforcements along the straps. I kept wanting to replace it, but the durable old green canvas refused to fall apart. It was the kind of thing a zoo patron might carry around without raising any notice, and I filled it with the things I thought I'd need. This included the atomizer of *aqua sapientis*, as well as some chalk, a couple of beeswax candles and my silver lighter, all wrapped in an empty potato chip bag just in case some zoo employee decided to get nosy. Most likely, I would only need the atomizer, but it wasn't like I'd be able to run out for supplies once I got started. I added two turkey and cheese sandwiches with Italian dressing, a bottle of water, the James Thurber book I'd been trying to finish all week, and a Swiss army knife. With this kit, I felt prepared for any eventuality.

Reflexively, I tapped my pocket to make sure the box with the blue bear was still there. I wasn't sure why, but I had started to like carrying it around. I wondered again why the huldra had given it to me. Was it a thank-you for releasing her? Or was there another meaning, something that made sense in her own alien logic but was completely unfathomable to a mortal like me? I didn't know. But I kept the bear in my pocket all the same.

Willard had retreated to the attic, having exceeded his quota of altruism for the next several days. I imagined he wouldn't be leaving his trains and his model kits before midnight at the earliest, so I wrote a note and put it under the statue of St. Genesius. Then I left for a trip to the zoo.

Melton Zoo is a lovely place, old and park-like, located on a wooded hill that used to be the edge of the city. It contained several century-old buildings that the administrators had wisely, if unexpectedly, decided to keep in service. Of course, beautiful historic buildings have their drawbacks, too, especially for someone with a job like mine. The ghost of an elephant is not something that anyone would want to deal with, take it from me.

I parked on a side street, so as not to arouse suspicion when the zoo closed and my car was still in the parking lot. As I walked to the entrance I noticed a couple of police cars in the lot, next to a pickup truck with the zoo logo on the side. Three cops and a handful of zoo employees in coveralls were intently kicking through the underbrush at the far side of the lot, where a triangle of woods abutted between the pavement and the zoo fence. Despite wanting to wander over and see what they were doing, I went the other way, up the slope to the ticket booth, where I paid my admission and went inside. I already had an idea what they were doing over there. If this was where the thorn weasel had been lurking, it had probably left some evidence of its presence. In the best case, they were inspecting property damage, like a couple of snapped trees or a fence that had been mysteriously pulled down. The worst case was that the police were there to seal off the area until the coroner's van could arrive.

There were a few hours to kill before the zoo shut its gates for the day, but wandering aimlessly around the zoo was less conspicuous than buying a ticket thirty minutes before closing time, and it was easier than trying to sneak over the fences once everyone went home. Besides, I liked the zoo. It was laid out around a small artificial lake, with the animal habitats radiating out from there, and I strolled along the paths like any visitor would. I watched the zebras and bought a bag of sweet potatoes to feed the giraffes. They didn't want to get close to me, so I left the potatoes on the railing of the overhanging platform and walked away, trying not to feel insulted when the animals came trotting over on their big spindly legs as soon as I left.

"Don't feel bad," said an older woman in a faded rugby shirt and bucket hat. She must have noticed me side-eyeing the ungrateful giraffes. "They're probably just spooked."

"Did I try to feed them the wrong way?" She had well-worn orthopedic shoes and a rolled-up bag of popcorn, and gave the impression of being a regular zoo patron.

She shook her head. "Usually, whenever anybody steps on the platform, the giraffes will come up and check if they've got food. Today, I think they're spooked about what happened to the bobcats. Animals can tell things."

"What happened to the bobcats?" I asked.

"One of them died last night."

"That's a shame," I said, while a queasy feeling grew in my stomach. "What happened to it?"

"Nobody knows. Not yet, at least. I was over at the enclosure earlier and I overheard the keepers talking. They think some outside animal got in and attacked it. But what animal around here could kill an adult bobcat and eat all the flesh off its head? They don't know."

I knew. But I kept that information to myself. I listened to her theories for a few minutes, then thanked her for her time and wandered off. I'd done enough sightseeing. The thorn weasel was somewhere in the area, but that still left a lot of ground to cover and I wanted to narrow down the search area. I could have used the nail again, but it's tough to keep up the requisite concentration when you're getting funny looks from passerby. Instead, I strolled purposefully through every area of the zoo, trying to find a location where the conditions felt right. It's not easy to put into words, but I like to think of it this way: If you spend enough time outdoors, in good weather and bad, and if you have somebody to show you the signs and if you practice long enough, you can eventually get pretty good at forecasting the weather just by watching the clouds and the wind and the quality of the sunlight. In this case, it's a similar phenomenon. Once you spend enough time dealing with powers that aren't supposed to be where they are, you start to get a certain sense when they're close by, whether you can see them or not. That's a long-winded way of explaining why, after taking a few steps down the densely forested path that led to the macaw enclosures, I checked to see if anyone was watching and disappeared into the trees.

This was the right place. I could tell. Reality was not quite right here. Something was pressing against it, changing it enough to notice. It was unnatural. This was where I needed to stay. I found a suitable tree, far from the path and possessing multiple low-hanging branches, and climbed it. Trees in general are excellent places to hide. Nobody ever looks up. Besides, sitting in a tree, seven or eight feet off the ground with my back against the trunk, is immensely satisfying.

Now, all I had to do was wait for dark. I unwrapped a sandwich and opened my book. At this time of the year, the late-afternoon light already was beginning to fail, but I read for as long as I could. When it got too dark, I kept myself busy trying to identify all the sounds I heard. There were the roars and brays of the big animals, and the occasional shrieks of the birds. The distant noises of the patrons got rarer and rarer until closing time arrived. I heard the squeak of wheeled carts, and the scrape and clatter of zoo employees pushing brooms and emptying trash cans. There was a rumbling whoosh that I couldn't place at first, then I caught a glimpse through a gap in the leaves and saw it came from a street-sweeper, about the size of a golf cart, with two whirling brushes underneath. Eventually, even these sounds of maintenance died away, and it was just me, the animals, and the sodium lights. I shouldered my pack and swung down. It was time to get started.

The sense of unnaturalness in the air had sharpened, and despite my best efforts I began to get nervous. My plan was to spray the thorn weasel with *aqua sapientis*, learn what it actually was, then make my escape and use my new knowledge to prepare something that would send it away for good. I had assumed I could escape because the weasel wouldn't be interested in pursuing me, but this hypothesis was starting to seem a little more tenuous than it had when I thought it up in my office.

After surveying the ground for a minute or two, I made a clear spot by kicking leaves and fallen brush out of the way, then took my chalk and inscribed protective symbols on a few flat rocks around the perimeter of the area. The symbols would keep out a lot of things, but the best they would probably do to the weasel is distract it while I ran away. I felt slightly guilty about doing this, since I didn't like the idea of zoo employees stumbling upon the scene after I was gone. They were probably on edge already after what had happened to their bobcat, and I didn't want to make them think they had a colony of warlocks on their hands as well.

I was tinkering with the arrangement of my inscribed rocks, adjusting them for maximum effect and—let's be honest—aesthetic harmony, when a cold rush of air made me duck. My first thought was that one of the zoo's birds had gotten loose and swooped low over my head. Then, belatedly, I realized this signaled the arrival of an entirely different kind of creature.

The thorn weasel was here. It hadn't pushed its way through the thicket, and it hadn't simply materialized in place. Instead, the creature took shape by flowing in from the shadows and drawing the foliage into itself, growing and coalescing until it loomed over me. It was massive. Much bigger than I remembered from yesterday. In the bright lights of the Peregrine perch, among the carpets and couches and discarded paper plates, it had seemed more contained. Now, I wasn't certain where it began or ended. Its eyes glowed green, like luminescent fungi. Its entire body rippled and twisted as it moved. The air was full of an earthy smell that combined both growth and rot. It made me think of an afternoon I'd once spent in an abandoned commercial greenhouse, where the plants had been left for months to live and die on their own.

The weasel tilted its enormous head, and I saw endless tangles of briars forming narrow jaws and fangs. It regarded me with something like curiosity, then gave a growl, a chilling sound that suggested imminent disaster, like tree limbs bending and grinding in a windstorm. Two thoughts occurred to me in rapid succession. One: I may have made a mistake by coming here. Two: I really, *really* did not want to see the true nature of this thing. It shifted its bulk from side to side, unpleasantly like a bull getting ready to charge, and I briefly considered running for my life. Then my better nature took over and reminded me that I was there to learn about the weasel, and despite my terror there was still only one way to do that. Without taking my eyes away from it, I crouched down and reached into the bag for my atomizer. I was going to have to get close enough to spray it, which had not seemed like a serious problem back at home. Now, in the moment, it felt a little more challenging.

While I hesitated, it reached out a paw and scraped away two of my inscribed rocks. I felt their mild protective energy deflate like a ripped balloon, but at least I knew the weasel was close enough now. I raised the atomizer, but before I could press the button a huge force slammed into my side and I found myself tumbling through the air.

The creature had batted me like a cat playing with a rolled-up sock. When I hit the ground, I gasped and croaked out an old charm that I'd heard Willard use a few times. It wasn't particularly powerful, but it had the benefit of being short, and it gave me time to drag myself to my knees.

Amazingly, I was still holding onto the atomizer, which I quickly pointed at the weasel, holding it out with both hands like someone pepper-spraying a mugger. I was now past the point of being frightened, and had shifted instead to wounded resentment. I was ready to be done. I wanted to get this over with, learn what I needed to know, and escape. A pessimistic voice in the back of my mind amended that last part to "escape if I could," but I didn't pay attention. I was too focused on lining up my shot.

The calculus of the next few seconds became clear. The weasel would close in again, I would spray it with the *aqua sapientis*, learn whatever there was to learn in a flash of magical inspiration, then tumble out of the way. This was going to work. I could feel it.

That was when the entire scene—the clearing, the weasel, the atomizer, and me—all began to flicker and glow with St. Elmo's fire. Both of us were frozen in surprise for a second, then the blue-green luminosity ignited with a bright light and a concussive clap of thunder. I stumbled backwards, slipped on one of my own inscribed rocks and hit the ground hard. When I looked up again, the thorn weasel was gone, with only a few broken branches and slashes in the ground indicating it had ever been here. Then I noticed, beyond the curls of ozone-scented steam, two people standing among the trees.

It was Lenora and Tim.

26

For a moment, the two of them looked like a pair of mythical creatures themselves, standing on a slight ridge, silhouetted by the zoo's lighting, and haloed by the mist. Then they saw me staggering to my feet and hurried over, becoming more human with every step.

"What the hell was that?" I demanded. I should have been more diplomatic, but being interrupted at the critical moment had rattled me more than I liked to admit.

"You're welcome." Lenora had on something that looked like a high school letter jacket, red and gray with a big white block capital "S" on one side. Next to her, Tim shifted from foot to foot in an oversized, paint-splattered brown work shirt.

"That thing would have killed you if we hadn't been here," Tim said.

I bit back a blunt reply and forced myself to be civil. "I appreciate your concern, but I knew what I was doing," I said.

"So you were *trying* to let it kill you? This was some sort of suicide?" Lenora asked.

I shook my head. "I needed to get close to it. I was going to use . . ." I found my atomizer on the ground and bent down stiffly to pick it up. "Oh, that's just terrific," I said. The liquid in the bottle had solidified into the consistency of sludgy gravy, and turned an unappetizing brownish-black as well.

Lenora moved closer to get a good look. "What is it?"

"It used to be *aqua sapientis*," I said. Whatever magical force Lenora and Tim had sprung on the weasel and me, it had thoroughly fouled the liquid I spent half a day brewing.

Lenora took the bottle and held it up. "Real *aqua sapientis*? You made this? Does it work?"

"It would have. Not anymore."

"What's *aqua sapientis*?" Tim asked.

"Did we screw it up?" Lenora asked.

I made an awkward face, attempting to communicate that she was completely right, but I was too much of a gentleman to say it out loud. I was rapidly recovering my composure and with it the understanding that nothing would be gained by shouting at these two. In fact, they might be able to tell me more than I could have learned by spraying the thorn weasel, and at a substantially lower psychic cost.

Lenora shook her head ruefully. "We thought it was going to kill you, and we did the first thing we could think of. There wasn't time for anything else. Sorry."

"Well, I appreciate the effort." I gathered up my things and started to kick the leaves and sticks around to disguise what had happened here. "Given how we left things last night, I'm a little surprised you took the trouble. Don't think I'm not grateful, though."

"It's time for you to go," Tim said. He had returned to Lenora's elbow and fixed me with a stern look. "This stuff is dangerous. We already told you that."

Lenora touched his arm. "Just a second, Tim." Then, to me, she said. "What were you going to do with the *aqua sapientis*?"

"I needed to find out about that thing. This was the quickest way."

"I thought it was dangerous, contact like that," she said. "Like it's a two-way street or something. You know about it, and it knows about you."

"That's possible," I agreed. "It's definitely not impossible. But it's quicker than four weeks of research. And the results are guaranteed. Assuming you don't go mad, of course." I leaned against a tree and exhaled deeply. "But there's still time for you to spare me all that work and just tell me what the damn thing is."

"It's not important," Tim said. "We'll take it from here."

"Can we not do this again?" I stretched. I was starting to feel where the weasel had knocked me around. "I'm fairly sure we all have the same goal here—to send the thorn weasel away. We're better off working together."

Lenora gave me a pugnacious stare. "You're just not going to give up about this, are you?"

"I am not."

"Neither are we," she said. "Come on."

Lenora led the way into the thickest part of the woods. I noticed she had switched out her Doc Martens for a pair of mud-encrusted hiking boots. I also noticed that Tim made a point of keeping himself between her and me.

"How did you know to come here?" I asked, having grown uncomfortable with the silence.

"We used a charged pendulum," Lenora said as we walked.

"What do you use for a focus?"

"A broken piece of glass with the edges filed down," Tim answered. "It came from a window in the foster home where Lenora grew up."

"Nice."

"The pendulum was really erratic at first, even after we shielded it," said Tim. "It kept oscillating around between different energy nodes on the map." It felt like Tim was making a point of showing how much he knew, demonstrating his qualifications to me, or maybe to Lenora. "Eventually it settled down over the zoo, so we figured this was the right place to look. We hid behind a building until everyone left, then the first thing we found was you and the thorn weasel."

"That's what you're calling it, too?" I asked.

"Your name was better," Lenora admitted. "A lot better than just 'the thing.' We didn't have a name for it before."

I stepped over a protruding root. We were descending into a ravine, away from the zoo's exhibits. "So you really don't know what it is?"

"Nope," she said.

"But we will," Tim added, taking Lenora's hand as she momentarily tottered on a loose patch of rocks.

"Just out of curiosity, how'd you learn to use your pendulum?" I asked.

Lenora shrugged. "The same way anybody does, I guess. Read some books, listened to all of Dennis Falco's friends talking, tried some things out, and all of a sudden we started to get results. What about you?"

"Believe it or not, this is the family business," I said.

We were now in sight of the brick wall that enclosed the zoo. Part of it had been shattered, making a ten-foot gap, with raw edges of bricks and mortar visible. Three strands of yellow police tape, originally connecting the two broken sections, now fluttered weakly in the damp breeze. I took a step back to survey the damage from a higher vantage. The wall had been breached from inside the zoo, and the assailant had obviously been something very large and very strong. Given this ominous scene, in addition to the death of their bobcat, I understood why the zoo management had called the police. If it had been me, I might have checked the national guard's availability as well.

Lenora left Tim, who was poking through the smashed bricks, and joined me.

"Look, I'm sorry about yesterday," she said. "I should have been honest with you back at the apartment. But I was freaked out from what Tim saw at the Peregrine building, and then you showed up, and I wasn't thinking right."

"It's okay—" I began, but she kept going.

"On top of that, I didn't know how much you knew, or even what you really wanted. I've heard some of Dennis's people mention your name, but I didn't know for sure if you were real or just another poseur."

"I understand," I said. "I give off that vibe. Whatever I'm talking about, people tend to think I just looked it up twenty minutes ago," I said. "I've got that kind of face. An amateur's face."

She unabashedly studied my features for a second, nodding slightly in agreement. She wasn't wrong. Sometimes, well-dressed amiability is as much of a liability as an asset. I've learned to live with it.

"Is there anything else you can tell me about the thorn weasel?" I asked. "You don't have any idea where it came from? Were you trying to call it up on purpose, or did something go wrong?"

Lenora sighed. "Oh, something went wrong." She shifted position slightly and the glow from the streetlight caught her face in full. Something about the tiredness under the eyes suggested she wasn't as young as I'd assumed. "Let me ask you something," she said. "What are you doing here? This isn't your problem, and it isn't your mess to clean up. Why are you making all this effort?"

I was taken aback for a second. Like most people, I found the simple question "Why?" tough to answer. Nobody was paying me, nobody had asked me to help, and yet here I was.

"If you were a firefighter and you saw a burning building, what would you do?" I asked.

She thought about this for a second, then finally said, "You really want to help? All right. Maybe we could use it."

"Lenora?" Tim called. He waved to get our attention before hurrying to join us. "Do you hear that?" he asked her.

I didn't hear anything at first. It was quiet before, and it was quiet now. Then I caught on to what he meant. It wasn't just "quiet" anymore. It was nearly silent. The chattering of night animals and the sounds of traffic had been ubiquitous background noise before, but now they were barely audible. It was as if some giant hand had turned down the universal volume control.

"I think it's coming back," Tim said.

Lenora glanced in my direction, and I could see the question "What do we do now?" forming on her lips before she choked it down. There may have been some understanding, possibly even respect, between the two of us now, but she was damned if she was going to ask me for advice.

I understood. Maybe if Tim hadn't been there, it would have been different, but he was and so it wasn't. I swung my rucksack off my shoulder and felt around inside, producing a piece of chalk and a couple of candles. It wasn't much, but every little bit might help.

"What kind of barrier can you make?" I asked Lenora.

She bit her lower lip, thinking. "Right now? I don't know. We'll give it a try."

"What do you want me to do?" Tim asked Lenora.

"Do what I do. Follow me." Lenora began a low chant, alternating between a few very close notes, some musical mode that I'd never heard before. Whatever it was, it touched a primitive chord in my mind. The language sounded like Latin, but she wasn't pronouncing it like any other Latin I'd ever heard. Was it Old French instead? Lenora turned to each compass point and repeated the chant. Tim did the same, saying the words with enthusiasm but less skill. I could feel something happening, an intermittent tightness developing in the air, but I doubted it was going to be enough. The impression I got was of a flickering oil lamp, giving a little bit of helpful light but not strong enough to cope with any winds that might blow up.

I started chalking helpful marks on the rocks around us, hoping to amplify the energies the others were summoning up. In general, it's not a good idea for two people to mix their magical work unless they're very familiar with each other. Even with the best intentions, the results were often unpredictable. Sometimes even explosively so. But given what we'd seen from the weasel so far, I felt it was worth the risk.

Lenora was concentrating on the invisible wall that slowly and jerkily began to surround us, but I saw Tim glance over in my direction a couple of times to see what I was doing. It was the same way you look over at the person next to you in a life drawing class to see if they're better than you are. I pretended not to notice.

After I had decorated every good-sized rock I could see in the immediate area, I returned to Lenora and Tim and took the blue plastic bear out of my pocket. I still didn't know if it had any real power or not, but it couldn't hurt. Occasionally, the mere fact of believing that an object is going to help you imbues it with a degree of potency. An occult placebo effect, so to speak.

Our preparations were as good as they were going to get. Now came the worst part: the waiting. All we could do was stay put until the thorn weasel decided to show itself. After a few minutes of nothing, I spoke up.

"Is it still out there?" I asked.

"Yeah. I think so," Tim said.

"You *think* so?"

"It has to be," Lenora said.

I was no longer convinced. This didn't feel right. The thorn weasel, whatever it was, was not subtle. If it was out there, it should have done something by now. More minutes ticked by.

"Are you sure it was here?" Lenora asked Tim.

"It was. It still is. I can tell," he insisted.

Eventually, though, we began to relax our guard. It's hard to maintain a state of hyper-aroused readiness indefinitely, especially once you start doubting there was any danger in the first place. I felt Lenora's protective magic fade away as her concentration wavered and broke.

Through the ragged hole in the brick wall, I could see the Granary Inn across the road. It was a gray stucco building that had at one point been a depot for farmers bringing their crops to the city, back when this area was a lot more rural than it is now. After sitting idle for who knows how long, it had been turned into a rustic restaurant. A dozen cars sat in the parking lot.

"We could check over there, I guess," I said. "Maybe it . . ."

"Wait." Lenora pointed to a tight cluster of several trees near us. The thin gap between two of the trunks was moving, wavering slightly as we watched it. Suddenly the gap widened of its own volition, and a voluptuous silhouette stepped through.

The huldra covered the distance faster than we could react, without ever seeming to change her languid pace. She was simply over there one moment, and beside us the next.

She remained breathtakingly beautiful, and I nearly took a step in her direction, like a moth hypnotized by a candle flame. She looked at me for an endless moment and I felt a clutching spasm of longing. Then she turned her attention to Lenora.

My instinctive reaction was to interpose myself between Lenora and the huldra, the way Tim had interposed himself between Lenora and me, and the way I always wanted to interpose myself between Sophie and her boyfriend whenever Carl visited Planet Caravan. It was jealousy—ridiculous, unreasonable, juvenile, and as unstoppable as a hundred-car freight train.

The huldra reached out and took Lenora's hand. Her tail lashed and she pulled Lenora away from us. As Tim and I watched, motionless, they left us behind and disappeared into the gap between the tree trunks, which merged together again behind them.

In the space of another breath, the spell was broken. Tim and I could think and move again.

"That wasn't the weasel," I said.

"Yeah, thanks," said Tim.

27

We stayed there for another half hour, studying the trees and trying to find a way of reopening the gateway through which Lenora and the huldra had disappeared. But the conclusion we grudgingly accepted after thirty minutes was the same one that had been obvious after thirty seconds. Lenora was gone, and there was nothing we could do to bring her back.

I could have sworn the thorn weasel was coming," Tim said for the tenth time. Maybe even the eleventh. Either way, I was certain he had said it enough.

"It's okay" I said. "It happens."

"No, it's not okay. It . . ." He waved his arms helplessly. Tim had been showing signs of increasing agitation, and it looked to me like he was only a few minutes away from full-blown panic.

"Look," I said, "we're not doing any good here. It's time to step back and think about the next move."

"Think?" Tim sounded like he'd never heard the word before.

"Think," I repeated. "Figure things out. Plan for the future. Ideally, somewhere else. Where's your car?"

"I . . . Um . . . What?"

I had overloaded what was left of his mind. Time to try again. I made a point to speak softly and clearly, the way you would with an agitated toddler or a nervous kidnapper. "Tim, listen to me. It's going to be okay. I know this looks frightening, but we're actually better off than you think.

Tim laughed at this. It was a borderline hysterical laugh, but at least it was a laugh, and I took it as an indication he was actually paying attention to me. "You saw what the huldra did at the Peregrine perch, right? She drained Eldridge Stamper into a husk. She could have done that to Lenora. The fact that she took Lenora with her means she wants Lenora alive."

"Really?"

"Yeah." I sounded more confident than I felt, but it was a necessary deception. If everybody freaks out, nothing gets done.

"We need to figure out what the huldra wants, and where we can find her. That's not going to be easy to do if the police find us trespassing at the zoo. Believe me, they do not take this stuff as lightly as they should. Now, where are you parked?"

"Up the street." Tim pointed past the Granary Inn, along the little side road that ran by the edge of the zoo and intersected with St. Albert's cemetery.

"So am I. We'll just slip through the hole in the wall and get in our cars. Sound good?" I checked my watch. It wasn't as late as I thought. "Do you know La Mancion on Green River Road? It's the one in front of the Home Furnishing Warehouse."

"Yeah."

"Let's meet there." I figured that if I picked a place close to Lenora's apartment, where I assumed he was staying, he'd be more likely to agree. "I don't know about you, but I'm starving. We'll eat, and we'll talk. Okay?"

Tim nodded numbly, like he'd just come out of a dental procedure and the nitrous oxide hadn't worn off yet.

"Good. Let's go." We hopped over the culvert on the other side of the wall, then hurried across the street and along the edge of the Granary Inn's parking lot, with the exaggerated casualness of two people trying not to be noticed. Having a plan and a place to go seemed to have stabilized Tim a little, but I wondered if I should invite him to ride with me. I didn't want him to freak out completely once he was by himself, and subsequently disappear into the night. At the same time, though, I had to admit I didn't want him in my car.

It wasn't because of his mud-spattered shoes and pants. After getting knocked around by the weasel, I probably looked even worse than he did. And it wasn't because of his slight but persistent odor of mushrooms, though that didn't help. I think the real reason was this: As long as I wasn't giving Tim a ride, driving him around and taking care of him, he wasn't really my responsibility. If I wanted to, I told myself, I could still wash my hands of this affair and go home.

Following Tim's car, I recalled the moment when the huldra appeared out of the trees. If we rescued Lenora, then we would most likely get to see the huldra again, and that thought gave me an unexpected tickle of anticipation. I tried to fight down the feeling, but met with indifferent success. That troubled me. Nothing good could come from letting my infatuation get out of control, but I didn't know if I could stop myself. Maybe when Willard had urged me to think of the huldra as an "it" rather than a "her," he had been acting from motives other than mere pedantry.

La Mancion was a small Mexican restaurant with surprisingly understated decor and excellent food. We ordered quesadilla variety platters, along with a Dos Equis for me and an iced tea for Tim. When the waitress brought us our food, I had a brief moment of deja vu, a memory of sitting down with Ollie Helfrich in the Executive Inn cafe, and the chain of events that ended with him in the hospital under a fake name. With an effort, I put it out of my mind.

At first, I just let Tim eat. I suspected he'd be more communicative on a full stomach, and I took the chance to surreptitiously study him a little more. He was younger than me, a fact which the massive Gettysburg beard and prematurely thinning hair did nothing to hide. That meant he was probably quite a bit younger than Lenora, too. After a few quesadilla wedges, Tim turned his attention away from his plate and said, "I probably ought to tell you some things, right? I mean, there's no point in hiding anything now, is there?"

I agreed.

"Lenora would hate me saying all this, but . . ."

"You're doing it for a good cause," I said. "Just tell me what you know. How did all this start?"

"I went to college at the University of Garvinville."

"You don't have to go all the way back," I said.

"No, this is part of it. I met Lenora my first semester. You know that used book place, the one that's just a few blocks from campus? We saw each other there a couple of times. We were always in the same part of the store. The occult books section."

The occult books at Book & Music Swap hardly merited the title of a "section," since they covered less than two shelves, but I'm sure they loomed larger in Tim's memory.

"We started to talk. I'd just gotten into this stuff over the summer, so I didn't know anything yet. She told me what books to get, what to pay attention to, who to ignore. Things like that. After a while, she took me to the meetings for her reading group. You know the one? They got together in the back of the knitting shop. I never understood why."

"The owner likes to think he's being secretive," I explained.

"I couldn't believe how serious Lenora was. With the rest of the people, most of them seemed like they were only there to show off what they bought, and convince everyone else how much they knew, but Lenora was different. She could actually make things happen. Do you know what I mean?"

"I do. Not just someone who liked the scene. An actual adept."

"I'd never met anyone like her in my whole life. I didn't know people like her really existed."

"She built up her own circle, too, didn't she?" I prompted. "Outside the reading group. Her own followers."

Tim handed his empty glass to the waitress, who took it away for a refill. "A couple of them were from the group, but the others were people she knew from different places. We would study, and we would practice, and sometimes we could get results when all the conditions were just right. I'll never forget the first time we made a crystal move from one side of the table to another. It sounds dumb, I know, but nothing was ever the same after that."

"The world had changed shape," I said.

"Yeah. Exactly. Lenora said that things were working better after she met me. She said I had some kind of natural ability." Tim glanced around to make sure no one was eavesdropping. "She said I could channel the magical forces."

I nodded sagely as I chased the last traces of salsa around with half a tortilla chip. Some people were like that. They had an inborn ability to focus occult power like a magnifying glass. However, like a magnifying glass on a sunny day, these people could also cause any number of accidental disasters if they weren't carefully supervised.

Tim watched the cars going by on Green River Road. Their headlights reflected off the wet pavement and made star-shaped patterns in the windows. "I stopped going to class. I spent all my time with Lenora. We were studying everything we could get our hands on, but it was hard, you know? So much of that stuff is just bogus. To find one book that really knows what it's talking about, you have to plow through two hundred that are nothing but garbage. And even then, you only know for sure after you've tried it out. That takes time."

I agreed. I could imagine how hard it was, knowing there was a whole other reality out there, but having no one trustworthy to help open the door enough to look through. As crotchety, uncommunicative, and just plain weird as Uncle Willard was, I felt an involuntary and embarrassing flash of gratitude for him.

"Lenora had been working at the rehab hospital over on Bellemeade Avenue—in the records department—but they were scaling back and she knew she was going to lose her job soon. We decided to find a way to make some money."

"With magic?" I asked. In the preceding few centuries, the amount of people who had used magic to make money could be enumerated on one hand. The successful ones, anyway. For some reason, it never quite worked out.

"She loved plants, and we were able to put charms on them to really make them thrive. You saw the ones in her apartment, didn't you? Winter or summer, good weather or bad, those plants always looked great. We thought people would pay for the same kind of service."

"Let me guess: When you described it to people, you used words like 'herbal treatments' and 'magnetic alignments,' instead of saying what you were really doing."

Tim nodded as he ate his last quesadilla wedge. Under the beard and the baggy shirt, he was awfully skinny. Despite myself, I hoped he'd been eating properly.

"We figured that people would be more willing to give it a try if we didn't call it . . ."

"Sorcery?" I said.

"Yeah. We did it a few times for people and it was all great. Lenora had worked out this whole ritual for raising spirits of nature and channeling them into helping the

plants. Then we got this new client—the mother of somebody Lenora worked with at the hospital. Some big house
in Riverside."

I sat up straighter. As a resident of a big house in the
Riverside neighborhood, I was curious who it could have
been.

"What was her name?" Tim said to himself, thinking. "I
guess it doesn't matter. Bates, I think."

"Loraine Bates?"

"Yeah, I think so."

"Oh, for crying out loud. She's my neighbor." Mrs. Bates
occupied the brick and slate Second Empire house across
the alley from us. She and Uncle Willard exchanged gardening suggestions every spring, and he adamantly refused her
invitations to join the Garvinville horticultural club.

"That's where it all started to go wrong." Tim glanced
down wistfully at his empty plate and I ordered some deluxe
nachos along with a basket of churros.

"So you've seen her house, right? It's huge. We thought
if we could make this lady happy, she'd tell all her rich
friends. Then we'd have more business, and maybe we
could start charging more. So Lenora wanted to try something special."

I worked hard to keep my expression neutral. Of all the
phrases that tended to proceed catastrophe, "try something
special" was probably second only to "just a couple more
beers."

"We told her we wanted to work at night, since some of
the 'treatments' were sensitive to sunlight. She watched us
for a while, probably to make sure we weren't doing anything weird, then she sort of lost interest and went inside."

For an instant I thought about all the trouble that could
have been saved if Mrs. Bates had possessed a higher
threshold for boredom.

"We laid down the herbal mixture on the flower beds
and made the signs in all eight directions, and went
through all the preliminary invocations like we always did.
After that, we started in with the new words Lenora had
worked out. At first, nothing happened. It just didn't feel
like anything, you know? I was about to ask Lenora if I'd
done something wrong, but then those big, dense bushes at

the back end of the garden started to sway. It was like there was a wind, but we couldn't feel anything. That's when she stepped out."

"The huldra?"

Tim nodded. "We didn't know what to call her then, but yeah. That's who it was. At first, I just thought she was some crazy naked lady, then I saw the tail."

Tim took a bite of churro and looked out the window again. "That was the point I started to think we'd fucked up."

28

I could picture the scene in my mind. There they were, crouching in the dark, working through their ritual and hoping Mrs. Bates wouldn't come back out and wonder what the hell was going on, when suddenly an uninvited visitor sends the whole project spectacularly off the rails. I tried to think about what I would have done in that situation, but nothing came to mind. Most likely, I would have run to Willard and asked for advice, but Lenora and Tim didn't have that luxury. They were sailing in dangerous seas without a chart, and had inadvertently encountered a monster.

Tim kept talking. "At first, I was more surprised than worried. Then I saw the look in Lenora's eyes. She was always the one who knew everything, the one who had things under control. When I realized how scared she was, I got scared, too. She stopped the ritual and said some words I only halfway recognized. They were part of a charm she knew, something to fight off harmful spirits. But as she was saying them, I kept thinking, 'Is this the right thing to do?' I didn't want to hurt the huldra. I mean, she didn't look evil or anything."

"She may not be evil, but she's not evil the way a shark isn't evil. That doesn't mean she's not dangerous."

"Maybe we should have done a different thing. Maybe we should have tried to communicate. I don't know," Tim said. "But the charm seemed to work. She stumbled a little bit, then Lenora said something else and the huldra sort of jumped back and limped away from us. It was like she'd gotten hurt. I remember that she was sort of leaning over, not standing up straight like before. Then she backed into the bushes and disappeared, but I knew she wasn't really gone. I couldn't see her, but I could tell somehow that she was still around. Does that make any sense?"

"It makes perfect sense," I said. "You were right, too."

So this was where the huldra had come from, I thought. I hadn't been sharp enough to put the pieces together before, but now it was clear. As clear as these things ever got, anyway. Lenora and Tim had been tinkering around with forces they didn't quite understand and weren't completely able to control. What was the result? Instead of vitalizing Mrs. Bates's flower garden, they drew into the world a dangerous creature that they couldn't send back. Their attempts to protect themselves—understandable in the situation—had injured and disoriented the huldra. The huldra escaped, most likely in some intermediate state between running free and being banished, and she happened to wander a couple of blocks over to the Peregrine perch. Why? It was impossible to say. As a creature of the forests, she might have been drawn to the dense bushes surrounding the building.

And who discovered her there? Eldridge Stamper. Did he happen to see a shape through the window and go investigate, or did his own peculiar hobbies give him a special sensitivity, a feeling that there was something exotic, unexpected, and possibly edible hiding nearby? Once he found the huldra, he bound her to his will with his magic silver chain and kept her hidden. Had he already constructed the talisman in his hidden workshop, or was he able to resist the power of the stunned huldra long enough to make it? Stamper wasn't around anymore to fill in that particular piece of the puzzle, but it didn't really matter. If this wasn't exactly the way things happened, it was close enough for me.

Tim was getting restless, so I paid the bill and we went outside. The drizzle had come back, and it was getting cold. Sooner or later, we were going to make the switch from "early fall" to "late fall" and it was going to be cold all the time.

"What am I supposed to do now?" Tim asked as we stood under the awning.

"We need to look in Lenora's apartment. I'm assuming you have a key, right?"

Tim hesitated.

"I know what you're thinking," I said. "You don't like the idea. That's perfectly reasonable. I wouldn't necessarily want some goofball poking around in the personal effects of my missing girlfriend, either."

"But I don't have a lot of other options, do I?"

"Don't think of it as 'no other options.' Think of it as 'the best chance of getting Lenora back'."

I doubt this speech took me out of the "goofball" category in Tim's mind, but at least he agreed to let me in. We got in our cars and I followed him back to Lenora's place. I was tired by this point, and trying not to think longingly of going to bed. I'd just switched out my summer sheets for thick flannel ones, and I imagined how comfortable and warm they were going to be, assuming I ever managed to get home. I felt bad for Tim, who was suddenly without his counterpart and unsure of what the future held. Then I realized I actually felt bad for a lot of people at that moment. I felt bad for Lenora, trapped and alone somewhere. I felt bad for Ollie Helfrich, recovering in a hospital bed. I even found myself feeling bad for the huldra and Eldridge Stamper. I shook my head and switched the Jag's sound system to some happy music. If I stayed on this train of thought much longer, I'd probably end up feeling bad for the thorn weasel, too.

Tim let us into the apartment with a key on a long lanyard. The luxuriantly blooming flowers still infused the air with their perfume, though they were starting to droop a little. Tim locked the deadbolt behind us and dropped onto one of the love seats. I sat on the other side of the room, facing him.

"Before we get started, let me ask you a few more questions. First of all, what happened when the huldra came to your apartment?" I asked.

Tim looked up, surprised. "How did you know that?"

"I drove her there." There was no point in hiding the truth now, I thought. "At the time, I didn't know that was where you lived, or even who you were. But when I found her at the Peregrine perch, that's where she wanted to go, so I took her."

"She told you?"

I shook my head. "She never said a word. I just knew where to go. I don't have any other explanation for it. What happened when she got there?"

Tim's shoulders slumped, as if recounting a trying day at work. "So, after she showed up in Mrs. Bates's garden and then ran away, Lenora and I tried to figure out what happened: What was she? What do we do about her? Why did she appear in the first place? Stuff like that. That day, Lenora was here, and I was at home. I'd just gotten out of the shower and I was in my bathrobe, having some cereal. She didn't knock or anything, but out of nowhere I knew for sure that there was something on the other side of my front door. I thought I was being paranoid, but I had to get up and look through the peephole. I couldn't help myself. There she was." Tim sighed deeply. "I freaked out. I never expected to see her again, and suddenly she knew where I lived. The scary part was that she didn't even look mad. She didn't look anything, really. She was just waiting."

"But she didn't try to come in, did she? I bet you probably set up some protective charms when you moved in."

"I must have," Tim said, "but I can't really remember. Anyway, she just stayed out there, standing in front of the door. For hours. Every five minutes I went back to the peephole to check if she'd gone away yet. I was a nervous wreck. You know, now that I think about it, I was probably less scared of her getting in than I was of one of the neighbor ladies opening their doors." He paused, considering. "If they had, would they have been able to see her?"

"Probably only if she wanted them to," I said. "They might have felt something weird in the hall, but to their eyes it would have been empty."

For me, that was the most unnerving thing, not only about this particular situation, but about my entire line of work: The idea that any number of immaterial creatures could be lurking nearby, unseen and unseeable, but perfectly able to watch you. And they rarely had your best interests at heart.

"She finally left, after I don't know how long. I ran down to the car. Every step I was terrified she was going to jump out of the shadows at me. I drove to Lenora's and told her what happened. After a while, we came up with an idea. We didn't know how to banish the huldra, so we were going to get something else to drive her away. Something stronger."

"Oh, dear." I knew where this was going. "So the two of you got Lenora's group together at your apartment, and you raised up the thorn weasel."

"We were sure we could control it," Tim said. "Things were going to be different this time. We were summoning it on purpose, we had our group around us, and we had all the magical wards set up. The conditions were so much better." Tim rubbed his eyes. "Then it just walked right through."

From here, I was more or less caught up with the chain of events. Lenora's group scattered, and she and Tim retreated to her apartment. Through the use of their magic pendulum, Lenora and Tim had detected a concentration of occult power around the Peregrine perch, and Tim had repeatedly staked it out in an effort to see if he could locate the huldra again.

"That's what we were doing at the zoo when we rescued you," Tim said. I let the ill-chosen word "rescued" slide and he continued, "We were trying to find the huldra, not the thorn weasel. We thought if we dealt with the huldra somehow, then that would take care of the weasel, too. We brought the weasel here to get rid of the huldra, and so if it didn't have any purpose anymore, we imagined it would go away."

That sounded like a slightly optimistic analysis, but I didn't say it out loud. We could dwell on the past later, once we'd gotten our future straightened out. I asked Tim if we could take a look at Lenora's notes now. He sort of flickered for a second, as if he wanted to change his mind, but realized he had come too far to back out. He went to a rickety desk by the sliding glass door, returning with an armload of books and papers, then spread them out on a trunk covered with an Indian-print shawl in the center of the room.

From there, he went into the narrow little kitchen and I heard him rummaging around in the cupboards, followed by the hissing sound of water. A minute later, he returned with a couple of steaming mugs. "It's just Tetley's," Tim said. "Lenora's got a bunch of herbal blends, but I always liked plain black tea better. It's what my dad drank all the time. Is that okay?"

Declining a belated offer of milk or sugar, I started to look through Lenora's notes. They were in a variety of formats, including loose-leaf binders, index cards clipped together, cheap drugstore spiral-bound notebooks, and fancy hardcover journals.

"It's all kind of a mess," Tim said. "She'd write in whatever she had laying around. I don't know how anybody could follow it."

"It comes with the territory," I said. "Whenever a wizard makes notes—"

"Lenora hated that word."

"What, 'wizard?' Most of them hate that word. I'd be lying if I said that wasn't sometimes why I use it. Anyway, their notes almost always look like gibberish."

"Is it on purpose?" Tim asked. "Like a magical defense mechanism?"

"Nope. None of them can ever be bothered to keep their things in order. If you wanted to be more positive about it, I guess you could say they're trying to put into rational shape something that's inherently irrational, and the presentation gets distorted because of that. Like when someone makes a flat map of the world and Greenland always looks wrong."

I flipped through Lenora's papers. They seemed more like word-collages than actual notes that another human being could follow. I was also very tired, and could easily have been perplexed by anything more substantial than a newspaper comic. At the very least, Lenora's handwriting was beautiful, swooping and decorative, almost calligraphic. This was quite a change from what Uncle Willard had in his binders. In the sections that weren't shakily typewritten, everything looked like it had been scrawled while he held the pencil in his teeth.

Eventually, after trying and failing to find any landmarks in the material that I could orient myself around, I passed the notes over to Tim. "These might make more sense to you than me. After all, you were the sorceress's apprentice, so to speak."

Tim unconsciously twisted the collar points of his work shirt. "Lenora didn't like me messing around with these," he admitted. "She said there was a lot of stuff in here I might misunderstand. It might send me down some wrong paths."

"Now's the time to start going down those paths," I said. "And since you knew her—know her, I mean—you have a better idea of how her mind works. It's going to be easier for you to piece this stuff together than it would be for me."

Tim gritted his teeth and began rearranging the materials. After a few seconds, he paused and looked over at me. "Do you really think we can bring Lenora back? You don't think she's . . ."

"I don't. I still think if the huldra had wanted to get rid of Lenora, she wouldn't have carried her off," I said. "So we can assume she's out there somewhere, and we ought to be able to bring her back. Stands to reason, right?"

"Yeah. Okay."

Now I was committed to focusing my attention on the huldra again, while postponing any action against the thorn weasel. To my mind, the weasel was still more dangerous, but if I didn't help Tim get Lenora back, there was a good chance he would go off and deal with the huldra on his own. In that case, if history was any guide, we would probably end up with three creatures lurking about instead of two, all of them uncontrollable and angry. My best choice, as I currently saw it, was to get Lenora free as quickly as possible before the weasel got around to rampaging again.

I stretched. There was nothing more sleep-inducing than watching someone else read. In addition, I was still feeling every knot on the tree trunk I'd bounced against when the weasel threw me.

"Look," I said, "I've got to get some sleep. We can pick this up in the morning."

There was a flash of panicked uncertainty on Tim's face, something similar to how I probably looked when I was dropped off at summer camp for the first time.

"Are you going to be all right?" I asked.

"Yeah." Tim nodded. "I've been staying here since the weasel-thing trashed my apartment. It just feels weird to be here alone."

"It's none of my business, but were you and Lenora . . ."

Tim nodded again.

"It's not just idle curiosity," I assured him. "Sometimes intimacy gives you a connection. You may be able to use that."

"I'll do whatever I have to do," Tim said. As goofy and scared and ineffectual as Tim looked, at that moment I believed him completely.

I stood up. All in all, the apartment was kind of charming. There was a view of the turreted recreation center through the sliding glass door, and the pennons, lit by a pair of yellow spotlights, fluttered softly in the night air. On a spring day with the breeze blowing, surrounded by comfy furniture, healthy plants, and beloved occult books, this must have been a nice little place.

"Look through those notes and see if anything jumps out at you. If there's something that might be useful, you'll know it when you see it. But don't try to do anything tonight, no matter what you find. We'll go over it all tomorrow and make a plan. Do you know the Planet Caravan coffee shop?"

29

In the morning, the iron-gray clouds outside my window were heavy and low. After verifying there were no panicked messages on my phone from Tim, I picked out a pair of olive-green pants and an old Judas Priest concert shirt that I'd found at a vintage store last month. Today felt like the right day to finally wear it. I was in the kitchen eating a banana when a voice echoed down the stairs.

"Dean! May I get your assistance for a moment?"

I found Uncle Willard at the foot of the ladder leading to his attic, looking up with a perplexed expression. Following his gaze, I saw a substantial wooden box perched on the lip of the opening.

"What seems to be the trouble here?" I asked.

Willard sighed, as if accepting an unpleasant truth. "You see that box? It's a layout module."

I had heard this term before. A layout module is something that model railroad enthusiasts build, a self-contained portable section of terrain and scenery with tracks entering and leaving at specified points, allowing it to be easily joined with other modules to make a much larger environment.

"A few months ago at the GMRHS, I allowed myself to get roped into building a module for their fall show," Willard admitted.

"The bastards," I said sympathetically. The Garvinville Model Railroad Hobby Society was one of Willard's few concessions to the existence of the rest of the human race, but for him it oscillated frequently between a pleasant gathering to discuss his specialized interest and an exasperating source of unwelcome obligations.

"They're setting it all up today at the old Armory, and I'm suddenly unsure how to get my module out of the attic." He shook his head in self-recrimination. "I should have built it in the garage or the basement, where it would be easier to transport, but I couldn't bring myself to do it. Working on a layout anywhere but the attic seems unnatural." He frowned again at the large box balanced over our heads. "Upon further reflection, I may have cut off my nose to spite my face."

For a moment he resembled a mournful old polar bear, watching a particularly tasty seal swimming away from him. I felt a sudden wave of sympathy. "You wouldn't have been happy anywhere else," I reminded him. "Besides, all your tools are up there. You would have been running up to the attic every five minutes." I put a foot on the bottom rung. "Come on, let's get this thing down. It can't be too hard."

After a quarter-hour of struggle, a few harsh words, and some serious consideration about installing a block and tackle, we got the unwieldy and surprisingly heavy module down the ladder. Carrying it out of the house and into the garage was an easier task, and once we had loaded it into the capacious trunk of his Mercedes, I felt an unexpected surge of pride. So far this week, I hadn't been able to protect Ollie from Stamper, I hadn't been able to keep Lenora from getting abducted, and the odds were good that I wouldn't prevent Tim from doing something stupid in the near future, but at least I had gotten Willard's model train module out of the damn attic unscathed. I was happy to take any victory I could get.

As we stood in the kitchen, celebrating our success, Willard picked up his tablet from the counter and tapped it a few times. "I saw this last night and meant to show it to you," he said by way of introduction, then loomed over me as I read it.

It was another brief paragraph from a Garvinville neighborhood news social media group. This one warned, in a half-joking manner, about a streaker running loose downtown. A naked woman had been seen by several people, and no one was sure if it was a prank, a protest, or the result of a mental imbalance.

Willard flipped through the posts and showed me a different one. It reported that the body of a homeless man had been found in an alley behind the Viceroy Theater, not too far from where the rampaging nudist had been spotted. According to the text, his body had been mutilated by an "animal scavenger."

"I'm starting to get the impression that time is running short," I said.

Willard nodded owlishly. "Whatever creatures your friends let loose, they're starting to feel more at home."

Willard returned to his attic, and I took my army jacket from the coat rack and left for Planet Caravan. It was chilly and unpleasant outside, with sharp, wet winds that whipped around the corners like assailants. Tim wasn't there when I arrived, which was fine with me. I waited while Sophie served a pair of ladies in tracksuits, then I let a somber-looking guy with a knit beanie go in front of me, so I could have more time for small talk.

At the counter, Sophie studied me for a moment, noticing my bedragglement. "You look like a man who could use a cinnamon coffee."

"And you look like a mind reader," I said.

She smiled. "Well, if anybody would know what a mind reader looks like, right?"

She handed my order off to Phillip, one of the baristas. Phillip was stocky, wore heavy glasses, and played a surprisingly soulful slide guitar at the Planet Caravan open mic nights. While he put my coffee together, Sophie reached under the counter and came out with a small pastry on a paper plate. It was crisply brown, with thick streaks of red through the center. Sophie cut off a corner with a wooden fork and held it out to me. "Taste that."

I followed her instructions. "Not bad at all. Raspberry?"

"It's a gluten-free tart recipe I've been tinkering with."

I made an appreciative noise. "No one loves gluten more than me, but that's darn tasty," I said, and she let me have another bite.

"So what are you doing out here today?" Sophie asked, leaning forward to brush a few crumbs from the corner of my lip.

"I knew you'd be here today."

"But I'm here every day," she pointed out.

"So am I, more or less. This morning, though, I'm supposed to be meeting somebody." I described Tim. "Big beard, kind of skinny, wears glasses, probably looks terrified."

"Is the 'terrified' part why he's coming to meet you, or is it because he's met you already?"

"Little bit of one, little bit of the other."

She shook her head, jangling her earrings. "Haven't seen anyone like that yet today."

Sophie put the rest of the tart away, despite my protestations. I'd get a full serving, she said, as soon as she was happy with the recipe. For the time being, she made me a breakfast sandwich, thick with avocado, bean sprouts, and other bounty of the earth that I couldn't immediately identify. I paid and picked up my coffee, then took everything over to a table that faced the front windows. Fifteen minutes later, Tim showed up, carrying a ragged black backpack. A night's sleep had done him good. He was standing up straighter, moving quicker, and there was a firmness in his expression that I'd never seen before. He got a matcha latte and we sat down to talk.

"First of all, I'm sorry for freaking out a little yesterday," Tim said.

"Don't worry about it," I assured him. "Perfectly natural."

"Anyway, once I started to think clearly again, I took a good look at Lenora's stuff." Tim unzipped his backpack and pulled out the papers we'd gone through last night. He had liberally embellished them with purple tape flags to mark important sections, and he also produced a folded quire of paper which contained a summary of his findings. "I thought it would help me if I wrote it all down in my own words," he explained.

We went over this information for a while, passing the papers back and forth. Tim's handwriting was surprisingly expressive, even better-looking than Lenora's. "I was an art major," Tim said when I pointed this out. "I could always do fancy lettering faster than most people could write."

Over his shoulder, I saw the garish photocopied flyers on the bulletin board by the door, announcing craft fairs and fund-raisers and community garage sales. I suggested he might be better off putting his artistic ability to work instead of trying to earn an income through the secret arts.

"Maybe so, I guess," Tim said. "Once everything is back to normal, I'll see what I can do."

Getting everything back to normal, though, looked like it would take some doing. According to Lenora's notes—or, more accurately, according to Tim's interpretation of Lenora's notes—she had been casting a wide net for "earth energy" to channel into the garden plots she and Tim had been hired to rejuvenate. Sometimes it's possible to draw energy from one reality to another and apply it for a specific effect, but in this case Lenora didn't seem to be making a distinction between the undifferentiated energetic force itself, and any creatures who might be composed of this energy. These creatures, if accidentally pulled into Lenora's sorcerous web, might not be particularly thrilled about finding themselves infused into a bed of nasturtiums. This, I believed, was what had happened on that night in Mrs. Bates's back garden. Lenora and Tim had reached out for any kind of magical force they could locate, and inadvertently pulled in the huldra. The huldra, understandably confused and irritated by this, had escaped before they could rectify the situation.

I had a brief, embarrassed realization that if I'd just let Eldridge Stamper and his friends eat the huldra, then this whole episode would have been over before it had a chance to get any worse. But I'm not that kind of guy and probably never will be. I sat back and took a long drink of my coffee before it got too cold.

"Look at this part." Tim took the papers from me and eagerly flipped to the back of a gray, spiral-bound notebook decorated with layers of stickers. He pointed to a page of instructions marked with two of his purple flags. "I found this last night, and as soon as I saw it, everything just clicked. It's a spell of binding and banishment, right?"

I studied the heavily abbreviated notes, two dozen lines written out in coppery fountain pen ink. The format closely resembled a recipe, but obviously written by and for someone who already knew how to make the dish. "Probably so. I recognize some of these steps."

"That's what I thought." Tim took off his glasses. Without the thick magnification, his eyes looked smaller, but bright and unexpectedly purposeful. "That's what I'm going to use on the huldra."

"Pardon me?"

Tim squinted at a well-dressed woman walking by the front window, then put his glasses back on. "Look, I appreciate your help, Dean. I appreciate everything you told me last night, but after you left I started thinking. This is my problem, not yours. It used to be Lenora's and mine, and now it's just mine. I have to do something. This ritual, if I get it right, it'll bring the huldra under my power. I can make her let Lenora go, and then I can force her to leave this world."

I was about to protest, but closed my mouth with a snap. Anything I said at this point wasn't going to make any difference. Obviously, Tim's mind was already made up. He was going to go forward with his plan whether I approved or not. What he had wanted this morning was confirmation, not advice, and I hadn't understood that until now. For a second, I thought about leaving him to succeed, fail, or be eaten on his own, but I couldn't bring myself to do it. After all, this wasn't entirely his fault. I had played a not-insignificant part, too.

With that in mind, I took another look at the spell in Lenora's notebook. "This might work," I said. "I've seen other formulas that are similar. There's a lot to do, though. A lot of components. Are you able to put all these together?"

"Yeah."

"Are you certain?"

Tim's voice got a little tighter. "Well, I have to try. I couldn't live with myself if I didn't."

I held up a hand. "I've got most of this stuff lying around the house. Why don't you come do the preparation there?"

"Really?"

"Sure." I checked my watch. With luck, Willard was going to be out of the house for hours. "I know you want to do this on your own," I said to Tim. "I understand. But you might as well make things easy on yourself, if you can."

Tim drank his latte and thought for a minute. Through the window, a gray-haired guy on a recumbent bike rode down the street, bright orange signal flag quivering behind him.

"All right," Tim said. "Let's give it a shot."

30

An hour later, I was standing at the top of the basement steps and dialing Dr. Helmbach's phone number. An acrid odor rose from below, as if someone were burning walnuts. Tim was down there, crouching beside a hot plate and carefully stirring a pan of various chemicals and powders as they slowly reduced down into a thin paste.

As soon as we arrived from Planet Caravan, I conducted Tim to the basement and retrieved the necessary substances from Uncle Willard's lab, while giving the impression that I was taking them out of storage. Tim was either too diffident or too stubborn to ask for any details, and that was fine with me. I didn't want to arouse his curiosity and run the risk of him wandering through the house. Not only would it have been inconvenient, but I was sure that Willard, once he returned from helping set up the model train expo, would have been able to sense that an intruder had been in his domain.

"Dr. Helmbach, it's Dean," I said into the phone. I could hear sounds of conversation and clattering glassware in the background. "Do you have time to talk?"

"Briefly. I'm at a luncheon for the hospital association, and I've got to give a speech in a few minutes."

"I can call back, if you want."

"Don't bother," he said. "It's nothing, really. They're giving me an award."

"Congratulations—what's the award?"

"Medical ethics." Dr. Helmbach hesitated for a second until the heavy cloud of irony dissipated. "You want to know about your friend, don't you?"

"As a matter of fact, I do."

"He's recovering. I think I can discharge him tomorrow if nothing changes. He was awake this morning, so I got the name of his wife and had the nurse call her for me. I believe she's coming to pick him up." He paused. "Maybe I should have asked you first. That's not going to cause you any complications, is it?"

"It shouldn't, but thanks for thinking about it." I congratulated him again on his ethics award and let him go. Now that Ollie was awake, I considered sneaking into the hospital to visit him, but decided to put prudence ahead of good manners for the present. Letting Tim out of my sight felt like a bad idea. Tim was hell-bent on confronting the huldra, and I wanted to make sure I was there when it happened. This was partly so I could provide assistance—half-assed though it may be—but also to ensure he didn't make things any worse.

Tim looked up from the steaming pan when I returned to the basement. "Is everything okay?"

"Sure. Just had to make a call."

The mahogany-colored sludge in the pan had assumed the consistency of yogurt. "Okay, I think that's good enough," I said.

"I'll add the yellow salt and a little pinch of those crystals, and say the next set of words," Tim said.

"After that, put it over there on the cinderblock to cool." I read Lenora's formula one more time and checked it against the bottles and tins I'd lined up on the old shelves that used to hold pickles and preserves. "When it solidifies, you can move on to the next section."

As Tim followed the instructions and I kept an eye on his progress, I was reminded of Uncle Willard watching and advising while I made the *aqua sapientis*. It wasn't a comforting thought. The last thing Tim needed was a teacher like me. Despite what I might look like to an outside observer, I was hardly an expert in this subject, and I didn't want to become one. In my experience, the more sorcery you studied, the weirder you got, until you ended up as a crabby recluse building models in your attic while sending your long-suffering nephew to run your errands. The others I knew who had also delved seriously into the hidden arts, people like Dennis Falco and his associates, were equally strange and off-putting in various ways. It came with the territory. Tim and Lenora were the first ones I'd met who appeared to have a normal, healthy relationship with another person. And look where that got them.

I appraised Tim's results with cautious optimism. The process was going without a hitch so far. Lenora's ritual was solid. If this worked with the huldra, I might even try it with the thorn weasel.

Tim was using my special French chalk to mark intersecting ovals of compact, elegant-looking symbols around the spot where he was going to begin the next stage of the process. When he finished a cluster of astronomical glyphs, he turned to where I was leaning against a support pillar nearby.

"Hey, thank you again," he said. "This is much easier than trying to mix it all up in Lenora's kitchen."

"It really does help to have the right tools," I said.

He looked away guiltily. "I kind of feel bad about some of the things I said earlier."

"Don't give it a second thought. I don't even remember it," I lied.

"Can I pay you for this stuff?" When I shook my head, he added, "At least let me clean it all up for you."

"Tim, don't worry about it. We'll deal with the cleaning when we get back."

He squinted at me. My use of the word "we" had bothered him, and he was unsure how to reiterate that he planned on confronting the huldra alone.

"I'm going with you," I said, handing him a jar of beeswax shavings. "End of discussion."

I could see him think about responding, but he finally gave up and took the jar from me, sprinkling the shavings into the pan.

Once the preparations were finished, we still had some time before it got dark. Lenora's spell appeared to be designed for use after sunset, so it made sense to wait. In addition, tonight was a propitious phase of the moon, and that certainly couldn't hurt. I opened the basement windows to ventilate the odors of alchemy, and we walked over to the river. This was mainly to get Tim out of the house, reducing the likelihood he'd start poking around and asking questions. But I also worried that if we were stuck inside all afternoon, I'd eventually get bored and succumb to the temptation to start showing Tim things. It was a possibility. Tim had an inquisitive, little-brother quality that made me want to impress him, despite knowing this was a bad idea. And, of course, I never needed much prompting to start talking about myself.

We crossed the four lanes of Riverside Drive and climbed the slope to the long, snakelike park that occupied the top of the levee. The Garvinville Museum of Art was here, along with a glass-walled, pagoda-topped little building that held the city visitors' center. Despite the October chill, a guy with a pretzel cart stood stoically on the sidewalk in front of the museum steps, so we bought a couple of pretzels and ate them while a train of barges steamed along on the Ohio River below us.

"It looks smaller," Tim said. "The river, I mean. When I was a kid, it was monstrous, like you'd have to swim all day to reach the other side. Now it feels like I could throw a rock across it."

"There's a lesson in that."

We ate in silence for a few more bites.

"Do you think we'll get Lenora back?" he asked.

"Yeah, I do," I said. "I'd be lying if I said I'd done this before, but the spell seems well-constructed. If we can bind the huldra, keep her from going anywhere, then I think she'll be willing to make a deal."

"How do I communicate with her?"

I thought about this. "We probably won't be able to have a conversation, but I'd be surprised if she couldn't understand what we want, and vice versa."

"I hope so." Tim brushed a few stray crumbs of salt out of his beard. "I love her," he said, looking out at the river. "Lenora, I mean."

"That's what I figured."

"I never told her, but I do. If I can't get her back, I don't know how I'm going to live with that."

"Don't worry. It's not going to happen." I tried to sound a little more confident than I actually felt.

"I should have told her," Tim said, ignoring me and following up on his own thoughts. "I should have told my family about her. They don't even know her name. Seriously. I never told them. I was so worried about what they'd think. She's older than me, and they'd probably imagine she talked me into dropping out of school." He sighed. "I never really knew what I was supposed to do—or how I was supposed to feel—until I met her. After I met her, life made sense. I should have told her that."

"You'll get a chance." I crumpled the waxed paper that had held my pretzel and tossed it at the nearby trash can. It missed by eight feet.

"So, your house is next to Mrs. Bates's, right?" Tim asked. "It's on the other side of that back alley?"

"Why do you ask?"

"I think her garden is the right place to try summoning the huldra. It's where she was brought over in the first place, and I figured it would give me an extra connection."

"That may not be such a great idea," I said.

"Why not?"

"For one thing, do you think Mrs. Bates is going to stand by if we tell her we're going to lure a dangerous, primordial nature spirit into her garden?"

"She was fine with the herbal treatment," Tim said.

"I don't think that compares. Besides, and more importantly, I live next to Mrs. Bates. If she sees me dancing around with candles and magic circles, I'm never going to hear the end of it. Whatever small advantage we'd get from using that same spot isn't worth the aggravation." Suddenly, I realized how much I sounded like Uncle Willard, and shuddered.

"Well, what kind of place should it be, then?" Tim asked. "It's got to have some connection with nature, right? We can't just try it out in an abandoned building somewhere."

"That's correct."

Tim pondered this while I tried to reassure myself that my uncle and I were nothing alike.

"I know where to go," he said at last.

31

Some time later, I stopped the car in the parking lot of an odd-shaped white building, sitting by itself on a spare stretch of Covert Avenue. It may have once been a nondescript house, but several phases of alterations had added a two-story ell onto one side, tall picture windows in the front, and a square extension topped with low crenellations. All the windows were coated with slightly shiny, ultraviolet-resistant plastic, and were plastered with gigantic cutouts of comic book characters and promotional posters for games featuring angry-looking elf maidens with bare midriffs. A sign on a rusty pole out front read "Book Baron" in nondescript commercial capitals, with "Used Books, Comics, Games, Cards, Records" underneath.

"Now I see why you wouldn't tell me before we left," I said to Tim. "Are you serious about this?"

Tim pointed. Behind the shop was a thick band of trees, dense enough that I couldn't see beyond it. "You've never been here?" he asked.

As a matter of fact, I had. One of the local adepts kept a discreet office here, preferring to do research and experiments somewhere other than his own apartment, and I had visited a couple of times to consult him on technical matters. I'd even stopped to browse through the cardboard crates of records once or twice, hunting for gems. But I'd never really noticed the woods behind the building. You don't pay attention to something until you're actually looking for it.

"I was here playing Magic one night, and some of us went out there to smoke a little between rounds," Tim said. "There's a gully with a stream running through it. You can hardly even see the road. I thought it might be a good place."

We were parked under the solitary old maple that grew out of a graveled square in the middle of the parking lot. Dusk was falling rapidly. The windows of the Book Baron glowed, and I could see silhouettes moving around in the upper story of the ell.

"They have games going on until eleven," Tim said. "Nobody's going to notice the car." He took his backpack from the seat behind us, and I buttoned up my jacket. It was getting cooler as the darkness encroached, but the rain still held off. It had been a wet fall so far, muting the colors of the leaves and knocking them off the trees earlier than normal. As someone who enjoyed both rainy days and autumn foliage, this gave me conflicting feelings.

Tim led us around the red panel fence bordering the parking lot, down a slope, and into the trees. In a month, most of the leaves would be down and this place would hardly seem like a wooded area at all. Already, I could see parts of the trailer park beyond the gully, and anyone in a hurry could have reached the other side within two minutes. Still, it might work for our purposes.

As I stood beside the thin creek I saw an old plastic grocery bag caught on a root, a cracked single-shot bottle of cinnamon whiskey, and some other miscellaneous detritus of civilization. Tim was already unpacking the materials, and I asked him to hand me one of the trash bags he'd tossed in before we left.

"Why?" he asked.

"I think the huldra might be more inclined to show up if there's not so much garbage around. You know, creatures of nature and all that. Besides, if we don't do it, who's going to?"

Tim shrugged, but handed me a bag. I picked up what I could while he got everything ready.

"You want me to help you with that?" I said as he marked out an eight-pointed star with the yellowish granules we'd cooked up in the basement. He refused, of course, so I stood back and let him finish the preparation. For want of anything better to do, I felt my pockets, checking that my match safe and various other essentials—phone, keys, penknife—were in their right places. For a moment, I thought a stray wire from Uncle Willard's train module had gotten into my interior jacket pocket, but it was actually the little silver chain I had lifted from Eldridge Stamper's personal effects. I unobtrusively transferred it to a side pocket while Tim worked. I was strangely nervous, and my mind was filled with curious police officers coming around the red wooden fence and waving their flashlights all over the place. I doubted my mind was currently nimble enough to spin an innocuous explanation for what we were doing.

Tim unwrapped a package of Hostess chocolate cupcakes and set them on top of a small cairn of rocks. Lenora's binding spell required a "desired offering," which I thought was an unhelpfully vague term. Tim was convinced it meant something that the magician in question especially valued, so we stopped at a convenience store on the way to the Book Baron and bought cupcakes.

He produced a brushed steel multi-tool and made a wry face. "I never liked this part," he mumbled as he unfolded the scissors. Usually, when blood is required, the traditional manner is to use a knife, but Tim gnawed at the side of his hand with the scissors until he got it deep enough, then dripped a few thin lines of blood over the cupcakes. In the gloom, the blood looked uncomfortably like cherry glaze.

Tim took a bandage from his backpack and stuck it over the cut. He referred to his notes and recited a series of phrases in a sing-song voice. When he was done, he said, "Now we wait, right?"

"Now we wait."

It's surprising the things you notice when you're standing around and being quiet. The noise of the street behind us, previously an undifferentiated hum, was now something I could break down into the sounds of individual vehicles. I could hear the talking and laughing through the walls of the Book Baron's game room, as good and bad plays provoked reactions from the players. The thin creek hissed as it splashed around a chunk of sandstone sticking out from the slope.

Without warning, there were three of us.

I didn't move, and I didn't make a noise. Tim stood next to me, breathing hard. The huldra watched us with her disinterested expression, which managed in its own way to be more terrifying than the thorn weasel's snarls and hisses. She took a step forward, hips and tail swaying in opposite directions. Then she stepped over the star Tim had made on the ground, crouched down, and picked up one of the cupcakes. She rubbed the blood on her lips, then ate the cake in two greedy, sensual bites.

Now was the time for the most difficult part. We had to bind this creature and force her to return her prisoner. What made it particularly challenging was that, at the moment, I had no desire whatsoever to send her away. In fact, I wanted her to stay. I wanted her to stay with me. We would get married and I would confine Uncle Willard to half the house and we would raise a family of happy little tailed babies.

Gingerly, as if struggling against great pain, Tim took two roughly-whittled rods of ash wood from his backpack. They were both about as long as a chopstick and as thick as a child's pencil. Tim held one in each hand, throwing his arms out wide. His arms shook as he angled the rods, turning them inward until they pointed at the huldra. She watched this performance for a few seconds, then turned her attention to me. Despite being fully aware of what was about to happen, I felt like someone had switched on an industrial fan made of pure desire. All I wanted to do was knock Tim over, run to her, and feed her more baked goods iced with blood.

Instead, I bit my lip and tried to redirect my mind. I thought about the chukka boots I had seen at Wegman's Shoes last month. I thought about the mixed lot of two dozen old tie clips that I hadn't bought at the antique store, but should have. I thought about 1950s Yugoslavian chess sets. I thought about Sophie.

The huldra turned her scrutiny back to Tim. Instantly, I felt the magnetism began to abate. Tim shuddered and made a slight moaning sound, and the rods dropped from his hands.

"Say the words!" I hissed. If Tim was going to restrain the huldra, he needed to recite the formula now, before she could get away.

Nothing.

Tim took a seasick step forward, and I knew the huldra had him. The critical moment was gone. She had gotten into his mind and was reeling him inexorably toward her. It was too late for me to take over the ritual, even assuming the huldra would wait patiently while I dug out Lenora's notebook, turned on a light, and found the proper page. Instead, it was time to improvise. I held up the tiny chain of silver links, the magical talisman that Eldridge Stamper had fashioned to keep her under control. I hoped it might do the same for me.

I gripped each end of the chain with a thumb and forefinger, and recited a few words that had worked for me in similar situations. The results were immediate. The huldra whirled as if stung. I felt a sharp burst of icy fear. I'd unquestionably succeeded in getting her attention, but now she knew I could be a threat. I frantically ransacked my mind for a charm that would keep her in place until Tim could repeat his spell, but then a hand reached out and tore the chain from my fingers.

It was Tim. Before I fully registered what he was doing, he had hauled off and punched me in the side of the head. I staggered. Getting punched by Tim wasn't on the same level as getting punched by Eldridge Stamper, but it was hardly a pleasant experience. As I straightened up, Tim stumbled past me, his hands extended like a man searching in pitch darkness. He was totally under her control now. I made a futile grab for the back of his coat, but it was too late. He was already beside her.

His arms went around her waist and she pulled him closer. Any thoughts of rescuing Tim suddenly went to the bottom of my priority list. Jealousy filled my mind like a rampaging flood. Every breakup, every betrayal, every declaration of just wanting to be friends, they all came rushing back to me when I saw that creature of incomprehensible beauty—tail or no tail—embrace the incompetent mope Tim. I had a quick impulse to pick up the wooden rods Tim had dropped and impale the both of them, vampire-style.

I gasped like a stranded goldfish under the weight of this supernatural jealousy, fighting off the images of vengeance and murder that raced through my mind. By the time I could think straight again, the huldra had already let him go. She stepped delicately backward as the pale, desiccated form of Tim Grimes fell to the ground.

32

The huldra was gone, melting into the tangle of weedy bushes before I got Tim turned over. I grunted involuntarily and mumbled something inane to myself when I saw his face. His hair and beard had become white and brittle, and his skin was deeply seamed. He had aged seventy years in the span of a few seconds.

Astonishingly, his eyes slid open. I managed to avoid screaming with shock.

Tim's lips worked noiselessly for a moment. Eventually, he croaked out, "What happened?"

"What do you remember?" I tried to remain professional. My sheer amazement that he was still alive would do Tim no good.

"She was looking at me. That's all."

"Can you stand up?" I asked. The broken pieces of the silver chain lay on the ground next to him. I scooped them up and grabbed Tim's backpack before helping him totter to his feet. When we reached the parking lot, now lit by pinkish-yellow security lights, he finally took a long look at his hands and realized that something wasn't right.

"Good God," he said, examining himself in the car window. He ran his gnarled fingers along his cheekbones and nose, as if to convince himself that the vision in the glass was real. "What happened?"

"It's the same thing she did to Eldridge Stamper," I said, opening the car door. "Only this time, the thorn weasel wasn't there to finish you off."

"Great. I guess." Tim slumped in the seat and I started the car. We drove in silence for a bit. I was still jittery from the emotional whiplash the huldra had put me through, and Tim, naturally, had to be feeling orders of magnitude worse. For a few blocks, there was nothing but the sound of the Jag's engine and Tim's labored breathing. Then he sat up straighter and coughed.

"I can't believe this," he rasped.

"We'll figure something out," I said. "Don't panic. Things that are done can usually be undone." The word "usually" was the key part of that sentence, but I kept this information to myself. There was no point in making Tim feel any worse.

"Lenora first," Tim said.

"Excuse me?"

"I've got to try again."

"You need to rest. We'll think about trying again later."

"No." Through the shaky voice, I recognized the same stubbornness, bordering on petulance, that had been a characteristic of Tim's ever since I met him. "I screwed it up, so I've got to try it again," he said. "The only thing that matters is getting Lenora back. That's what I'm going to do. You can help me or not. I don't care."

I checked my blind spot and changed lanes. "All right. Fine. We'll try again," I said. Tim's insistence on re-trying the ritual was insane, but I wasn't heartless enough to drop him back at his car and let him figure things out for himself. So we returned to the house. I dreaded the idea of having to explain Tim to my uncle, but when we arrived, Willard's Mercedes was still absent from the garage. Either the installation of the train layout had taken more time than expected, or his associates from the club had talked him into some social event afterward. Either way, there was no one to peer suspiciously at me over reading glasses while I helped Tim inside and installed him in my office.

Tim moved gingerly, unsure how much stress he could put on his withered and gnarled body. I helped him onto the couch and threw a blanket over his knees. "Wait here," I said. Before he could protest, I added, "I'll get us something to eat, and we can work out what to do next. Rest your eyes. I'll be back in a minute."

In the kitchen, I switched on the electric kettle and shook some crackers onto a plate, then prospected in the fridge for some cheese. I attempted to slice up some fruit and summer sausage while I waited for the water to boil, but stopped when I noticed how badly my hands were shaking. I had done my best not to let Tim's transformation freak me out, but now a wave of revulsion rolled over me, and all I could do was breathe deeply and wait for it to subside. Fortunately, shocks like this never stuck around too long. This is either due to my innate mental fortitude or my extreme shallowness, but in any case, I was largely in control of myself again by the time the kettle clicked off. I tossed some Assam in the teapot and poured in the water, then took a pair of mugs from the cupboard.

When I returned to the office, carrying the refreshments on a tray, Tim was asleep. For a few seconds I watched him, just to see if he was resting comfortably. His skin was papery and spotted with freckles. His white hair and beard were disheveled, giving the impression that he'd dozed off under a tree a hundred years ago and had yet to be woken up.

I put the tray on the side table within easy reach of the couch, took a pear, and quietly left the room. I went upstairs to Willard's lab and turned on the light over his work table. While Tim was asleep and Willard wasn't around to ask questions, I could make use of the time. At the sink, I washed off the broken strands of Stamper's silver chain, then dried them with a shop towel and arranged them under the adjustable magnifying lens. This chain had bothered the huldra enough to have Tim tear it out of my hands. She still appeared to be in the mood for vengeance, so it was worth keeping the chain in our arsenal, assuming I could get it back together without damaging the magical potency. I found a set of small tools in a drawer and got down to work. Each of the links had a few runic symbols, ridiculously small, carved on them, and I made a transcript of each link as I went along. It was obvious that the pieces had to go back together in the right order, and with luck the pattern of the runes would show me where to re-attach each section.

It was slow work, meticulous and painstaking. Those aren't necessarily my strengths, but I was happy to have something to concentrate on to keep my thoughts from wandering back over recent events. Tim had gotten in over his head and had his life drained away by the huldra. Ollie had gotten in over his head and had nearly been murdered by Stamper. I couldn't help but reflect that the common factor in both incidents was me. I had gotten Ollie enthusiastic about investigating Stamper, and I had let Tim go through with a ritual he didn't fully understand and wasn't ready to perform. They were, of course, grown men who were capable of making their own choices, but that didn't make me feel much better. I couldn't shake the impression that I should have done more.

I forced my mind back to the task at hand, moving the chain fragments around with a pair of tweezers, checking my transcriptions against some of Willard's reference books, and hoping to find a configuration that made sense. When inscribing his marks, Stamper had used some abbreviations and shortcuts that were highly idiosyncratic, to say the least, but eventually I got a sense of how the pieces could be put back together. I just hoped that I hadn't lost any links in the mud when I recovered the fragments. About halfway through the delicate process of reconnecting them all, a loud noise from somewhere outside made me jump.

It was a metallic clatter, a noise that sounded very much like the trash cans by the patio door falling over, perhaps knocked over by a large man unwilling to move them out of his way like a normal person. I abandoned my project and raced downstairs, wanting very much to catch Uncle Willard before he started interrogating Tim. When I reached the kitchen and looked out the window, what I saw wasn't my uncle lumbering in from the garage. Instead, it was something much worse.

A white-haired figure stood in the back yard between the flower beds, sprinkling powder on the ground from one of my jars. A battered black backpack slouched at his feet, and several books were propped open on the birdbath, which had been covered with a trash can lid and converted into a makeshift lectern. I recognized Lenora's notebook, as well as a pair of old Spanish demonology manuals from the bookcase in my office. I, of course, also recognized the white-haired figure chanting formulas in a raspy voice. It was Tim.

"Hey!" I called, rushing outside. I was about to follow this up with several more indignant statements, but I immediately tripped over the trash cans that lay abandoned at the bottom of the patio steps. The racket I caused, followed by heartfelt and expansive cursing, was enough to get Tim's attention.

"What are you doing?" I demanded as I got myself vertical again, hopping on one foot and trying to ignore the pain in my left shin.

Behind his glasses, Tim's blue eyes were bright with enthusiasm. "I'm bringing the huldra here," he said. "This time, it's going to work."

"Are you insane?" I asked, hobbling forward as quickly as I could manage.

Tim shook his head. "I know what went wrong last time. I didn't protect myself well enough." He pointed to my books, currently held open with a couple of damp half-bricks from the flower beds. "When I saw these, I realized I could do the same ritual all over again and it would work the way it was supposed to, as long as I built a strong enough wall between me and her."

"And my back yard seemed like the best place to try this out?"

"Sure," Tim said. "Why not?"

"We have neighbors, you know." Most of the yard was enclosed with a stout wall, and ornamental trees provided additional screening, but the privacy was hardly comprehensive. A quick check to the left and right didn't reveal any curious faces in the windows of the next-door houses, but that was no guarantee Tim's antics had gone undetected. I sighed. Life was easier for everyone if the rest of the neighborhood continued to see Willard and me as essentially harmless, and shenanigans like this didn't make the pretense any easier.

"Why didn't you come get me before you started this?" I asked.

Tim coughed. "You wouldn't have helped. You would have told me to wait." While I sputtered, pinned by his impeccable but exasperating logic, he continued. "Don't worry about it. I'm almost done."

I dragged the trash cans back to their proper positions and joined him. "How far did you get?"

"Pretty far, I think." Tim ran his finger down the page of Lenora's notebook, checking the entries. "Where did I stop?" he said to himself.

"You stopped at a safe place, right?" Working with sorcery was a little like driving: There were certain times when you could let your attention drift and certain times when absolute focus was required. Mixing those times up was a recipe for disaster.

"Of course I did." He checked the notes. "I must have. I mean . . ."

As Tim's voice trailed away, I looked out across the garden to the row of decorative shrubs along the back wall. Beyond the wall was the old brick alley, and then Mrs. Bates's house, where all of this had started. A breeze agitated the bushes for a moment, then died out. The bushes, however, continued to move.

It was much colder now. I saw flashes of pale skin through the leaves. Next to me, Tim's startled gasp rattled in his chest.

She's here, I thought. Tim brought her back, she's probably not happy, and Tim hasn't finished the spell. I dried my sweaty palms against the sides of my pants. Something bad was going to happen very soon, and if I was going to rescue the situation I had to do it in less time than it took for her to step into the open.

But what emerged from the bushes wasn't the huldra.

33

A dark mass pushed itself toward us. It was wholly too big to have hidden behind Willard's row of well-groomed azaleas, and the discrepancy gave my mind a sickening twitch of incredulity. It was enormous, as broad as a garage door and undulating restlessly. A pair of bright green eyes trained themselves on me. It was the thorn weasel. My concerns about Tim's antics startling the neighbors were now fairly inconsequential.

Behind me, I heard Tim whisper, "Oh, no."

"Get back in the house," I hissed.

Every time I saw the weasel, it was more horrible than the last. I wasn't sure if it was changing with each encounter, molding itself to match my subconscious fears, or if I was just getting more afraid of the damn thing. I struggled to move, to make noise, to do something, but the monstrous intruder had me paralyzed with fear.

The weasel's massive head swung from one side to the other, sniffing the air to get a better impression of the entire back yard. It was searching for something, I thought. It was probably on the trail of the huldra. A moment ago, I thought I had seen her through the bushes, and the weasel must have homed in on her as soon as she appeared. Had it been lurking in the area? Was that the reason why she fled so quickly? What was the weasel going to do now that its preferred prey had escaped?

It lumbered forward, the vines twisting into an extended paw and the rest of its mass forming up in the proper orientation behind. I thought about the dog with the flesh ripped from its skull, the dead bobcat in the zoo, the poor homeless guy, and Eldridge Stamper, but forced myself back to the present moment. Now was not the time to be distracted by fear.

"What do we do?" Tim asked.

My heart-of-hearts answer was "we should run," but I knew that wasn't the solution. Running away would only put the confrontation off until another time. But, more to the point, I would have felt incredibly guilty outpacing wizened old Tim and leaving him to be shredded by the weasel.

"We've got to send it back," I said. "Back where it came from."

"Now?" Tim asked.

"I wasn't planning on it, but here we are."

I averted my eyes from the weasel's and took a step forward. The overgrown-greenhouse odors of vegetation and rot rolled over me. I wished I'd had a chance to go over those demonology books that Tim had pulled off my shelves, since there were a number of things in them that might have been useful. Instead, I had to rely on the scraps of lore that happened to be stuck in my mind already. I rattled off a string of incantations, alternating between three languages: Latin, Old Dutch, and some Enochian for good measure.

The weasel shied backward like a surprised animal. While I knew its hesitation was only momentary, I thought I might be able to keep the upper hand if I worked quickly. But then, without warning, something pulled me forward, nearly knocking me off my feet. The creature had extended its tendrils around to either side without me noticing, then lashed them around me before I could react. Their brambly embrace hurt like hell, driving any further magical formulas out of my mind. Now, it was all I could do to dig my heels into the ground and slow the inexorable pull toward the thorn weasel's jaws.

My left arm was still free, and I dug into my pants pocket before the thickening strands of vines and thorns made it impossible. I retrieved the little brass match safe and slid open the cover with my teeth. Inside was the blue plastic bear. Back at the Peregrine perch, the weasel had backed off when I confronted it with the blue bear. It was possible that the same thing might happen here, freeing me from its grasp and allowing Tim and I to escape into the house, where Uncle Willard's carefully-fabricated occult wards would prevent it from following us.

First, though, I had to get the bear out of the box. I tilted the match safe to shake the plastic trinket into my hand, but at the same moment a band of viciously-barbed thorns dug themselves into my ribs. I flinched involuntarily, and the bear went flying. I had a vision of the future, some point long after the weasel had killed me, long after Willard had grudgingly mourned, when a garden center employee delivering a load of mulch would find the blue plastic bear in the flower bed. He would hold it between his thumb and forefinger for a second, letting the plastic sparkle in the sun. Then he would shrug, toss it into the trash can, and go about his day.

I saw the miniature bear tumbling through the air on that distant day, just as it was tumbling through the air right now, like a dark meteor in the light from the patio. I dropped the brass match safe and threw my arm out. The blue bear landed in my palm.

The vines continued to tighten, but not fast enough to keep me from raising the tiny bear and brandishing it at the weasel. Everything stopped for an instant. The tendrils relaxed slightly and even the weasel itself ceased to undulate. I think it was waiting to see what I did next. Actually, so was I.

I don't know where my subsequent idea came from, but it doesn't matter. I've always felt that the surest way to choke off the flow of good ideas is to worry too much about where they come from. It's much better to just let them happen. That's what I did this time. Without pausing to think about why, I raised the blue bear over my head, as far as my vine-tangled arms would let me. Then I slapped it down hard on the thickest mass of tendrils I could reach.

The effect was instantaneous. With the sensation of being in an elevator and suddenly dropping five floors, my senses shifted. The thorn weasel and I were the only two things in the universe. An instant later, we were no longer two things at all. We were connected. I was briefly conscious of the weasel as a massive swirling mountain of green, alongside a much smaller blob of yellow, which was me. Then there was nothing but a singular green-and-yellow mixture, a giant multi-hued marble that contained both of us. At first, I felt like drifting in that storm of color and pattern forever, not entirely me and not entirely the weasel, and not giving much thought to the world I'd left behind.

Then my mind cleared and I realized what had taken place. The weasel and I knew each other now. We were aware of each other. It knew what I felt, and I knew what the weasel felt. I knew it was hungry, not just for food, but for destruction. It wanted to scrape the flesh from my skeleton and scour the bones not only because I was delicious, but also because it was satisfying, in the primal, atavistic way that smashing a priceless vase is satisfying. Destruction was its mission, its purpose for existing.

Beyond that, there was something else, too. One more secret I wasn't expecting. When it registered on me, I nearly cried out with surprise and recognition. I felt like my mind had been torn open, stuffed full of knowledge, and crudely sewn back together. Now I didn't just know the weasel. I *understood* the weasel.

This revelation, however, was going to be of little use if the thing killed me, which it clearly still wanted to do. Apparently, what the weasel learned about me was nowhere near as fascinating and mind-altering as what I learned about the weasel.

At this point, as I grew dimly aware that my physical self remained standing in Willard's flower bed, wrapped in thorny vines and about to die, I began to register a vague figure a few feet away. He was frail and slight and wobbling unsteadily, but he was still there. He hadn't run away. I had the impression he was flipping madly through the pages of a book. I heard his voice drifting through my consciousness, and I pushed myself toward it like a swimmer pulling for shore against a current.

"What do I do?" Tim called. "Do I banish it?"

"Yeah, sure. Sounds good," I mumbled. The vines were tightening around my chest, and it was hard to get the words out.

My vision of the normal world was returning, and I could see Tim holding up my irreplaceable demonology book by its cover. "Which one? There's like a dozen versions."

"Pick one."

"Really?"

Tim correctly interpreted my strangled grunt as a confirmation, and began chanting. His Latin was still a mess. If I were a creature from beyond I would have been humiliated to be driven off by it. But it had an effect. The thorn weasel loosened its grip on me and I dropped to my knees. There was an awful sound, the moan of an enormous tree just before it toppled over, and the weasel leaped at Tim. Fighting my disorientation, I tried to speak another charm of protection. Based on what I now knew about the weasel, I didn't want to chase it out of this world entirely, but I still needed to drive it away from Tim. And I wouldn't have minded removing it from the back yard, too.

The thorn weasel reared up, lurched away from Tim, and fixed me with a glowing-eyed expression of malevolence. I could hardly believe it, but the combination of our two incantations, poorly-performed as they both were, was enough to keep the weasel at bay. It gave one more lunge, as if still thinking about tearing me into pieces, then was gone.

Everything was quiet. I fought the impulse to drop to the ground and lay motionless, staring up at the night sky while I got myself reoriented. My mind raced. Connecting with the weasel had made several things clear, and I knew I had to act on this new information while there was still time. I took stock of the yard. Where Uncle Willard's garden had been, there was now only a thoroughly torn-up area of ground, as if a pack of rambunctious dogs had been digging around in it. Off to the side, halfway across a ravaged flower bed, a thin figure lay stretched out and motionless.

I drew in my breath, then knelt on the ground beside Tim. I tried to find a pulse, but couldn't concentrate. Between the weasel's attack and my subsequent mind-altering experience, nothing seemed real. Eventually, the cold dampness seeping through the knees of my pants reminded me to get busy. I put my arms around Tim's wasted frame and carried him unsteadily into the house. The closest, most comfortable place to set him down was the ornate couch in the living room. When I manhandled him onto it, he let out a grunt and took a shallow, uneven breath.

"You rest here," I said. There was no response, so I left him in the living room and raced around the house, gathering up my jacket, my keys, and anything else I thought I might need. Thanks to the weasel, I now knew where to find the huldra, and I knew where to find Lenora, but I had no idea how much time I had to act. Through all of this, I was still clutching the blue bear in one hand, just like the huldra had been when I rescued her from Stamper. I forced my fingers to uncurl and dropped it in my pocket. Would I need it again? I wasn't sure, but I didn't want to leave it behind.

Then a voice from the hall interrupted my frenzy.

"Why is there a dead man on my couch?"

34

Uncle Willard stood in the doorway connecting the side hall to the living room. A paper bag with the logo of the Garvinville Model Railroad Hobby Society dangled from one hand, and he gazed in alarm at the still figure on the couch.

"He's not dead," I said.

"Are you certain?"

"Check him yourself, if you're curious."

"I would prefer not to," he said.

My mind squealed with frustration at having to slow down and explain myself. I had been hoping to get out of the house and do what I had to do immediately, before either the revelation faded or Willard got home to ask questions and sniff disapprovingly. But since Willard now stood before me in the doorway, questioning and sniffing, my plan was shot to hell and I had to make the best of it.

"He's okay, really." I crossed to the couch and nudged Tim with my knee. Tim obligingly produced a rattly groan and shifted slightly. "See?"

Willard condescended to enter the room and frowned at Tim. "Do you need to call a doctor?"

"I don't think a doctor could fix what's wrong with him."

"What would that be?"

"Well, for starters, four hours ago he was in his twenties."

"I see," he said.

"Exactly. They haven't covered this kind of disorder in medical school for about a thousand years."

"What's the matter with you?" Willard demanded. "You look maniacal. Are you drunk?"

"Not yet, though it's on the list."

"What did you do?"

"Funny story," I began, then realized that my post-revelation buzz wasn't helping my credibility. I made an effort to tone it down, and gave Uncle Willard a precis of what Tim and I had been doing today, from studying Lenora's notes, to failing to control the huldra, to encountering the thorn weasel in the backyard flower beds.

By the time I stopped to take a breath, Willard was glowering. I knew what was on his mind. Over the years, I had gotten pretty good at reading his glowers. He was annoyed not because I had let a dangerously untrained practitioner run amok, but because the untrained practitioner had ended up unconscious in his living room. One of Willard's guiding principles was to keep a distance. Home was not the place to conduct dangerous experiments, it was not the place to invite the forces of the outer worlds, and it was not the place to let people—or things, for that matter—wander around unsupervised. When that rule was broken, the result was the particular kind of glower I was seeing now.

I steered Willard to the kitchen and got a beer out of the fridge as an initial peace offering. It would have been gauche to re-use the plate of abandoned snacks I had left out for Tim, so I prepared some pumpernickel and a wedge of cheddar. Willard set his paper bag on the table, and I could see a few slim bundles wrapped in newspaper, just the right size to be swap-meet rolling stock, and a stack of *Model Railroader* magazines from the 1970s.

"I hate to do this to you," I said, "but could you keep an eye on Tim for an hour or two?"

This time, Willard's glower said "Have you lost your mind entirely?"

"Just until I get back," I added. "I was going to leave him by himself, but since you're here . . ."

"Do you seriously expect me to sit in a chair and make sure your friend doesn't die while you're away?"

"I'm not sure I'd call him a friend," I said.

"He's comatose on the couch," Willard pointed out. "What should I call him? A stranger? An enemy?"

"I know where the huldra is," I said.

That was enough to startle him out of his tirade. "How?" he asked.

"When the weasel attacked us, we connected in some way."

"Did you use the *aqua sapientis*?"

"No, that got ruined yesterday. But it was the same effect, more or less. I knew what the weasel knew, and the weasel knew what I knew. One of the things I learned about was the huldra. I know where she—"

"—it," he corrected.

"You know what? You're right about that," I said. "Either way, though, I know where to find the huldra, but I may not have much time."

"Where is it?"

"Wellman Woods. When the weasel and I were, you know, *together*, I saw the tree where she'd hidden herself."

"You recognized the tree?" he asked.

"Well, no. One tree looks a lot like another, but I recognized the area. And I also saw the Wellman Woods entrance gate and the nature center, so I'm pretty certain about the location. The huldra's been moving from place to place. Wherever the trees are right, that's where she—it—whatever—goes. But she doesn't always stay. That's why I've got to leave right now."

Willard drank his beer and made a show of resigned acquiescence. "All right. Go."

"Thanks." I bounced up from the table, not wanting to think about the favor I was going to owe him at the end of all this. I detoured upstairs to pick up something from Willard's lab, then slipped out to the garage.

I tried not to think about Tim during the trip to Wellman Woods. If his condition took a turn for the worse, would Willard let him expire on the couch? Probably not. Calling Dr. Helmbach again, or even an ambulance, was less of a hassle than dealing with a dead body, and my uncle was nothing if not a shrewd calculator of his own personal inconveniences.

I was going to need all my energy for the upcoming confrontation with the huldra, and a positive mental attitude was a large component of that, so as I drove I made a point of considering all the things that had gone right recently. Had Ollie actually been eaten by cannibals? No, he had not. He was currently recuperating, receiving what I assumed was excellent medical care. Was Tim dead? No, he was not. Despite his best efforts, Tim had somehow managed to not get himself killed. Granted, he currently looked like a shrunken apple doll, but things could have gone a lot worse for Tim overall. In addition, Eldridge Stamper would be eating no one else, and his pack of associates had been scattered to the winds, leaderless. Really, I told myself, there were a large number of praiseworthy elements in my current situation.

I turned onto Morgan Avenue, feeling undeniably better as I passed by XYZ Hobbies. This was the only shop in the city selling the model parts and miniature tools that met Uncle Willard's standards. Eventually, I saw the tall trees of Wellman Woods on my right. Wellman Woods was an enormous nature park, two hundred incongruous acres of old-growth forest in the middle of the city, accidentally left undeveloped by a series of failed business ventures and eventually sold to the Garvinville parks department. Being the middle of the night, the place was closed, with a pad-locked metal gate across the cheerfully rustic entrance. The whole park was enclosed by high fences. The sections near the entrance were made of wood panels, but elsewhere it was chain link, topped with a coil of barbed wire. This was an imposing and near-impenetrable barrier, unless you happened to know another way in. Which I did.

Seward Road ran along several commercial blocks whose backs abutted against the Wellman Woods fence. At the halfway point, I turned and parked in front of Big Hat Willie's country music club, then walked purposefully around to the other side of the building. I made sure that no one was loitering in the area, then pushed a wheeled dumpster up to the fence that protected the woods. My aim wasn't to climb the fence, but to reach the electrical junc-tion box riveted halfway up one of the posts. I fiddled with the latch for a few seconds before it finally popped open, revealing a number of wires and fuses, and a tarnished key in a yellow plastic holder. I grabbed the key and slithered back down to the ground. This key opened the emergency access door twenty yards down the fence. The last time I'd had to sneak into Wellman Woods, to surveil a congregation of devil-worshipping lawyers (a smaller group than you might expect), I'd torn a favorite pair of corduroys hauling myself over the fence, so I found this hidden entrance and contrived to make a copy of the key, stashing it in the junc-tion box for future use.

The emergency door led to a maintenance trail, a grav-eled path used by the employees of the park to move around lawn mowers, fertilizer carts, or anything else that was in-convenient to drag into the depths of the forest. From there, I reached the network of walking trails that meandered through the woods. The ambient light from the surrounding city dropped sharply once I was among the trees, but I wasn't particularly worried about getting lost. As a kid, I had been here for little league games and nature hikes. As a teenager, I had been here for illicit drinking and hanging out with girls. As an adult, I usually came here to spy on someone or something, so by this point I had a pretty reliable understanding of how the trails were laid out.

Moving as fast as I could in the dark, I worked my way toward the cluster of oak trees around Goodacre Pond. That was the area I had seen when the thorn weasel and I were entangled, and as I got closer the sense of familiarity increased. Near the pond, I stopped to study one of the larger trees, an elderly specimen slightly apart from the others. Its trunk was gnarled and wavy, the way oak trees sometimes are, nearly giving the impression that the tree had a face. I stepped off the path to get a better look. This was obviously more than just an impressive old oak. I could feel the difference. This tree contained something, and I was pretty sure I knew what it was.

I put my hands on the bark and for an instant thought I felt something squirming underneath. About a foot above eye level was a scar, where two sections of the trunk had grown together and made an uneven spot. Moved by an irresistible impulse, I reached up and tried to pull the edges apart. I don't know if I'd been charged with magical potency after my experience with the thorn weasel, or if the tree was just ready to give up its secret, but the bark actually started to move under my hands. I extended the fissure downward, peeling it back as if it were wet canvas. Soon I had widened it enough to see a figure inside, a dark shape that looked both human and botanical, like the root of a mandrake. Exposure to the cool night air made it squirm and twist slightly, like a sleeper on the edge of waking up.

Before I could reach in, I noticed that the crickets and night birds had all fallen silent around me. I straightened up and turned around, knowing what I was about to see.

35

The thorn weasel stood out sharply from the surrounding gloom, illuminated by a green fire glowing somewhere deep inside the monster's body. Muscles and tendons continuously knotted and dissipated, and its jagged, dagger-like fangs grew larger as I watched. It took a heavy step in my direction, then another, its motion as ominous and unstoppable as the first moments of an avalanche.

"Hi there," I said.

I took out the thin silver chain that Eldridge Stamper had made. Before leaving the house for Wellman Woods, I had quickly closed up the last few open links I had abandoned when I heard Tim thrashing around in the back yard. My workmanship was pretty shoddy, but it was enough to keep the chain together, and that was enough for my purposes. I held it up by the ends, just as I had done in the gully behind the Book Baron a few hours ago.

The weasel stopped. As I stood my ground, its vines undulated and twitched, and the monster slowly began to shrink. Its color lightened and it took on a different outline. It drew in on itself, compressing its bulk and hiding the green fire. The multi-legged beast re-formed itself into something much smaller: a familiar, human-like shape. When the metamorphosis was finished, the huldra stood before me.

This was the secret I had learned when the weasel and I were connected. The huldra and the thorn weasel were the same thing. There had never been two creatures. Lenora and Tim had accidentally summoned the huldra in Mrs. Bates's back yard, and later, when they tried to dispose of her through the invocation of a second force, all they had done was compound their original mistake. Once again, they had confused "energy" with "being" and the creature that tore its way through their protective circle, and then through Tim's apartment, wasn't some new entity pulled up from a deeper plane of existence. It was the huldra herself. Their ritual had endowed her with a vast new infusion of esoteric power, giving her the ability to assume either form at will. After that, she appeared as a beautiful woman with a tail or a horrifying thorn weasel at will, according to her own unguessable whims.

This understanding, though, did not make the two of us friends. I was as vulnerable to the huldra as I ever was. For a second—maybe a little longer than a second—I longed to feel that perfect skin under my fingers, to inhale the hypnotizing mix of animal and vegetable scents, to lose myself in a cold embrace. I knew now my uncle was unquestionably right, and the creature in front of me was an "it," not a "her," but I could hardly bring myself to care.

Behind me, the figure inside the tree shifted. The wooden creaking sounds reminded me why I was here, and helped me to shake off the enchantment. Before the huldra could reach me, I held out the chain again, forming as taut a line as I could manage without risking the integrity of my inexpert repairs. The huldra stopped her advance. Her expression didn't change, but at the same time I knew that something was different. She was concerned.

Stamper's magic chain now made sense to me as well, another result of my connection with the creature. Having been inside the huldra's mind and memories, I understood how Stamper had used this magic object against her, and I now knew how to use it myself. I formed the chain into a loop, keeping the edges open with a couple of fingers, then carefully began to pull the loop shut.

The huldra stumbled. She was trapped, encircled by the power Stamper had infused into the chain. Ironically, Stamper had managed to fashion a stronger, more effective charm than Lenora and Tim, despite his minimal training and rudimentary equipment. Not for the first time, I was reminded that magic isn't easy, doesn't make sense, and usually isn't fair.

I shrank the loop of chain, narrowing the supernatural walls around the huldra even further. Now there was resistance as I slowly pulled the links through my fingers. This wouldn't send the huldra back to where she came from, but it would keep her from escaping, and I could reduce the circle until she was crushed like an old car in a compactor.

The huldra pushed against the air in a gesture that would have seemed comical, a parody of mime, in some other circumstance. The noose of chain got progressively harder to tighten, until it felt like I was cutting into something hard and nearly unyielding.

She dropped to a crouch. I took a deep breath. A little more effort—assuming the chain didn't snap—and this would all be over. I was glad for that. I didn't want to draw out the process any longer than it had to be. Then, through her disheveled hair, the huldra's eyes met mine.

I felt the same impulse as before. The same desire and the same willingness to do whatever she wanted. But I knew it was just an illusion. She wasn't a beautiful, helpless woman any more than she was a ravaging conglomeration of thorns and vines. She was a force from Outside, and the only way I could deal with her was to destroy her. There was nothing left for me to do besides carry on with the job.

But I didn't want to do it.

Despite what she'd done to Stamper and to Tim, and to that poor guy behind the Viceroy Theater whose name I didn't know, and the animals, and any other victims who might have crossed her path, I still didn't want to crush the life out of this beautiful, sinister creature. She hadn't asked to be here. She'd been summoned by a couple of boneheads who had more technique than ability, then captured by a lunatic who wanted to eat her in order to make himself more powerful. She had definitely caused problems, and she was too dangerous to leave at large, but I didn't have it in me to kill her. Uncle Willard, I'm sure, would have had no problem with it. He would have pulverized her to dust and gone back to his basketball and his model railroad without a second thought. But Willard wasn't here. I was, and I wasn't going to do it.

Slowly, I relaxed the loop, then snapped the chain and dropped the fragments to the ground. The huldra tilted her head in animal curiosity. The crushing, suffocating pressure had lifted, and I think she wondered why.

The huldra stood and held out her arms to me, as she had done to countless lonely shepherds and nighttime wanderers over the course of the centuries. Centuries? Millennia, probably. Without me noticing, she had glided forward on her delicate, bare feet. She was close enough to touch now. All I had to do was reach out.

Instead, I reached into my pocket. My fingers closed around a mud-spattered lump of hard plastic. The blue bear seemed almost to shimmer in the darkness. I still had no idea what the odd little thing was supposed to be, and it was unlikely the huldra would ever explain it to me, but this tiny gumball-machine toy was something we had in common. It was a token indicating our relationship was more complex than simply predator and prey, or hunter and hunted. I held it out, resting it on my open hand like I was offering a carrot to a horse that might bite me.

She broke her gaze and looked down at the blue bear. I thought I saw a flicker of emotion, delicate as a watercolor wash, cross her exquisite face. I held my breath as she reached toward me, but all she did was pluck the bear from my hand. She regarded the thing impassively for a moment. Then her eyes rose to meet mine again, and I braced myself for another wave of irresistible magnetism. But then her attention shifted back to the bear. Her hand closed around it, making a fist.

I wondered how she would respond. Were we making a deal? She must have been aware at this point that I could have destroyed her, but didn't. For a second, I worried I had merely given her a final opportunity to reduce me to a dried-out husk, but then she glided past me. She put her hand on the trunk of the massive oak and the fissure widened to the size of a door, like time-lapse film of a blooming flower.

The huldra reached into this impossible cavern with her free hand. The muscles of her shoulders and her extraordinary legs tensed, like she was struggling against a weight, and I realized what she was doing. She had taken hold of the figure encased inside the tree and was pulling it loose. With a graceful motion, she freed the figure and let it collapse to the ground. Then she stepped over it, entering fully into the tree. She looked in my direction once more. Those fathomless indigo eyes were the last I saw of her before the bark closed up between us, taking the huldra out of my world for good.

I was so engrossed in watching the huldra that when the figure at my feet began to move, I was startled. Hurriedly, I dropped to the ground beside it, smashing my left knee against a knotted root, an injury that I wouldn't notice until later, when I tried to get out of bed and found I could hardly bear to put any weight on it. The figure was slick with some sort of viscous oil, which I soon realized was tree sap. It was a woman, and I noticed idly that she was just as naked as the huldra had been. With my handkerchief, I swabbed as much of the sap away from her face as I could manage. It was Lenora.

She coughed, first weakly and then with growing strength as she drew more air into her lungs.

"Nice to see you again," I said.

"What happened?" she said thickly.

"The huldra let you go. She's gone now. So's the thorn weasel. Both of them together. Do you think you can walk?"

She sat up. I wrapped my jacket around her shoulders and helped her stand. I had doubts about whether supernatural tree sap was going to wash out, but chivalry does what chivalry must.

By the time we retraced the path back to the access door and emerged from the woods behind Big Hat Willie's, the clouds in the east were starting to lighten. I drove Lenora back to the Medieval apartment complex so she could shower and put on some clothes. While she was cleaning up, I discreetly retrieved my Czech army jacket from her hallway floor and wrapped it into a bundle. My dry cleaner, Mr. Van Helden, had been able to rescue a fair percentage of my clothes from various fluids and oozes in the past, so I hoped he might have another miracle up his sleeve. I made a point of not sitting down while I waited for her, because I knew sitting would lead to resting my eyes, and resting my eyes would lead inevitably to sleep. To keep myself awake and occupied, I drifted into her narrow kitchen and surveyed the contents of the fridge. When Lenora emerged from the shower, with her hair still wet and her customary makeup unapplied, looking like someone who'd just recovered from a week-long fever, I held out a plate with an egg-white omelet and a small pyramid of Hydrox cookies.

"This was going to be toast," I explained, indicating the cookies. "But I couldn't find any bread."

"It's on the shopping list." She took a bite of the omelet. "Thank you."

"You were gone for about a day," I said, setting down a mug of tea. "Do you remember any of it?"

She shook her head. "Hardly anything. It was like I was dreaming. The creature—the huldra—she would be there for a while, and then she'd be gone. I wasn't sure if she was angry with me, or was trying to protect me, or what," Lenora said. "I never knew what she was thinking. She was just . . ."

"Inscrutable," I suggested. "Alien."

"I guess so. What happened to her?"

"As far as I can tell, the huldra and I eventually came to an understanding. She decided to leave."

"How'd you do it?"

"I wish I could say exactly." I sighed and took a cookie from the package on the shelf. "We made a connection. Sort of. More or less."

"What about the big thing? What did you call it? The 'thorn weasel'?"

"It was the huldra," I said. "Different forms of the same creature."

Lenora thought about this in silence for a moment. Then she rubbed her eyes and pointed at the omelet with her fork. "This is good."

"Imagine how much better it would have been with toast."

"Where's Tim?"

"Why don't you get dressed first, then I'll tell you every-thing."

36

Twenty minutes later, Lenora had dried her hair and put on some crimson lipstick. She wore black tights, boots, her motorcycle jacket, and a t-shirt with the neckline hacked into a deep V and a portrait of Aleister Crowley silkscreened on the front. We were on the way back to Uncle Willard's house. Since my passenger seat was still sticky with sap, Lenora sat in the back and leaned forward to talk to me through the gap.

I had summarized the events of the past twenty-four hours, including Tim's dogged attempts to locate the huldra, and his valiant effort to help fight off the weasel. I may have emphasized Tim's heroism a little more than I would have if I'd been talking to someone else, but it seemed like the right thing to do at the time. While we waited to make a turn, I told her how the huldra had drained Tim, leaving him withered and frail.

"All he wanted to do was learn things," she said quietly, just as we started moving again. "I should have been a better teacher. Our results were so good when we started working together, so I kept trying more and more. I never thought about slowing down. And then all this happened." She sighed. "Poor Tim. He didn't deserve this."

"I'll say this, though: If anyone else—Dennis Falco, to pick a name at random—went through what happened to Tim, their first priority would be trying to get their life back. But I don't think it even crossed Tim's mind. All he cared about was trying to find you." I coughed uncomfortably. "He's in love with you. He may not have ever said it to you, but he is. The only reason I bring it up now is in case he forgets to mention it later."

Lenora nodded. "I think I love him, too."

I paused at a stop sign. "Well, good. At least something positive came out of all this."

Upon reaching the house, I unlocked the side door and we went in. It wasn't until I noticed Lenora tiptoeing behind me that I realized I was walking with equal caution. My subconscious dread of what I might find in the living room suddenly rushed to the front of my mind. Any number of horrific scenes were possible, ranging from Tim dead on the floor to an empty house and a note on the coffee table reading, "I'm taking care of it. Details to follow." I was definitely not expecting what greeted us when Lenora and I turned the corner. Tim lay on the couch, still sleeping, with a red down comforter tucked up to his chin. A heavy, wide-bottomed mug, a plate of saltines, and a bowl of ice cubes sat on a folding TV tray nearby. Willard had pulled the best chair over to the side of the couch, and was dozing in it, his feet up on the ottoman. His biography of Jack Parsons lay open, face down, over his ample midsection, and a copy of *The Hobbit* rested on the coffee table.

Despite the cautious entry, our presence in the room set off Willard's finely-tuned sense of personal space. He woke with a snort, pulling his feet down and sitting up straight with the exaggerated dignity of the startled.

"This is Lenora," I said. "She's here to pick up Tim. How is he?"

"As well as can be expected, I suppose." Willard stood, grimacing as he unkinked his lower back. "He was wakeful a while ago, so I gave him something to eat and he drifted back to sleep." Willard nodded at Lenora. "Pleased to meet you."

I glanced down at the table. "Were you reading *The Hobbit* to him?"

Uncle Willard's eyes narrowed. "I assumed he needed rest after all he'd been through. Reading aloud seemed like the most expedient way to induce it."

"I see," I said. I moved the TV tray out of the way and Lenora knelt at Tim's side.

"Tim, it's me," she said quietly. "How to you feel?"

Tim was still white-haired and frail, but under Willard's care he had lost some of the unhealthy gray color he'd had when I dragged him inside after the weasel's attack. He blinked a few times, then cautiously propped himself up on his elbows.

"You're back," he said weakly.

"Yeah, I'm back. Thank you, Tim." She wrapped her arms around his thin shoulders.

I lifted the mug from the tray and sniffed its contents. "Ginger ale," I said.

"I believe that's traditional when someone is bedridden." Willard's voice was heavy with dignity.

"And a bendy straw. I didn't know we had any of these in the house."

"Shut up."

Lenora and I helped Tim into the back seat of the Jag, leaving Willard free to clean up the evidence of his compassion and prepare a suitable denial. They sat together on the ride back, with Tim leaning against Lenora. Occasionally they talked in low voices, but a newly-developed rattle under the dashboard made it difficult for me to make out what was said. That was probably for the best. When we arrived at Lenora's place again, Tim felt able to walk on his own, with Lenora a few steps away, watching intently for any signs of faltering.

"Call me," I said to her once she had unlocked her door and escorted Tim to a chair. "Let me know how he's doing."

"Thank you, Dean. Thanks for everything."

"Any time."

Lenora hesitated, then asked, "What are you going to do now?"

"Do about what?"

"About me. About what Tim and I were doing. Are you going to tell people?"

"Who would I tell? I'm not the sorcery police, and even if I were, what good would it do? It's over. The huldra is gone, and nobody's going to try to bring her back. I'm right about that, aren't I? I don't know what state Mrs. Bates's garden is in, but I think it can be left to rise or fall on its own merits without any more treatments."

"Yeah, probably so."

"Dennis Falco wanted to know how this all worked out, but I'll leave that to you," I said. "You can tell him whatever you think he'd enjoy hearing."

"I'll come up with something," she said.

There was no point in me lecturing her further on the responsible practice of the occult arts. If she and Tim hadn't learned their lesson by now, they weren't going to learn it.

"Next time, though, we can talk about my fee," I added.

In a week, I would stop by Knit Now to check on Lenora, and she would show me a long, wispy white hair. Noting my expression of confusion and disgust, she would direct my attention to the end of the hair, where it had been recently plucked from Tim's beard.

"See that?" she would say. "The root is black. The rest of it's white, but it's growing in black again. His face is starting to fill out, too. I think he's recovering."

With that happy news, I would buy a handmade scarf for my mom's upcoming birthday, and fervently hope Lenora and Tim would keep themselves out of trouble in the future.

But that would all happen later. At the present time, I dragged myself upstairs and fell into bed as soon as I returned home. Not only had I been up all night, but my knee had begun to throb ominously. Sleeping for half the day also gave me an opportunity to avoid Uncle Willard, who was probably going to be tough to deal with until he'd had a chance to work off some irritability up in the attic with his trains. Even then, I doubted he was going to let me forget about all this for a long time.

A short while later, I was awakened by my phone chirping next to my bed. It was a text from Ollie. "They're letting me out of the hospital now," it read. "I wanted to say hi again before my wife drove me home. Are you available?"

I briefly mourned the rest of the nap I wasn't going to get, then replied that my schedule was wide open.

"Awesome. How about that little coffee place by your house?"

This was ideal, since I was confident Willard was in no mood for another round of guests. My knee, where I had fallen on the tree root in Wellman Woods, had developed an angry, purple bruise, and it had stiffened to such a degree that walking was a painful challenge. An Ace bandage helped, as did the silver-headed ebony cane we kept in the umbrella holder by the front door. I debated for a moment about the best way to get to Planet Caravan, and whether operating the Jag's manual transmission would be more difficult than walking. In the end, I decided to risk the walk and hope the knee warmed up with use.

Sophie was behind the counter, wearing coppery hoop earrings and a plaid shirt over a tank top. "I'm guessing there's a story behind that," she said, noticing the cane when I leaned it against the counter to get my wallet.

I shrugged modestly. "Nothing much. Just had to go down to the basement of one of Uncle Willard's buildings and kill some rats. Things got out of hand."

"Mm-hm." She gave me my coffee and a pair of raisin molasses cookies from the jar on the counter. Watching me hobble over to pick up a napkin, she asked, "Does it hurt?"

"A bit. But I'm being exceptionally stoic about it."

"You want me to make it feel better?"

"I'm open to suggestions," I said.

She disappeared behind the counter and returned holding a small blue-glass bottle with a cork stopper. "My friend Elyse makes this. She calls it 'Burning Spirit muscle tonic'." Sophie uncorked the bottle and held it under her nose to inhale the fragrance, brushing her lips against the glass. "It's got witch hazel, capsaicin, magnetic oils, plant extracts, and some other stuff. I'm thinking about selling it here. Apply it to whatever's hurting you every couple of hours."

What could I do? I bought the bottle.

37

A blue Subaru pulled up across the street as I finished my second cookie. A blonde woman in a pastel sweater got out of the driver's seat, then went around to the other side and helped a man in a red t-shirt and gray track pants onto the sidewalk. It was Ollie, and he didn't look great. There were ugly remnants of bruising around his cheekbones, and he walked with a hesitancy that suggested his internal injuries weren't completely healed yet. But he was still the same Ollie Helfrich, and managed to appear surprisingly chipper despite his infirmity.

"Dean! How are you?" he said as soon as they were inside. "This is my wife Denise. Honey, this is Dean Sherwood. He's the guy I was telling you about. He was the one who called the doctor after my accident."

"Thank you so much," Denise said to me after we sat down. Denise was fresh-faced, no-nonsense, and like her husband, not the kind of person to get involved with cannibals, warlocks, or creatures from beyond. "We're so lucky you were there when it happened. I mean, you always hear about hit and run drivers, but you never think it'll happen in real life."

Ollie winked one slightly puffy eye in my direction, indicating that this was the story we were going with.

"I'm glad I was able to help," I said.

Denise saw my cane and asked if I'd gotten hurt helping Ollie.

I shook my head. "Unrelated injury."

"He's a private detective," Ollie volunteered.

"So, Ollie, how are you feeling?" I said, before Denise could ask about the kinds of things I usually investigated.

Ollie thought about this for a second. "Pretty good, actually. Sore, but not too bad, all things considered. According to the doctor, I've got a ridiculously tough spleen."

"They want him to get checked out by our regular doctor in a couple of weeks, but he's okay to travel," Denise added. She stood up to go order sandwiches, giving Ollie and me a few minutes to talk without being overheard.

"I can't remember very much about what happened," Ollie said. "I think Stamper told me he had a set of Peregrine financial records at his house, and there was something in them I needed to see." He paused, considering. "You know, after all we learned about him, it probably wasn't too smart to go to his house. But since my audit showed he might have been misusing club funds, my instinct was to give him a chance to clear his name. I guess I wasn't thinking."

"You'll do better next time."

"There may not be a next time," he said. "No more weird stuff for me. I'm sticking with the spreadsheets from now on."

"See what I mean? You're learning already. Next time, you'll just say 'forget it' at the beginning and save yourself a lot of trouble."

Ollie's subsequent clear memory was waking up in the hospital. As soon as he was lucid, the nurse on duty summoned Dr. Helmbach.

"He said not to talk to anyone about what happened. If anybody asked, I was supposed to say I couldn't remember anything. So I kept my mouth shut and played along. When he called Denise, he said I'd been run over by a hit-and-run driver on some street near the Peregrine perch. A car whipped around a corner, knocked me in the air, and kept on going."

I marveled once again at Dr. Helmbach's unexpected skill at duplicity. He'd told the hospital that Ollie had been in a home-repair accident so they wouldn't be tempted to investigate. Then he told Ollie's wife that he'd been a victim of a hit-and-run, because she'd know that the home-repair tale was bogus. It was an impressive web of cover stories.

"He also told me not to worry about getting a bill."

"Absolutely right," I said, making a mental note to get Ollie's account number from Dr. Helmbach and run over to Priory Hospital with a fat stack of hundreds and a winning smile for the financial services clerk.

In the short time we had left before Denise returned, I filled him in on what had happened since his injury. I let him know how Stamper had gotten his gruesome comeuppance and how the huldra had returned to where she came from.

"What was she?" Ollie asked.

"I guess you could call her a forest creature, although that doesn't really do her justice. She got dragged here, wasn't happy about it, and started taking it out on people. In the end, though, we managed to communicate a little bit. Though, I have to admit, I could hardly tell you exactly what we said to each other."

Denise returned, carrying two plates. She and Ollie ate while I sipped my coffee and told stories about the history of the neighborhood. I focused on light, entertaining topics such as local architectural follies and the great riverboat bordello fiasco of 1905, which happened three blocks from where we were sitting. Once the turkey sandwiches and kettle chips were polished off, Denise mentioned they had a long drive ahead, and I escorted them out to their car. Ollie stopped me as I assisted him into the front seat.

"You know, Dean," he said, "the Peregrines really are a great organization. I love working for them."

"I'm glad you still feel that way. Given everything that happened, I was going to see if you wanted me to burn the place down. I could make it happen. I know a guy."

"Really?"

I shook my head. "No. I don't know a guy. It would have been me." I hated the idea of torching a historic building, but I felt like I owed Ollie, so I would have done it.

"That's why I wanted to say something before I left," Ollie said. I don't want you to have a bad impression of the Peregrines just because of a few bad apples."

It isn't often you meet someone with enough innate positivity to refer to a nest of cannibals as "a few bad apples." I took a moment to savor the experience.

"Those are good guys over there," Ollie said. "I think they'll police themselves pretty well after this. But, you know, if you happen to be walking by . . ."

"I'll keep an eye out," I assured him.

Ollie eased into the seat and opened the glove compartment. He extracted a card and handed it to me. Like the first one he had given me, it had the official Peregrines' logo embossed on it, with Ollie's name and his contact information.

"We can always use more good guys, Dean. And this way, you can keep an eye on them from the inside. Think about it. I'll even be your sponsor."

I thanked him for the offer. The odds of me joining the Peregrines weren't high, but it seemed ungrateful to not even pretend to think about it. Denise started the engine, and I waved as they drove off. I wasn't sure I would voluntarily set foot inside Peregrine perch 47 ever again, but if I did, and happened to see another naked woman tied to a table, I was going to keep on walking.

Probably.

Back at home, Uncle Willard was in the back yard. He had changed into his overalls and arranged a selection of gardening implements—more than one man would need on his own—ostentatiously along the garage wall. I walked carefully up the path, the ferrule of my cane tapping against the bricks, and I saw him stooping slightly to study the ruined flower beds. When he saw me, it took him several seconds of concerted effort to straighten up.

"What's wrong with your leg?" Willard asked.

"I hit my knee on a tree root last night. What's wrong with your back?"

"I slept in a chair, the victim of a misguided sense of duty."

"Well, don't think it's not appreciated," I said. "Here, I've got something that'll fix your back right up." I handed him the bottle of Burning Spirit muscle tonic.

Willard's nostrils formed steep arches as he regarded the bottle with suspicion. "What is this?"

"Tonic. Liniment. Folk medicine. Something like that. Hand-made by artisans. You can't go wrong with artisans."

"This wasn't made by the same people who let that creature escape, was it?"

"Would I do that to you?" Before he could attempt an answer, I redirected the conversation. "Do you want some help with the flower beds?"

Willard frowned at the sky. "At least until it starts raining again, yes."

"Give me two seconds," I said, and went around to the front of the house. My work boots were in the vestibule, and I wanted to return the cane to its customary place. I figured leaning on a cane while raking dirt was a little bit excessive, even for me.

A few leaves drifted down from the Japanese maple, and I brushed them aside as I ascended the stone steps to the front porch. My hand was on the doorknob when something caught my eye. To the left was the diamond-paned window that opened into my office, and a small object sat on the sill. I gingerly stepped off the landing and onto the muddy ground behind the bushes to get a better view.

I stood there for a long time, staring at what I found, not sure what to think. In the center of the sill, facing inward so it could look through the glass, was the blue bear.

About the Author

In addition to *The Blue Bear*, Quentin Dodd has written several books for young readers, as well as the screenplay for the independent horror-comedy film *Zorg and Andy*.

Quentin lives in Indiana with his wife, two children, a large collection of antique cameras, and several homemade musical instruments. He is not certain if he has ever seen a ghost.

For more information, including updates on new books and a free Dean Sherwood short story, please visit

www.QuentinDodd.com

www.ingramcontent.com/pod-product-compliance
Lightning Source LLC
Chambersburg PA
CBHW070343200726
48294CB00003B/772